THE GRAY AREA BETWEEN

The Gray Area Between is a work of fiction. References to real people, names, characters, places, and incidents either are the product of the author's imagination or are used fictitiously, and any resemblance to actual persons, living or dead, business establishments, events or locales is entirely coincidental.

ACKNOWLEDGEMENTS

Thank you to my friends and family members who accompanied me on this journey.

To the established and aspiring authors at the New England Crime Bake. You gave me incentive to push forward with my story.

Special shout out to Judy Baker, Jo-Anne Williams and Steve Souza for their encouragement to write this book and interest in my historical research.

Heartfelt appreciation to my first readers – Denise Morin, Ann Marie Marcotte, Lorna Currier, and Jean Klimm Bowie

A special thank you to my husband, Phil, who donated *my* time to write. LOL

Cover Design by Kevin Bujold
Cover Photo of Robert Bowie by Phil Perrotta
Cover Photo of USS Lejeune - Courtesy of US National Archives

DEDICATION

For my mother, Doris

Men and boys all drifters alike know
Winds of change are blowing, trees are bowing
Dark clouds are gathering, a storm is coming
My wandering days will soon be done

Chapter 1   Myles 1957

Confidence was something Myles Bingham had an abundance of, although some called it arrogance. A mentor taught him any journalist worth their weight in gold knows walking into an establishment with an air of purpose is the key to getting what you want.

He approached the young lady behind the desk of the third floor nursing station at Beacon Marine Hospital. She was deep in thought, intently focused on her task. He cleared his throat, so as not to startle her. The receptionist raised her eyes and smiled brightly at him. Myles thought this woman was a breath of fresh air in this depressing, antiquated building.

"Hello. May I help you?" Her syrupy voice threw him off kilter for a moment, but he quickly recovered. Beautiful women had always been his weakness, and many times they were his downfall in life. After the last one, he vowed never to let a woman get in the way of a good story again.

"Is Dr. Daniel Templeton available?" he asked in an authoritative voice.

"Is he expecting you?"

"No, I was hoping to speak with him. Tell him I'll be brief, but if I need an appointment I'll be happy to make one."

"I can check, sir. May I please have your name and nature of business?"

"My name is Myles Bingham, and I'm with the *Courier*." He puffed his chest a little, as he clarified his introduction. "I'm a reporter."

One delicately penciled eyebrow arched her surprise, as she brought the phone up to her ear. "Oh, THE *Courier*? I love to read that magazine," she whispered, holding her hand over the mouthpiece. "You may have a seat over there, sir." She pointed to a backless brown leather bench near the window.

"Thank you." Myles sat on the bench and picked up the competition's rag to thumb through while he waited.

The receptionist spoke for a moment, listened, hung up the phone and called over to him. "Mr. Bingham, Dr. Templeton will be with you soon."

"Thank you, Miss…? I'm sorry I didn't get your name."

"Thomas. It's *Miss* Thomas." Her eyelashes batted like butterfly wings against her cheeks.

"Thank you again, *Miss* Thomas." He grinned and went back to his reading. Every now and then he would sneak a peek at the pretty receptionist.

Ten minutes passed. He was about to ask Miss Thomas if the good doctor was still coming, when he saw a tall, willowy man in a white medical coat approach. Despite his lankiness, he moved gracefully in long strides across the waiting room. Myles stood to greet him.

"I'm Dr. Templeton. How can I help you?" The doctor towered over Myles as he thrust his large hand downward to shake hands.

"Dr. Templeton, I'm Myles Bingham, from the *Courier*. Thank you for seeing me. I promise I won't take up too much of your time."

"No, that's quite all right, Mr. Bingham. I have a few minutes and was just heading to the cafeteria for coffee. Join me?"

"Just what the doctor ordered."

"Good," Templeton wrapped the ends of his stethoscope around his neck. "Follow me."

Myles stood in line behind Dr. Templeton, waiting to pay the cashier for his coffee. He looked around at the drab surroundings. *At least they were trying,* he thought. The hanging baskets of plastic flowers were a poor attempt to beautify these walls that contained such horrific results of trauma. The mint green walls meant to soothe the patients and visitors failed miserably.

He was in deep thought about the hospital décor when the cashier caught his eye and waved him through. "You're all set, sir. Dr. Templeton took care of your coffee." She turned her attention to the next customer in line.

They found a table in a quiet corner of the cafeteria. Before speaking, Myles prepared his coffee with cream and two sugars. Dr. Templeton took his strong and black, no doubt to bolster his energy for his long shift.

Dr. Templeton took a case from his pocket and put on a pair of horn-rimmed glasses, which framed a receding hairline with tufts of gray-brown hair above his ears. Myles knew right away he lucked out. Dr. Templeton was approachable and had a soft, compassionate manner about him, unlike some others in the medical field he had dealt with in the past.

"Now, what can I do for you, Mr. Bingham?"

"I am intrigued by one of your long term patients I recently read about in the *Boston Globe*, and I would like to do an interview with him for a feature article in my magazine."

"You have to be talking about Charlie," Templeton grinned. "He's the only patient of intrigue in this hospital. He's definitely our man of mystery."

Myles nodded, "Yes, my editor thought a living unknown soldier would make a great human interest story. So, as his doctor, are you granting my request?" From the surprised look on the doctor's face, Myles thought he may have overstepped his bounds. The doctor drank his coffee, obviously sizing Myles up before he answered.

"Mr. Bingham, to be honest with you, that's up to him, not me. This isn't a prison, it's a hospital, but I don't think a one-sided interview will be very exciting. You see, Charlie doesn't speak much. He can speak, but either chooses not to, or he has nothing to say, most of the time."

"Well at any rate, it couldn't harm him, right?"

"There's no way of knowing that for sure. Last time he was in the headlines we had to weed through a lot of publicity hounds. But, I guess at this point it will be good to have the media reach out to the public again. We may get a clue to the poor man's identity."

"When can it be arranged for me to speak with him? I may also want to talk to his primary nurses or any of his other caregivers as well. Can you tell me about his current physical condition and what it was when he was admitted back in '45? What he can and cannot do now?"

Dr. Templeton leaned back and took a sip of his coffee. "Whoa, slow down. I'll give you a brief rundown of what we do know."

Bingham took his pen and notepad out of his suit jacket and nodded a go-ahead to Dr. Templeton.

"Well, Charlie has been a mystery right from the beginning. Apparently, according to our records and my memory, he came in with the wounded from the USS *Lejeune*, which came into port from Southampton, England in February 1945. He became my patient on day one, and for the first year he was in and out of a comatose state, riddled with infection from his wounds.

"What type of wounds did he have?"

"Shrapnel wounds which developed deep layered infections resulting in severe bone disease. This has paralyzed him from the waist down. Charlie endured many surgeries to safely extract what shrapnel we could. As a matter of fact, he still has some in him."

"How much time went by before the hospital tried to identify him?"

"In all honesty, it was nobody's fault that it took quite a while."

"What do you mean? Can you set the scene for me Doc?"

Dr. Templeton sat back in the chair. Everyone knew the days when a transport pulled in were not hard to recall. On the contrary, they were hard to forget. He gathered his thoughts and cleared his throat.

"You had to be here to understand what it was like. Boys, men wounded, maimed, were being brought here in droves. These men were the cream of the crop, America's manhood. Neighborhoods were decimated, only the women and children remained. Sure, the war was over and the men were coming home, the war was over, but they were broken. It was over a year before things slowed down enough to put the word out on Charlie."

The doctor's voice lowered. "Although, I don't think the time made a difference," he added.

"Where did they search?"

"We, as in the hospital staff, started with the help of the Red Cross around early 1947. An extensive investigation with the aid of the Immigration and Naturalization Office began, and a set of Charlie's fingerprints were sent to Washington, but they were not on file with any of the armed services or any criminal base they had at the time. They, in turn, sent the prints overseas, and the Brits came back empty-handed as well."

Myles wrote furiously in his notebook as the doctor spoke.

Dr. Templeton drained his coffee and checked his watch. "Sorry, I have a meeting at eleven o'clock. After the meeting, I will visit Charlie to let him know what you want to do and gauge his response. Leave a number where you can be reached with Miss Thomas. I'll have her call you if he's receptive to an interview and, if so, Miss Thomas will check the nursing schedule and set up a time." He stood and reached out his hand. Myles shook it, and thanked him for his time and the coffee.

"Mr. Bingham, don't be mistaken about Charlie. He doesn't speak much, but I believe he is fully capable of communicating more, and he's aware of what goes on around him. He has a charming way with the ladies. The nurses dote on him night and day."

"So you don't think Charlie is an amnesia victim?"

"I didn't say that. Talking and remembering are two different things. Regarding your question, in my opinion, no, I don't believe he is an amnesiac. I think he's made a conscious choice to live this way."

"A choice?"

"Yes, I also believe at one point he may have been able to walk again. I'm not a psychiatrist, but I've studied him for years, and I think he feels this is his punishment for whatever he did in his life. He feels it's warranted. That not only goes for me. A lot of the people around here believe Charlie is hiding something."

The doctor started to walk away, when he suddenly stopped and turned back to Myles. "Mr. Bingham, please remember one thing."

"What's that?"

"No matter whether Charlie is hiding something or not, he is still a human being who needs our help. He's not just a human interest story." Dr. Templeton was paged on the overhead system, and he hurried away before Myles could say anything.

Myles received a call around late that evening from Miss. Thomas. She informed him Dr. Templeton thought Charlie was all right with an interview, and he could meet Charlie at one o'clock tomorrow.

After he confirmed the time and thanked her for the call Myles attempted to engage her in conversation, but she politely bid him a good night.

Miss Thomas calling this late at night made him smile. He considered himself a good reporter, and a good reporter is intuitive. If he picked up on anything at all with her, it was the fact that Miss Thomas was flirting with him.

It was after midnight before he retired to bed. He spent the last couple of hours nursing a whiskey, his mind swinging like a pendulum between the lovely Miss Thomas and preparing for the interview. Miss Thomas won out.

Chapter 2   James 1916

The old man didn't agree with the adage, 'People don't change, they are who they are.' Regrets can change a person, and he had his share of them. Charlie thought back, as he often did, to the day James's life started on a downward spiral. His memory as a young man, walking home after a long day working on the waterfront, was so vivid he could still smell the noxious fish effluent in his nostrils. Those memories played out on center stage frequently these days. The memory of James tugged at Charlie's mind, like brittle film pulled taut on a motion picture projector before snapping and unraveling to the floor. They pulled him back to the day he wished he could live over.

***

James rubbed his forearms in an attempt to shed the small, bone-like shards stuck to his skin. Silvery scales fluttered in the wind, shimmering in the last rays of the setting sun, before dropping on the frost-covered leaves in the gutter. He pulled his coat sleeves down and quickened his pace home.

His hate for gutting fish started at a young age after a dock boy pushed him into the barrel of toxic soup called chum. While other eight year old boys prepared for their maiden voyage with the fleet, James chose to help keep the docks and marine equipment from disrepair. He took odd jobs scraping barnacles and painting the hulls of boats floundering on their wooden ribs on the sand like a pod of beached whales. Cleaning the catch couldn't be avoided, especially if he wanted to earn enough money to leave Gloucester. James Lawson just turned twenty, and he wasn't about to get stuck in this town for the rest of his life.

His father was disgusted when James refused to crew on a trawler. The old man drank heavily and blamed his wife for raising "a mama's boy." No matter now, James thought, he's gone. A smile crept onto his lips, but it was short-lived when he remembered his stepfather lived here now.

He leaped up the rear steps of his family's Massachusetts row house and opened the kitchen door. James's stomach growled when the aroma from a kettle of stew, rolling gently over a low flame, hit him. He picked up a wooden spoon from the counter and plucked out a potato. As he brought it up to his mouth he sensed something was wrong. He put the spoon down and crossed the kitchen to the parlor.

Then it struck him. His mother always yelled at him for tramping through the house stinking of fish. "That's what the mud room is for," she'd tell him, as he attempted to sneak up the stairs to his room. They acted out this scene every day. Not today.

Thud, creak, creak. James stopped and listened. Angry voices rose from below the floor planks, muffled by the wool rug. He ran across the parlor to the hall and turned the doorknob on the basement door just as his mother screamed.

"Stop, no, no! Don't do...." There was a loud *crack* and then silence. James grabbed a monkey wrench from the narrow shelf above the railing. The skin of his knuckles rubbed against the cement wall as he closed his fist around the tool's cold, iron handle. The rickety wooden stairs bowed under his weight. He jumped the last two steps at the bottom of the stairs to the dirt floor of the musty basement.

An oil lamp hung from a rafter swinging back and forth like a pendulum. The flame cast dancing shadows across his stepfather's back, as he stood over his wife's lifeless body.

The bastard killed her!

The basement floor seemed a vast span to cover, but it took only seconds for James to reach his stepfather. His body flew through the air toward Alfred Lorentzen's back. James's right arm arced downward and the wrench made full contact with his stepfather's head.

The sound of bone crunching was the last thing James remembered until he found himself standing in his attic bedroom. Dazed, his hand shook as he slicked back his black hair with the sweat from his brow and caught a whiff of a sweet, ferrous smell. His stomach tightened as he turned his palm over and saw a red, sticky smear. His temples pulsated with rage when he looked at the wrench A scream echoed in the stairway, startling him He lost his grip on the bloody monkey wrench and it hit the floor with a thud. *She's alive.*

Chapter 3   Annie

Annie Lorentzen lifted her aching head. Tears streaked her dirt-caked face. She rolled onto her side, pulled herself up to a sitting position and wiped her face with her apron. Blood trickled from her split lower lip as she spit out the grit lodged in her teeth.

Alfred. Where is he?

Bile burned her throat as her panic rose. Annie struggled onto her knees, teetering for a moment, waiting for the dizziness to pass. She grabbed onto an oak barrel and pulled herself up to a standing position. Annie stood, wavering slightly before taking a step. Her eyes focused and she gasped. Alfred was sprawled face down, three feet away, blood seeping into the soil around his head.

Annie kept her eyes fixed on his body, as she stepped back toward the stairs. She thought Alfred moaned, but she was too frightened to check.

James should be home soon, and she wanted to see her son. She needed him. Annie summoned her strength and held onto the wall, as she made her way up the stairs in the dim light. Trembling, she crossed the hall into the parlor and leaned over the back of a chair to rest. She lifted her head, and that's when she saw them.

Drops of blood crisscrossed the floor and glistened in the last rays of the setting sun filtering through the parlor window. Annie straightened and followed the wet spots to the bottom of the attic steps and looked upstairs.

A chill rippled up her spine, and she screamed, not out of fear for herself, but of what she might discover up there, at the end of the blood trail, in James's room.

Chapter 4   Annie and James

The screaming from the stairway stopped, replaced by footsteps coming up the stairs towards James. He watched his mother enter his bedroom. She took in the scene — the blood on his hands, the wrench lying on the floor at his feet. Their eyes met. She went over to him, picked up the blood-covered wrench and left the room.

She returned empty-handed, and he didn't ask any questions. Annie took her son's hand and walked him over to the bed. She sat beside him, shaking, and didn't speak for a few moments. Finally she broke the quiet.

"James, we have to go to the police," she pleaded. "We can't leave him lying down there moaning."

"I'll kill him if he hits you again. I swear, I will," he whispered.

"We have to go to the police for help, James. I'll tell them he was drunk, and he fell and hit his head."

James studied her face, watching her eyes flit side-to-side, wringing her hands in her lap. No tears fell from her soon-to-be-black eyes. He would never understand why she always excused Alfred. He took her hand in his, edged her to her feet, and helped her downstairs and out of the house.

A colony of gulls circled high above the town's harbor. Their screeches punctuated the two-block walk to the police station. In his youth, James often thought their bloodcurdling cries resembled the keening of funeral mourners. They were saltwater vultures, pecking at decaying things.

He could relate to their prey. At times, he felt he was dying in this town, suffocating, but now his plan to leave was in jeopardy. How could he leave his mother here alone with that monster? Peter, the youngest, was already out to sea, and their sister, Catherine, and her husband moved up the coast to Rockport.

The ancient brick police station had seen better days, but money was scarce and manpower more important, especially during those days when the fishing fleet was in port, and the men needed to blow off steam.

James and Annie stopped as they reached the entrance and looked at each other. James held her gaze until Annie broke away. James stepped forward and opened the door for her.

An officer sat behind a large oak desk. They approached the desk with no apparent urgency and waited to be addressed. He glanced up, made a quick assessment, and he put his head back down to finish his paperwork.

Finally the officer looked up again. "How can I help you?"

James felt his face flush. He knew once he told the police what happened, he would be in trouble. They would blame him, not Alfred, because of his past history, but he had no choice in this matter. He had to protect his mother.

"Look here son, I don't have all day," the officer grumbled.

Annie started to say something when James cut her off. "I'll handle this, Ma." He turned back to the officer. "I came home from work and found my stepfather beating my mother."

The officer addressed Annie. "Alright then, are you hurt, ma'am?"

James interrupted, "Look at her face. Of course she's hurt, so I hurt him. I'm telling you I need an officer to accompany us back to the house. If you can't talk to that bastard, I'm going to kill him. I swear I will."

"Whoa, boy, slow down." The officer's fist pounded on the desk as he stood. "Look, have yourselves a seat on that bench, and I'll get an officer to go with you to check the situation out."

Two patrolmen, Officer Parson and Officer Russo, accompanied them back to the house on Railway Avenue. Officer Parson motioned to James and Annie to wait on the porch as he stepped inside. The officer pushed open the unlocked door and listened from the threshold before going in.

"Mr. Lorentzen, it's the police. We're here to help you!" Parson shouted. His head cocked sideways as he waited for a reply. Nothing. "We're coming in," he said. Before he crossed the threshold, he asked Annie, "Where did you last see your husband?"

She took a step toward the front door and pointed in the direction of the basement door. Her voice wavered. "Down in the basement."

"Russo, stay with them. I'll go down below and check it out."

Parson entered the house, crossed the parlor floor to the opened basement door and bellowed, "Hello? Mr. Lorentzen?" No answer.

He descended until he heard a moan and then hurried to Lorentzen's side. The man was sitting up, holding the back of his head with his left hand. He was steadying himself with his right hand flat on the floor, trying to roll onto his side to stand up. Parson squatted down and took Lorentzen's right arm, put it over his shoulder and pulled him to his feet.

"Let me take a look." He removed Lorentzen's left hand from his head.

Blood had stained the dirt floor, but the wound was no longer flowing.

"Well, looks like you took a good one. Let me help you." He put Alfred's arm around his shoulder and braced him up under his armpit.

"We'll get that looked at."

Once upstairs, Parson sat Alfred in a kitchen chair and found a towel to wrap around his head.

"What happened?" he asked Lorentzen.

"My wife and I were talking, and my stepson came in and attacked me for no reason."

James exploded in the doorway. "You lie, old man." He stepped through the door, carrying an iron bar. Officer Parson moved fast and blocked James's path. "Put it down. Now."

The eight to ten seconds seemed a lifetime before James lowered the bar to the floor, backed out and stood beside his mother.

Officer Russo motioned James and Annie to step back when Parson and Lorentzen reached the porch. James and his stepfather glared at each other, as Parson guided Lorentzen by the arm down the front steps.

Lorentzen stopped and threw his arm back against Parson. "I don't need to get checked out," he slurred. He glared at James. "We take care of our own. Don't we boy?"

Officer Parson ignored him and kept moving. "Yes, you do need to get checked, sir. In fact, we're all going to the station to straighten all this out. The doc is right next door to the station. He'll come over and take a look at you."

As the police ushered James and the Lorentzens down the walkway, Edward Paulson, the next-door neighbor shouted, "You're in for it now, kid!" His wife's sympathetic eyes asked Annie if they could do anything for them.

Annie shook her head "no" as she untied her apron and draped it over the porch railing. She patted her hair, stiffened her shoulders and followed down the steps behind her husband.

After giving their brief statements, James and Annie sat in silence on the station bench as Dr. Hubbard examined Alfred. The water in the washbowl swirled with blood as the wound was cleaned. The doctor prodded, Alfred winced, and James grew angrier.

Finally, Dr. Hubbard picked up the washbowl and placed it on the sink. He updated Officer Parson on Alfred's condition, washed up and left the room.

Annie and James stood as Officer Parson approached.

"Mrs. Lorentzen, the doc put a couple of stitches in the wound. Your husband will have a good headache, but the doc said you can take him home now."

"What do you mean take him home?" James lurched forward off the bench. Annie grabbed his arm to stop him, but she was not quick enough. The short burst from Officer Parson's fist disappeared in James's abdomen, knocking him off balance.

"Better start thinking before you jump, boy. I don't want to hear of another problem with you."

James doubled over. His hands clenched around his middle, knuckles blanched white, "But what about...."

"You've been warned. Shut your trap, boy. Now, you take your mother home. Both of you need to learn a little respect for the head of your household."

James's eyes pleaded as he searched his mother's face waiting for her protest. She averted her eyes and said nothing. He walked out of the station alone.

***

Well into the night, Annie sat by the fire to ward off the chill. Her fingers moved deftly over her neglected darning. The house was quiet, too quiet. When they returned from the station, Alfred retired to their bedroom. She assumed he went to sleep because of his headache. James was not home yet, and she welcomed the mindless work and tried not to think about the day's events. Eventually exhaustion crept over her and she fell asleep in her rocking chair.

A noise startled Annie awake. She sat up straight and glanced at the Chelsea clock on the mantel. She picked up the darning, placed it in the basket of wool scraps beside the chair and got up. She tiptoed to the bedroom and opened the door. From a distance, she saw Alfred lying half on, half off the bed. He had vomited in the porcelain bowl on the night table.

Her fingers gingerly touched around her blackened eye and throbbing cheekbone before she shut the door and returned to her chair by the fire.

Two days later Alfred Lorentzen developed a fever and became too weak to leave his bed. He didn't appear to be making a recovery; in fact, his condition was deteriorating. Dr. Rowley was called to the Lorentzens' home. After an examination, the doctor recommended that Alfred be transferred to the hospital, and town officials determined that James should be arrested.

Officers Russo and Parson were sent back to the house to make the arrest. The two rounded up James and Annie and told them to sit at the kitchen table.

Parson looked down at James, "James, according to the statement you made the other day, you assaulted your stepfather."

"What about it?"

"Doc said you didn't do that damage with your fists."

"Didn't say I did."

James never saw Parson's foot coming. Air exploded from his lungs as the chair teetered on its legs before collapsing and dumping him on the floor.

"What are you? A smartass?"

James held one arm across his chest as he struggled onto his knees. "What difference does it make what I hit that bastard with?"

Parson's nightstick smacked down on the table. "We're here to tell you Mr. Lorentzen is not recovering. Seeing that it is now a grave situation, City Marshal Marchant sent us to bring you in as well as the weapon you used. It will be entered in as evidence."

Before James could answer, Annie stood and gasped, "I threw it away."

"Threw what away? Why? And where did you dispose of it?"

"It was a big wrench. It frightened me, and I didn't want such an ugly thing in my home. I threw it away in a trash barrel down on the docks."

This surprised James. He searched his mother's face, but she turned away, avoiding his eyes.

She lied…that was a lie. She hadn't the time to do that after she picked it up. Maybe she did it later in the night, he thought. He was so mad at the police station that he left without her. Yes, maybe she went down to the docks after she returned home.

Officer Parson turned to his partner, "Russo, check the house out."

Russo left the kitchen. He was annoyed with domestic disputes and was more than happy to let his partner deal with those two. He observed the tools on the cement ledge at the top of the stairs and decided to search the house from the bottom up. *The Lawson kid probably grabbed the wrench from here.* Every step creaked as he cautiously made his way to the basement.

As he descended the stairs, a draft of cold, damp air sent a chill through his body. The small, rectangular windows were up high on the wall and didn't allow much light into the basement, but they were not tightly sealed against the outside elements. The glass was opaque from years of dirt and dust.

Russo took out a match and struck it on the rock wall. He cupped one hand over the other as he walked over to light the lantern. The lantern glow did nothing to warm the room, but it did highlight the area where Alfred's blood had seeped into the compacted dirt floor.

"Jesus," he muttered as he stepped around the imprint of Lorentzen's body still visible in the dirt beside an oak barrel. He walked the perimeter of the room, discovering canned preserves and other provisions squirreled away for the winter months.

Russo went back upstairs and searched the two small bedrooms off the hall. He checked the parlor sideboard, pulling the linen out of each drawer.

As he turned around, he saw the trail of dried blood leading to the attic. He made his way up the attic stairs to James's bedroom. The small area was furnished with a dresser, trunk and standing mirror. In the front corner, under the eaves, stood an undersized bed covered with a horsehair mattress over a rope-strung box frame. He inspected a dark, rust-colored stain in front of the mirror and checked under the mattress and in the dresser for the weapon. He was about to go back down when he noticed a smudge on the hallway wall at the top of the stairs. It was to the right of a hanging curtain, used to cordon off the eaves which Annie used as extra storage space for linens.

It was a partial fingerprint, as if someone had leaned against the wall. Russo pulled the curtain aside and found various things stored in boxes on makeshift shelves. A basket full of wool scraps was on the floor. The one on top had a familiar rust-colored spot. He bent down and picked up the pile. The hairs on the back of his neck tingled. He threw the scraps to the side and squatted to get a better look at a blood-stained wrench. He took a breath, sucking air deep into his chest. Russo wrapped a piece of cloth around the wrench, stood up and carried it downstairs to the kitchen.

Annie, James and Parson watched as Russo placed the bundle on the kitchen table. He looked at each of them before he flipped the cloth aside, exposing the monkey wrench.

The uncomfortable silence was broken by Parson. "Mrs. Lorentzen, is this the wrench you told us you threw away in a barrel down at the docks?"

Annie looked over at her stove, ignoring the officers.

"Answer the question, Mrs. Lorentzen."

"Yes." Annie's insolent answer was a surprise to the officers, but it hit James like a slap across the face. Questions began to spin around in his head.

Parson refolded the cloth and nodded to Russo. "Well, it looks like you'll both be accompanying us to the station."

Annie thought that, in time, her second husband and son would get along, but James resented Alfred's presence in the house and, as the neighbors were well aware, there had been many violent outbursts in the home. Annie sat at the police station on the hard oak chair, knowing her loyalty would soon be tested. She would have to make a difficult choice between her husband and her son, but the truth was she had already made it when she picked up that horrible, bloodied tool.

***

Chief of Police Charlie Figgins wanted a signed, sworn statement regarding the events from all the people involved, including the victim when he was able to do so. James had already admitted the act, but according to the officers on the scene there were some discrepancies, like the weapon being found hidden in the closet, after Mrs. Lorentzen asserted that it had been thrown away.

James was kept in a holding cell until the next morning when they planned to escort him to the hospital so his stepfather could identify him as the assailant in front of witnesses. James wondered why there was ever a question. He had told them he was protecting his mother, but he had a questionable reputation around Gloucester, where his behavior was known to be as predictable as the tides. He was trouble, a brewing storm on the horizon, bound to hit the mainland. Some of the townsfolk thought it was only a matter of time before he was in serious trouble.

James's hands were handcuffed behind his back. One of the policemen held his right arm and forced him through the hospital door. They stopped to inform the nursing station they were taking him to face his stepfather and be formally identified as the perpetrator who assaulted Alfred Lorentzen. A nurse motioned the solemn group to follow, and she led them down the dingy hall to Ward 201.

The dim light cast eerie silhouettes on the sheer white curtains that separated the patients. The officer maneuvered James toward the second bed. James's mouth went dry. The silence became an uncomfortable hum that vibrated his ear canals.

The man on the bed was frail, his gray pallor merged with the dingy white sheets. James thought for a minute this wasn't his stepfather. *This couldn't be that monster, Lorentzen.* He stopped moving forward and stared at the withering figure on the bed, until the cop pushed his baton into his lower back. "Move, boy, right up to the bedside. Stay on the left."

Six people stood on the right side at the head of Alfred's bed. He knew City Marshal Marchant, Inspector Sullivan, Dr. Hubbard and Dr. Rowley, and he guessed the sixth person standing beside the nurse was a lawyer. All eyes were on James as he inched up along the rail until he was parallel to Alfred Lorentzen's head.

The lawyer leaned forward. "Mr. Lorentzen, open your eyes, please. Mr. Lorentzen?" Lorentzen's eyes fluttered before they opened.

It was obvious he struggled to focus them.

The policeman holding James's arm asked a question. "Mr. Lorentzen, sir, we need a moment of your time. Do you recognize this young man?"

With great effort, Alfred Lorentzen turned slowly toward the voice. His eyes widened when he saw James.

"Yes," he whispered.

The officer leaned closer to Lorentzen's face and asked his questions in a slow and clear voice. "Is this your stepson?"

"Yes," Lorentzen answered.

"Was this the young man who attacked you and hit you over the head?"

Alfred's eyes taunted and held James's gaze. He didn't say anything for a couple of seconds; he watched James stare back at him.

James felt a defiance rise up inside. He would not allow himself to be unnerved by this bastard.

Alfred's flat, raspy voice seemed to rally when he responded, "Yes, that's him, he did this to me. James Lawson attacked me."

Infuriated, James pulled and twisted his shoulders against his cuffs. "I'll do it again too, old man, if you don't leave her alone." The officer jerked him around and pushed him to the door. "Another outburst from you and you'll feel *my* baton on the side of *your* head!"

Chapter 5   Annie

Annie Lorentzen's life was falling apart, one piece at a time. Her son was in jail, she had perjured herself, and she sat at her husband's bedside watching his life slip away. His consciousness was fading minute by minute, announced by the loud, irritating tick of the clock on the hospital room's wall.

If he dies, I will have lost two husbands, and I'm getting older. There is no glow to my skin, my eyes. Who will want me? How will I be able to support the house?

She had been holding his hand for hours, with her head hung down, too weary to hold it up, when she noticed a change in the room. It was getting colder. No, wait, she thought, it was Alfred who changed. The warmth in his hand was gone. She felt the room was getting cooler, but didn't understand the implications of this right away. Suddenly the reality of what was happening hit her all at once. Alfred was gone. One minute he was here in the room with her and the next, he was gone. Dead. She was a widow.

Annie was surprised she didn't feel the way she expected; instead she felt guilt that her sorrow wasn't for her deceased husband, but rather for herself and her son. What would happen now?

They'll charge James. They'll charge my boy, my James, with murder. I'll be alone again.

She put Alfred's hand gently on his chest, stood and walked out to the nursing station.

The hospital informed the police of Alfred's death, and they contacted the district attorney's office. The DA instructed the hospital to arrange for Alfred's body to be taken to Greeley's Undertakers, a local funeral home. An autopsy was scheduled for later that morning.

When the initial formalities were done, Annie stood on the front steps of the hospital and contemplated what to do next. There were people to contact, a funeral to arrange, but she couldn't think straight, knowing James was sitting in a jail cell. The walk home in the cold air would help clear her jumbled thoughts.

With each aimless step she took, she sank lower into the dark recesses of her mind where all she wanted to do was survive. No matter what, she always survived. She made it okay after she buried her first husband, and she would this time too.

Once Annie confirmed this to herself, she became aware of her surroundings. She was already downtown, standing in front of the mercantile window. The furious whispering of two women standing in the doorway brought her out of her musing. They threw furtive glances her way, and it was obvious they were discussing her. The townsfolk had been acting like she had the plague, and Annie would not succumb to humiliation. She stiffened her shoulders and raised her head up high as she walked by the old biddies. This would pass. She would show them all.

Chapter 6   Myles Meets Charlie

Myles made sure he was early for his one o'clock meeting with Charlie, so he could enjoy a few moments speaking with the beautiful Miss Thomas. He walked to the nursing office and stopped short inside the waiting area. Behind the desk was a woman in her sixties, batting her false eyelashes behind oversized, turquoise, jeweled glasses. She reminded him of a strutting peacock in heat.

She looked up at him. "How may I help you, sir?"

He walked up to the desk, disappointment evident on his face. "Uh, hello. I'm Myles Bingham. I have an appointment in fifteen minutes with a patient here. Charles Lawson. His charge nurse is supposed to do the introduction."

The peacock thumbed through the appointment book. Her face wrinkled when she snapped her gum, causing her glasses to slide down her nose. She pushed them back up with her index finger and answered, "Yes, you're on the schedule with the head nurse, Jean Harrington. Have a seat please. *Snap.* I'll give her a call to let her know you're here. You're a bit early, sir."

"Yes, I am." Myles blushed, and he cleared his voice and looked around the room. "Where is Miss Thomas? She made the arrangements for me, and I'd like to thank her."

"Oh, yes, she asked me to cover her for an hour or so. *Snap, snap.* Her fiancé came to take her out to lunch. Isn't that sweet?" *Snap.*

"Yeah, sweet," he grumbled. "I mean, that's nice." He went over to the chair and sat down, slowly shaking his head in disbelief.

Fiancé? Boy, am I off my game.

A couple of minutes later Head Nurse Jean Harrington came and introduced herself. Myles could smell the starch from the matron's crisp uniform as the no nonsense nurse spoke with a cordial, but direct voice.

"Hello, Mr. Bingham." She addressed him with a curt nod of her head.

"Miss Harrington, thank you for your time." Myles put his hand out, but dropped it quickly when she didn't reciprocate.

"No problem, but before we get started, Mr. Bingham, I want you to be aware of the men you'll see here. A 'casualty of war' is such a broad statement. Their wounds could be life-taking, or life-threatening, but they are *always* life-changing. Wounds can be so visible that people will shun you or so invisible that other people cannot comprehend or understand you. These men are fine human beings. I take it that you will remember those points on this visit."

Myles didn't know why she seemed to be chastising him, but he quietly complied. "Yes, I understand. Thank you, Miss Harrington."

He followed her to the third floor, down long hallways lined with haunted faces. Someone was visiting Charlie, so they waited a couple of minutes outside his room. As the man was leaving the room, Myles heard him say, "Confession is good for the soul, it heals what ails you. No worries my son, St. Patrick was a sinner and look at his legacy. See you tomorrow, Charlie."

A priest came out to the hall. His shoulders were stooped and bent forward as if he carried a heavy load on his hunched back. Despite the physical challenge of this deformity, his head was held high, and the first thing Myles noticed were his watery blue eyes, sparkling brightly against a tanned face, covered by a crown of thick, white locks.

"Good afternoon. Excuse me." The priest nodded them.

Myles and Miss Harrington acknowledged him and stepped aside to let him pass when Myles decided to speak to him. "Good afternoon, Father."

The priest stopped and turned with surprising agility, "Mulcahy is the name, Father Mulcahy. I'm the hospital chaplain. Is there anything I can do for you and this lovely lady?"

"I'm Myles Bingham. Pleasure to meet you, Father. Do you have a moment to speak after my visit with Charlie?"

"Of course, I have a small office, more like a closet than an office," he winked at Miss Harrington. "You'll find it down on the first floor, in the building's bowels, next to the chapel," he said with another wink. "I think they want me close to the enemy, if you know what I mean." He turned and shuffled off, his hand waving goodbye in the air.

Myles stopped Miss Harrington before she crossed the threshold of Charlie's room.

"Dr. Templeton said he can speak, is that right?"

"Yes, Charlie can speak. We believe he either can't hear well or he chooses not to. I believe it's a little of both." She opened the half-closed door, and he followed her into a cheery, brightly lit, private room with a bed, a chair near the window and a dresser. Toiletries covered the top of the dresser along with a checkerboard, a vase with some wilting flowers, and a deck of playing cards. A calendar hung on the wall with the days past crossed out.

Charlie was sitting up in a reclining chair by the window, his legs up, covered by a plaid, wool blanket. On his night table between the chair and the bed were a pitcher of water, a glass and a radio.

Miss Harrington made the introductions.

"Good afternoon Charlie, Mr. Bingham is here to do a feature article on you in his magazine. We're hoping someone will recognize you." She stepped back and let Myles approach him.

Myles began, "Charlie, do you mind if I call you that?"

He waited, but didn't receive any kind of acknowledgment from Charlie, only a curious tilt of the head and a suspicious look. Bingham pulled over the visitor's chair and sat facing Charlie. Miss Harrington stayed standing by the dresser in case her patient needed something.

Myles looked around the room approvingly. "Nice accommodations." Charlie looked at him and then turned to stare out the window. Myles took a small notebook and pen out of his jacket and cleared his throat.

"Ok, let's get started. My name is Myles Bingham and, as you were told by Dr. Templeton, I'd like to do a story on you in my magazine to see if anyone recognizes you. You've been here since 1945, so that's, let's see, twelve years now. That's a lot of time lost, although I know from Dr. Templeton that many agencies attempted to ID you about one year in, but to no avail."

Charlie's mind was churning as he turned away from the window to look at the reporter. What difference does it make anymore? I'm good here, can't do it on my own anymore. There's nothing out there for me, only trouble. His face was flat, emotionless, but his brown eyes were sharp, which did not go unnoticed by Myles.

"Let me go over how you got here." Myles flipped through papers he brought with him. "You were one of the wounded that came in on the USS Lejeune in '45. The paper in your pocket and the ship's manifest both stated that you were Charles A. Lawson, from Boston, forty-nine years old, and had served on the *Cutty Sark*. Is that right?"

No answer. Myles looked at Miss Harrington, who shrugged her shoulders.

Charlie smiled and nodded. He could string this man along to break the monotony and he might like the publicity. Being a mystery to people was the only con he had left to play.

Of all names, the Cutty Sark. That was surely Lefty's warped sense of humor since it was his favorite beverage of choice. I wonder what ever happened to Lefty.

In the past twelve years, Charlie had all the time in the world to reflect on his life, the people who were in the past and the people who surrounded him now. Sometimes he felt like two different people who took turns watching the other one and their reactions. He wasn't sure why he chose not to speak at times. Maybe it was a way of holding people and memories at bay.

In the beginning he was too ill, but as time went by, he had no choice except to hide, and Charlie soon became aware of how different his life was going to be at the hospital. But now, this was a game. He was just an old man living in his head and he didn't have to hide from anyone.

Everyone had their own speculations about him. The years were passing quickly and people accepted that he was Charlie, a nice old man, a mystery that would never be solved and would someday fade away only to be known as an urban legend.

Charlie would replay his life in his head over and over again, changing parts and thinking how it would have played out if he had made different choices. *It all came down to making choices, like Mom had told him when he was a young boy.* Charlie was getting tired and found himself drifting off into the past, the reporter's voice droning in the background, until he heard Myles clear his throat.

"Charlie, are you with me?"

Charlie opened his eyes and spoke. He recited his name, age and ship in a haunting monotone. "Charles Lawson, forty-nine years old, *Cutty Sark.*" As Charlie spoke he flashed back to 1929 to a man named Jones, who kept stating his name over and over. Jones was the man James had run down with his taxicab who couldn't be identified. Repeating his name and with no family to claim him. Charlie remembered thinking back then how nice it would be to disappear. *I got my wish. I turned into him. Ironic.*

"The war is over Charlie. You're not a prisoner of war. You are safe here. Myles continued, "Charlie, the *Cutty Sark* is a training ship in England. That ship wasn't in active service when you came here. It hadn't been for years."

"I crewed on the *Himonea*," Charlie flatly recited.

"Charlie, the crew of the *Himonea* was interviewed after you made that statement a year ago and no one knew or recognized you."

No answer.

"Were you in the Merchant Marine?"

No answer.

"You have tattoos that a mariner would have."

No answer.

"What about when you were a boy? Do you remember your parents or where you grew up?"

No answer.

Myles thought he saw a flicker of something in Charlie's eye. He wasn't sure what sparked, but his question about his parents had resonated with him. He watched Charlie's eyes glaze over and realized Charlie was somewhere else. Somewhere in his mind. Not in this room.

***

Charlie's parents were more visible in his mind than ever. He especially had vivid dreams of the day his father died. They bothered him terribly, which was one of the reasons he spoke to Father Mulcahy so often. The priest was the only one besides Charlie who knew what happened that day out in the waters off of Gloucester.

Charlie Lawson's father had been a strict disciplinarian with rigid household rules that his family was expected to adhere to without question. Their relationship had always been volatile, and the harder his father was on him, the harder Charlie would try to figure a way back into his good graces, but nothing seemed to work.

On the day his father died, thirteen-year-old James, a.k.a. Charlie, was helping him pull their lobster traps to re-bait them. While teetering on the edge of manhood at times, James would feel waves of uncontrollable rage and, unsure of how to handle his emotions, he frequently flew off the handle. The one thing he did know was he would not take any more beatings at the hand of his father.

Charlie never talked to anyone about what happened that day, until he told the priest. His nightmares were coming to the surface, and the priest told him this was his brain's response to the private war within him. He thought the priest a perfect confidant, tied by his own vows of silence; he in turn could only listen. The same as Charlie had done for the soldiers here for many years. Father Mulcahy could not divulge Charlie's most private confessions and Charlie liked the priest's Irish brogue, which reminded him of Lefty.

Charlie was vaguely aware of Myles's voice droning in the background, but he couldn't focus on what he was asking him because he kept drifting into the past. Drifting to his mother's kitchen table when she asked him how his father died. *James, what happened that day?* He remembered what he told her. *It was an accident, Ma. Pa's foot got tangled in the trap lines.*

The memory of that day played like a movie in Charlie's mind. He saw the small boat off the eastern point. At dawn the water was like a mirror reflecting the rising sun. James had expected a beating that morning when his father had dragged him out of bed, his breath sour with moonshine. Instead he was told they were going out to pull traps. James did the heavy pulling while his father drank and preached.

After the fourth trap was re-baited, his father was slurring his words and he took a step toward James. He said something about how James didn't do it right. James angrily pushed the trap overboard just as his father stepped inside the coiled rope. The line spun over the side pulled down by the weight of the trap. James's father lurched starboard and tumbled into the water.

Charlie saw the water splash up over the side of the boat and watched his other self, James, the boy, lean over the gunwale above his father, knife in hand prepared to set him free from the rope, until he remembered. Remembered all the beatings, the name calling, his fear and moments later realizing it was too late. He had waited too long and in slow motion, ever so slowly, he watched his father's wide-opened eyes sink below the surface, the salt water blurring his view, distorting his father's face, revealing the monster he truly was. Then, James took a deep breath in and cut the line. He did cut it. He showed his mother the cut rope. He didn't understand what the problem was, he showed all of them. *I meant to cut it off faster. I meant to…*

***

"Charlie? Charlie, are you with us?" Myles looked at Miss Harrington for help. Her only response was a shrug of her shoulders. He stayed with Charlie for a little over an hour and got nowhere, but Myles had a keen eye for deception, and as he observed Charlie, he knew Charlie was as sharp as a tack. He was curious to see what the priest had to say about the old man.

Miss Harrington and Myles said their goodbyes to Charlie even though they didn't know if he heard. They left the room to talk out in the hall.

"What do you think, Mr. Bingham?" she asked him.

"I don't know. As you saw, I didn't get far. He seems to remember some things, but those things don't add up to his age or the dates the ships were active. He does enjoy the company, but after a while he would seem to drift."

Nurse Harrington smiled, "Oh yes, in the last couple of years he's loved the attention. He gets cards from people who have heard about him. Someone left that radio at the nursing station as a gift. He even has a daily checker game going with one of the nurses, but even with the attention to keep his mind active, we've noticed he is drifting off more frequently."

"I noticed Charlie is missing one of his index fingers. Was that injury from the war?"

"No, it wasn't. There's a notation on that in his admission chart. The doctor believed it looked like an old surgical amputation. It was nicely healed, maybe done a couple of years before he was admitted here. Lord knows we get our own share of finger amputations from the shipyard."

Shipyard, Myles muse. "I just don't know what to make of Charlie. My intuition says Charlie knows he's got quite the life here," he said. As soon as the words were out he knew he overstayed his welcome with nurse.

She looked sharply at him. "Yes, Mr. Bingham, it's a good life if the price you want to pay for it includes your legs and your independence. I'm sure you can find your way out. Good day, sir." She left him standing there as she walked away in a huff.

29

Myles watched her go and thought she was too close to the old man. Too emotional. A nurse needs compassion, but a reporter, a good reporter gathers only the facts and works with logic. You answer the questions—who, what, why, where and how? —without emotion. There is an inbred intuition that someone with the nose for news listens to, and Myles Bingham had this. He would bet the Pulitzer that this man, Charlie, was the best con man he ever crossed paths with in his career.

***

Myles followed the signs downstairs to the chapel and found Father Mulcahy's office. Even though the door was opened wide, he knocked gently, so as to not startle the old man.

"Come in, my son, come in. Have a seat." The priest gestured to a chair that was beside his bulky wooden desk, not in front of it. The placement alone was inviting and promoted communication. Myles thought Father Mulcahy may be a wise man. He could give him valuable insight into the mysterious unknown soldier.

"Can I get you a cup of tea?" he offered. "Or coffee, if you prefer?"

"No, thank you, Father. I'll get right to the point, so I don't waste your time."

"Time is all most of us have in here. We have to make the most of every day until the day we meet our maker. Now what can I do for you?"

"Yes sir, ahh, I mean Father, well, I would like to ask you about Charlie."

"Aha, yes, Charlie. He's a character, that one. What about him?"

"I think he may be manipulating people. He's shrewd, has a roof over his head, three meals a day."

The priest sat back in his chair, fingertips tented, tapping gently against each other. "Are you judging your fellow man, Mr. Bingham?"

"I don't like the public being played. What do you make of his amnesia?"

The priest's eyebrows arched, "He has amnesia? I'm not privy to all of a patient's medical records. Only what I need to know, but amnesia? You could have fooled me. From what I've heard, people have made all kinds of speculations about Charlie. Some have said he may even be a Nazi. It was well known that Hitler put older men who knew English in dead soldiers' uniforms behind enemy lines as spies. What do you think of that?"

"I've heard the rumor and I wouldn't dismiss it, mainly because government resources couldn't locate any records on him. How long have you been at this hospital, Father?"

"Only eight months, so I'm still feeling my way around. Charlie has been here twelve years, and he'll probably meet his maker here. He comes to me because he has things to reconcile in his life."

"Why do you say that, Father?"

"My forte is the soul. If it was only up to his physical body, I believe we wouldn't be having this conversation now, would we?"

Myles pondered that statement before he answered, "I suppose not."

The old priest shook his head. "I can't imagine what he is going through. I'm humbled though."

"Humbled? By Charlie? Why's that?"

"Charlie wouldn't have anything to do with Father Robillard, whom I replaced, or the one before him, for that matter."

Puzzled, Bingham asked, "Why do you think that is? What reason would he have to speak with you and not the others?"

The priest sucked in the air as if he were about to say something, but the room stayed silent. Myles watched the priest's face knowing that he was searching for solutions to an internal, obligatory struggle between the mind of the man and the mind of the priest. Father Mulcahy blew air out of his lungs and slapped the desk as if he had an epiphany.

"I can truly say our unknown soldier is dogged by remorse. This man, known to us as Charlie, has unlocked many questions in my own heart regarding redemption." Myles raised his eyes hearing this. Father Mulcahy continued, "Yes, it's an interesting word, isn't it? I think when it comes to redemption, he is asking himself a common question all mortals ask."

"What question is that, Father?"

The priest searched Myles' face. "How much goodwill balances the scales? Is it measureable? Does it matter?"

At this, Myles looked up sharply, trying to get a good read on the priest. He thought priests probably made good poker players.

Father Mulcahy leaned back in his chair and folded his hands across his robust chest. "You want a reason he has decided to speak to me? It's simple. It's a reason I think that we all have to come to terms with some day. Age, along with the futility of his situation. Charlie is getting older, and without family and useful legs he knows he will never leave these hospital walls."

"So he is looking for redemption?"

"Yes, I told him a man is a reflection of the events in his life, and how these events are handled gives you the view into the soul of the man. There comes a time where a man has to face the man looking back at him from the mirror."

Myles agreed, "True statement, Father. Can you tell me anything else he brought up in your conversations?"

"Surely, you know I cannot speak of anything revealed to me in confession. I hope you are not asking me to violate a sacramental seal."

"No, of course not, but are all your talks conducted as priest and penitent?"

"It hasn't been all confession, you know. We have had some mighty interesting philosophical discussions as well."

31

"That's strange. Considering Charlie is a man of few words, it seems he shared most of them with you."

"Yes, I suppose you're right." His eyes twinkled. "Must be the collar." Father Mulcahy's index finger and thumb tugged gently on the white hair in his beard. Myles noticed this habit emerged when he seemed engaged in deep thought or possibly in a moral struggle.

"So what *can* you share regarding your time with Charlie to give me some insight into the man?"

The priest sat back in the chair, fingers as busy as a quilter in a quilting bee, and proceeded to share his thoughts with Myles.

"Let's see, one interesting talk we had involved memory. I would like to get another opinion on this subject, so I guess I can tell you the generic gist of the conversation." Father Mulcahy got up from his chair and paced as he spoke. "Charlie has a lot of old memories he has been dwelling on over the years, and I asked him if his perception of those memories was accurate. He took his time and thought about this and honestly didn't know if they were real, or they had been distorted by his trauma or passing time."

"I'm not following you," Myles said.

"Well, it has always fascinated me because I believe the course of your life could be affected by distortion of a memory."

Myles contemplated the priest's explanation. "Interesting, are you suggesting that one could create their own reality, and for that matter, it could keep changing depending on what they forget over time?"

"Yes, it happens with some people who have had hardships in their life or possibly abuse in childhood. It's a theory. When Charlie spoke with me in the confessional, the events he disclosed happened. Or so he believes they happened in the way he told me."

"Forgive me for playing devil's advocate, Father. That's his reality, but couldn't that also be a cop out? I mean the truth is black or white, or so the saying goes. I would think that you of all people would think this way."

"Even in my profession, lines get blurred, Mr. Bingham. Man is complicated and…yes, there are gray areas."

Myles took a moment to think about the priest's words and then asked, "You say Charlie only speaks on the up and up to you, as a man of the cloth?"

"Yes, he always insists I listen to him within the guidelines set for the sacrament of confession."

"Charlie *insists*?" Myles pointed out, "Is his insistence based on religious grounds or is he a man who makes sure there are no loose ends?"

The priest looked over his glasses at Myles and answered the question in an unwavering voice. "Have faith in your fellow man, son. Some men have dark roots that go deep, but some have stronger wings to rise above. My job is to guide them to reach high."

Father Mulcahy raised an eyebrow, and when he spoke again the tone of his voice was direct and resolute. "Listen, you can look at it whichever way you want. It's not up to us to judge, but oh yes, he insists he be heard under the sacrament. Every day, *every* conversation."

Chapter 7   The Townsfolk

Mary Pickford and Charlie Chaplin were making a huge splash on the big screen, and people were thankful for a distraction from all the bad news around the globe. The world was at war, and this New England fishing town was additionally rattled by Alfred Lorentzen's death.

The winter had been kind to Gloucester's fishermen. Normally, the end of March would be the first time the ice-bound harbor would be clear enough for the fleet's first trip out. Fortunately, due to an unusual early thaw, the fleet left the first week of March and beat the other coastal towns to the fishing grounds. After a bountiful catch they returned to port to find one of their own dead.

Gloucester was a close-knit community, with families entwined by marriages and hard work, so gossip was flowing when the newspaper's headline hit the street the morning after Lorentzen died.

Local Fisherman Dies after Brutal Assault at the Hands of Stepson

James Lawson is being held on a five thousand dollar bond for an assault charge with a dangerous weapon charge; could now be facing manslaughter. Alfred Lorentzen, the victim, received a fractured skull at the hands of his stepson and succumbed to his injuries yesterday. The young man admits the attack and claims he had provocation.

***

Simon McBride, the proprietor of the local bait and tackle shop, held court with local fishermen gathered around his store's potbellied stove. He read the article aloud to Alfred Lorentzen's former shipmates, the crew of the fishing schooner *Esperanto*. The mood in the room was ugly. In their eyes, James was already found guilty and sentenced.

An old-timer in the back yelled, "That kid was trouble since the day he was born."

A young man about James's age made his way up to the front where Simon stood. "Well, you know how Alfred got when he tied one on, meaner than a bluefish in a school of porgies."

Simon shook the paper in the air. "That's no matter to anyone. What a man does in a man's home is his own business, I say."

The first mate of the *Sea Scup* stood on a crate to be heard. "You know how womenfolk air their dirty laundry out for the world to see. Like Simon said, that's nobody's business."

"Now it's James we're discussing here, not Annie. That Mrs. has had her share of misery in past years," argued an unidentified voice from the back of the room.

The captain of the schooner *Ella Dora* faced the men. "That's the point, isn't it? Who was with her first husband, Big James, when he died? The answer seems as plain as scales are slick, if you ask me. The boy was with him. I lost a good crewman that day and no one knows what happened except the kid. Would you trust him working beside you out on Georges Bank?"

The crowd murmured their agreement. Simon shook his head. "Yes sir, you're right about that. That Lawson kid is a slick one."

Once again, the young man braved his elder mates' opinions. He stood on a chair and shouted above the din of the crowd, "Lawson had a reputation as a troublemaker, but who's to say, on that day, he may have been justified in his actions. No one knows for sure. That's for a jury to decide."

No one was listening.

Gloucester was a town divided. This act of violence upset everyone, and they all had an opinion. News of the crime was made worse by an unprofessional reporter, who described a horrific crime scene in his article after talking to his brother-in-law, who lived next door to James. The neighbor never liked James, and he embellished his story when he told his wife's brother about the bloodbath, after referring to James as a punk and a hooligan.

***

Frank Lorentzen, Alfred's brother, was on the crew of a fishing trawler that had returned to port. Harbor Master Spurr met the trawler as she docked to deliver the bad news. Upon hearing the news of the demise of his brother, Frank marched downtown and barged into the police station, determined to see justice done.

The bulging veins on Frank Lorentzen's weather-beaten face were purple. He tried to control his anger as he approached his old schoolmate, Chief of Police Charlie Figgins. Frank resembled every other fisherman in the area. His head was covered by an oilskin hat that gave protection from the brutal winds and salt spray. Wool nippers, which gave the men a solid grasp on their fishing lines, were hanging out of his pockets. It wasn't until he whipped the hat off that the chief recognized him.

The chief held his hand out to his friend. "Frank, I'm so sorry. Mora said to send her condolences when I saw you." Frank did not reciprocate; he stood his ground like a raging bull, head down, eyes glowering, shifting his weight menacingly from one foot to the other.

"Charlie, I want that boy held accountable for my brother's death, or else." Frank's words were slow and deliberate.

"Hold on there, Frank." He attempted to explain the legal process and quickly saw this was futile. "We're holding him, Frank. Let the law handle this."

"That Lawson kid better hang for this!" The vein on the side of Frank's forehead swelled and pulsed, his face contorted in grief. The chief was afraid Frank was going to have a stroke. In a compassionate gesture he put his hand on Frank's shoulder, but it was instantly cast off.

"Hold on, Frank. He'll be indicted, and he'll get a fair trial. That's the way it works."

"Fair!" Despair from his howl hung in the air like a shroud. "How fair do you think he was to Alfred? Charlie, that kid bludgeoned my brother to death."

"Look, we don't know that. James told us he was protecting his mother, and it was the only way he could stop Alfred from beating *her* to death."

"And you believe him?" Frank spat, spraying the chief with his spittle.

"I didn't say I believe him, but it's my job to see he gets a jury to decide what happened."

Sweat rolled down Frank's face, and his grief was palpable. The chief felt bad for him, but he had a job to do. He knew the Lawson kid had a history of being a troublemaker. There had been incidents when he was younger—stealing from the corner store and breaking into summer houses. He had warned Annie Lorentzen that she couldn't let her son run wild, but she had chosen to turn a deaf ear. After his father's accidental death in the outer harbor,

James's behavior had gotten worse. James defied anyone with authority and took to committing more serious crimes, one of which the chief was thinking of now. He had picked up James for assault and battery in the past, but nothing came of the charges because the victim left town.

As the chief thought about what he could say to appease the situation, Frank's body deflated. His shoulders slumped and the fight went out of him. Charlie was at a loss about what to do next. He was torn between doing right for his friend and doing the job that he was appointed to do by the townsfolk.

"Frank?" The chief reached out and touched Frank's shoulder with a large beefy hand in an attempt to reassure him.

The old salt's eyes filled with tears. Frank turned, walked toward the door and stopped with his hand on the doorknob. Quietly, without turning around, he whispered, "You know my brother was upset about the goings-on in that house. Things were not right."

Chief Charlie Figgins wanted desperately to console his childhood friend, but his words sounded hollow. It wasn't only his problem; the whole town was divided on this case. The Lorentzens happened to be a well-known family in Gloucester.

"Frank, I can assure you we'll take great care with the investigation."

Frank waved his arm in disgust at the Chief and walked out the door.

Chapter 8   James Receives Counsel

Carlton Baker took his hat off and waited patiently for Chief Figgins to open James's cell door. Baker was a tall, willowy man, his soft-spoken manner sometimes mistaken as sullenness until his conversations revealed intelligence peppered with empathy. James watched Baker bend his head to enter the cell, walk over and sit on the lower bunk bed beside him.

"Hello, James. My name is Carlton Baker. The court has appointed me as your counsel."

James studied the grave look on Baker's face. Suddenly he felt trapped. His eyes darted around the cell, and his heart pounded. "Is my mother...? Is she okay?"

"I've got bad news, James. Your stepfather took a turn for the worse and passed on this morning," Baker informed him.

James looked down at his shoes and said nothing, but he hoped Baker did not notice his eyes filling up. He swallowed hard and wondered if he was feeling sorry for his stepfather or for himself. Maybe both, but probably not.

James lowered his head into his hands. He mumbled, "What happens now?"

"Well, it's not likely this will stay local because it's no longer an assault case. The court will bring a substitute complaint of manslaughter at the hearing."

James stiffened, his voice quivered, "Will I be able to get out of here?"

"Not unless you can procure bail. They haven't changed it yet, it's still five thousand dollars."

"For what? He got what he deserved. That bastard was beating her."

"James, calm down. Let me handle this. I argued for a lower bail and suggested two thousand as a reasonable amount. Judge York, however, felt the current bail was a fair sum."

"Can't you ask again? Tell them I'm not going anywhere."

The counsel shook his head. "James, you were lucky. The judge alluded that he had initially considered making the bail even higher."

"It's useless anyway. I can't do five hundred, never mind five thousand." James glared straight ahead at the drab, gray wall.

Baker got up and put his coat and hat on, walked over and banged on the bars of the cell to notify the Chief he was done. He turned back to say something but James was lying on the bunk bed, an arm covering his eyes.

"I'll let you know as soon as I get the hearing date."

The cell door opened, Baker walked through and the Chief clanged it shut and turned the key. The sound of the door closing reverberated off the walls of the small cell like a bullet ricocheting until spent before the finality of dropping to the floor.

Chapter 9   Trial and Exile

Assistant District Attorney William McSweeney of Salem arrived at the police station, where he met Marshal Marchant and Inspector Sullivan for a conference on the Lawson case. Later, Mrs. Lorentzen was summoned to meet with them where she was examined at great length as her answers were recorded by a stenographer.

The day of the hearing arrived, not soon enough for James. Townsfolk filled the courtroom, leaving standing room only. Similar to a wedding, people gathered on one side of the center aisle or the other depending on their opinion of James's guilt or innocence.

Among the people testifying were James's mother, Annie Lorentzen; Alfred's brother, Frank; Chief Figgins; Walt Hillstrom, owner of the trawler James worked on; and neighbors abutting the Lorentzen residence.

All eyes were on James when he was led into the courtroom and directed behind a table that faced the judge. He kept his head down and turned his back against the rail that kept everyone on the other side of the courtroom, separated from him. *What else was new?* he thought. It was always him against the crowd on the other side of the tracks.

He was dressed in a black suit, white shirt and tie that his mother had brought to the jail. Upon Annie's arrival, the guard had taken the items and informed her she was allowed five minutes with James, but in that short time James noticed his mother did not meet his eyes. After she left, the guard brought the suit to the cell for him to change into for the hearing. He stared at it. This wasn't his, he didn't have a suit. His mother didn't have the money to procure one. He reached out and fingered the lapel and ran his hand down the breast of the jacket.

Repulsion overwhelmed him. *This was his suit.* His mother had brought him that bastard's suit for him to wear for the court hearing of Alfred's death.

James suddenly found this funny, so funny he laughed out loud. The guard heard him and walked over to the cell to check on James. The hair rose on the back of his neck as he watched James throw his head back in a manic roar of laughter, all control abandoned and tears streaming down his cheeks.

Murmurs and whispers filled the courthouse as the sheriff brought James in and led him over to the defendant's table. The gavel pounded as the court was called to order and the buzzing of voices dimmed. Several witnesses were sworn in by the government, including City Marshall Marchant; Inspector Sullivan; Officers Baker, Bickford and Cronin; Drs. Hubbard, Finnegan and Rowley; and others. James and his counsel conferred and waived the reading of the complaint.

Assistant District Attorney McSweeney opened the case for the government by outlining it for the court. He stated the purpose of the hearing was to assess if there was probable cause to hold James A. Lawson over for trial.

City Marshal Marchant was the first witness called. He was sworn in and ADA McSweeney asked him to recount to the court the events of Friday, March 24th.

Marchant spoke clearly. "The defendant, James Lawson, came to the station on Friday, March 24th, at about 4:45 in the afternoon and said that his stepfather had been beating his mother, he hit him to make him stop and wanted an officer to go to his house right away."

"And did you abide by his request?"

"Yes, I sent Officer Parson and Officer Russo there."

"Could you clarify where 'there' is, Marshal Marchant?"

"Yes, the Lawson-Lorentzen house at 3 Railway Avenue."

"We'll ask Officer Parson what he found when he arrived at the home, but for now please tell us what you know transpired."

"I wasn't on the scene, but I was back at the station when the officers brought back Alfred Lorentzen, the head of the household, after he was allegedly assaulted by his stepson, James."

"Did you get a statement from Mr. Lorentzen?"

"Yes, he told us his stepson hit him over the head."

"Did Mr. Lorentzen say if there was any provocation leading up to this incident?"

"No."

McSweeney frowned, "No? Is that 'no' to any provocation or 'no' to he didn't say?"

"Mr. Lorentzen told us he could think of no reason James had to do this. His quote was 'the kid is a bad seed'."

James's face burned red with anger. He attempted to jump up in protest but his attorney grabbed his arm and pulled him back down.

ADA McSweeney continued the questioning. "What happened next?"

"We called Dr. Hubbard to the station to dress Lorentzen's wounds, which he did."

Nearly every question from ADA McSweeney's mouth was objected to by Counsel Baker and every point was bitterly contested during the city marshal's testimony. The latter was given extended cross-examination and on redirect testimony he recited a statement to the effect that Lawson heard his mother and stepfather arguing and went in the room and hit Lorentzen over the head with a monkey wrench.

James jumped to his feet and shouted, "I didn't say anything of the kind. He was beating her to a pulp down in the basement." He was quickly quieted by the court officers, and Counsel Baker immediately held a consultation with his client.

Officer Frank Parson was the next witness and gave what proved to be important testimony. The ADA asked the officer to give his account of his role that day.

"On our first visit, Officer Russo and I accompanied the defendant and Mrs. Lorentzen to their house on 3 Railway Avenue on Friday, March 24th, and I engaged Lawson in a conversation on the way there. He told me his stepfather, Alfred Lorentzen, had been pounding his mother and he hit him with a monkey wrench."

"What did he say Lorentzen was doing to his mother when he approached them?"

"He said his stepfather was standing over his mother and had been beating her. He told me, 'I'll kill that bastard if he doesn't leave my mother alone.'"

"What did you find when you entered the home?"

Officer Parson glanced across the courtroom before answering. "When we arrived at the house, the door was open. I called out to Lorentzen, but he didn't answer. I found him in the basement. After helping him upstairs, I asked him what happened. Lorentzen informed us that they, his wife and he, were there talking things over when Lawson came in and hit him over the head with something."

"And what did you say?"

"I asked why James would hit him. He told me his stepson was always causing trouble in the household and he wanted him to leave. If I may quote Mr. Lorentzen, he said, 'It was all because of that little prick, he doesn't want to work and he's no good.' The wife said Lawson was her son and he was going to stay there."

"And where was the defendant at this time?"

"Lawson was extremely agitated. He had been standing in the doorway, but when Lorentzen said he was no good, I heard a noise," said the witness, "and when I turned, Lawson came into the room with an iron poker from the hearth, raised in a threatening manner."

"Show us how he held this poker, please."

The witness raised his hand up over his head and showed the court how the bar was held.

"Officer, please tell the court how you responded when he entered the room holding the poker in this manner."

"I jumped and grabbed him and told him to lay it down on the floor and to get along out of there. I informed him the police were in charge now and that his mother would not be hurt as long as I was on the scene. I found a towel to wrap Lorentzen's head and a washcloth to clean his face which was covered with blood. I told him to get his coat and hat on and come with us to get his head fixed up."

"Was this the weapon Lawson used to strike Mr. Lorentzen?"

"No, sir, it was not."

The witness testified that he took Mr. Lorentzen to the medical room at the police station and that the wound was dressed by Dr. Hubbard.

Dr. Hubbard was called to the stand and testified that he had dressed Lorentzen's head and had placed three stitches in the wound. He said it was possible for a man under those conditions to have a fractured skull, but not as a rule, as some symptoms of it generally would show immediately. After treating him on Friday, March 24th, the next time he saw the patient was on the following Monday night at the hospital when Alfred was failing. He agreed the blow on the head might have been caused by a monkey wrench as originally stated.

Under cross-examination, Dr. Hubbard stated again that no fracture of the skull appeared when he dressed the wound at the police station. He testified he saw a marked depression in the skull about the size of the end of his finger which was not there on his prior examination. On the following day, Tuesday, he received notification from the hospital to be present for the police interview of the dying man.

Dr. William Rowley was the next witness. He testified that he treated the patient on his removal from his home to the hospital. At that time he was in a declining condition. Dr. Rowley stated that great force caused the wound, and that on examination of the skull, he believed that the monkey wrench displayed as evidence could have produced this wound.

Marshall addressed the court and announced that Officer Russo was not available to testify, and then turned back to Officer Parson. "On your second visit to the residence, Officer Russo checked the house. Please inform the court of his findings."

"Yes, sir. Officer Russo had found dried blood drops in the parlor and followed them to the defendant's attic bedroom where he located a larger stain, possibly indicating where the weapon had been dropped. In a storage space in the hall, he located a large mechanic's monkey wrench, stained with dried blood, hidden under a pile of fabric scraps."

"What had Mrs. Lorentzen told you about the weapon?"

"When we asked her where it was, she told us she had thrown the wrench in the trash on the docks."

ADA McSweeney went over to the evidence table, picked up the monkey wrench and turned to address the court. "Let it be in the record that this piece of evidence is the weapon that caused the injury on Mr. Lorentzen and that upon his imminent demise this was found with blood on it at the home when it was searched. In an interview with Mrs. Annie Lorentzen, she stated she had thrown the weapon away, when in fact it was found in the back of an upstairs closet hidden under a pile of scrap material and horsehair blankets."

Annie was called to the stand. Counsel Baker approached the bench. "Mrs. Lorentzen, could you please explain to the court why you informed the police you threw the weapon away after your son, James, assaulted your husband?"

Annie dabbed her eyes with a handkerchief. "I was distraught, sir. I wanted it out of my sight so I buried it deep in a closet I don't use."

Counsel Baker attempted to show that one of the three stitches of the wound was broken when patient was brought to the hospital and asked Dr. Rowley if he had brought this fact to anyone's attention. Counsel indicated this could have been an entry for infection or a second blow to the head, suggesting perhaps the victim had been weak and fell and hit his head. Dr. Rowley testified that he did not recall that any of the stitches were broken or that he had spoken to any person in connection with the matter.

James listened intently to his counsel's theory of a second blow to the head. James was confused. What were they saying? He loosened the borrowed tie that suddenly felt tight like a noose around his neck.

Why did mother hide the wrench? To use it again? Is it possible that she...no! He flinched and looked around hoping he hadn't spoken his thoughts aloud. Surely a doctor would have noticed a broken stitch. Was it possible someone hit him on the head again after he was stitched up? James had been disgusted with everything that day, including his mother, and he had made himself scarce when he left the police station. He didn't know Alfred was brought to the hospital until they came and arrested him.

In answer to a subsequent question, Dr. Rowley stated that it was possible for death to result from infection of the wound. When called to testify to the holding of the autopsy, Medical Examiner Finnegan agreed with Dr. Rowley's statement that an infection could have been a contributing factor, but he saw no outward evidence of this. At this point, the defense counsel and Mr. Sweeney came to an agreement.

James's knees went weak. He exhaled and held onto the table to steady himself as Judge York addressed the court, "Probable cause of guilt has been found by the court and James A. Lawson is to be held on $5000 bond for his appearance before a jury in Newburyport, on Monday next. After interviewing witnesses, gathering evidence and receiving the initial results of the autopsy of

Alfred Lorentzen, ADA McSweeney has made the recommendation that the complaint against your client, James A. Lawson, be changed to murder. Mr. Lawson shall be held in custody without bail until the grand jury convenes. Bailiff, take the prisoner back to his cell."

The courtroom erupted in cries, most for and some against the ruling. Judge York beat the gavel furiously in an attempt to regain control. He gave up and walked out of the courtroom.

After the proceedings concluded, Counsel Baker met with James in his cell. "James, you have admitted to taking a life. We could probably stop this now."

"What do you mean?"

"As your counsel, I am suggesting you plead guilty to a lesser charge of manslaughter. Your mother's testimony of abuse is evidence enough for me to ask for a manslaughter plea."

"How long will I go to prison for?"

"I'll ask for the court to be as lenient as possible. I'll be straight with you, James. I don't know if they'll go for it, but I don't see where you have a choice, boy."

James sat on the edge of the cot, his head in his hands as he considered his options, but when he lifted his head up and looked around the small, dismal cell he quickly made his choice. "Okay," he agreed, his voice weak with resignation.

The next morning, the Gloucester front page read:

Lawson pleads guilty to manslaughter

A strong recommendation of leniency was returned by the court at the conclusion of a hearing on the charge of murder against James A. Lawson, following the death of his stepfather, Alfred T. Lorentzen, at 3 Railway Ave. on March 28, 1916.

A week later, James was sentenced by Judge Aiken to five years imprisonment, which term was suspended on his entering upon a bond to be of good behavior and an indefinite term of probation. Judge Aiken strongly suggested, in light of the strong emotions and division of the townsfolk in this case, that Mr. Lawson be of service, enlist in the war effort and go do something productive with his life.

Carlton Baker congratulated James on the outcome and advised him to read between the lines, get out of town and bid farewell to Gloucester.

***

Annie Lorentzen stood on the platform at the train station and watched her son throw his duffle bag up into the car before climbing aboard. For the first time in her life there was nothing left inside of her. The void left by the events of the past few months seemed insurmountable. On top of her many losses, she had been ostracized from the community.

The platform was crowded for a Tuesday. People scurried about checking the arrival/departure schedules, pulling luggage, greeting passengers and saying goodbye to family.

James turned to his mother and she rushed forward and hugged him.

"Oh James, you promise to write soon, won't you?" She didn't wait for an answer. Instead she dropped her arms, stepped back and smiled at two women standing near them.

"Good day, Mrs. Gardiner, Mrs. Blanding."

The women gave Annie a look of revulsion. In unison they turned away on their heels and walked off in the opposite direction, arm in arm and whispering.

Annie was outraged. A scarlet flush crept up her neck and consumed her face. "Did you see that, James? Those old biddies."

She knew she should feel loss, sadness, something, damn it, and she anguished over her lack of every emotion except anger. Seven years ago, it was her first husband, then Alfred and now James is going away. How could this happen to her?

Of course now that James is off to war, the family can put it behind them and won't suffer any more tragedy. Sorrow always seemed to follow her boy from such a young age. Maybe the townsfolk will be kinder to her now. James would be fine. He's young and will be off seeing the world, having adventures she would never have. Yes, better that he be gone from this town. Annie had no choice, she had to live here.

James boarded the passenger car. He chose a window seat, settled in and looked out at his mother as the whistle announced the train was ready to depart the station.

"All aboard."

Annie's gloved hand lifted in a ceremonious farewell wave to her son, possibly for the last time. She continued to watch James until a newcomer by the ticket counter caught her attention. Her hand dropped when the man smiled and tipped his hat toward her. Her transformation was seamless, yet at the same time, astounding.

A girlish smile snapped tight to her lips, like a corset on a mannequin as she raised a hand to primp her hair. Her thoughts were off and running in a whole different direction. She forgot about being at the train station to say goodbye to her son. Forgot she recently buried her husband. She smiled coyly at the man who politely held the door for her and she knew at that moment things were already looking up.

***

James sat on the train, his forehead pressed on the cool morning condensation that covered the window. This helped to lower the heat rising inside him as he tried to control his anger. A lump in his throat prevented him from a long goodbye. He was going to war and wasn't sure if he'd be back, but his mother seemed oblivious to this fact.

He watched his mother's every move as she turned to leave the platform. He saw the man and saw her face, then realized she never looked back at the train, never met his gaze for their final goodbye. Probably better that she hadn't, he thought. If she had, she would have known. She would have known her son inside and out. She would know he hated her at that moment. She would know that she had given birth to a monster.

Doesn't it take a monster to make one?

James wondered why she had hidden the wrench. Had she planned to use it? Did she use it? He would never know the truth. He opened his eyes for one last look at his home, but saw only his youth left behind in a gray blur of the train's motion.

He closed his eyes and listened to the train chugging out of the station and as the speed built up, the tighter he squeezed his eyelids, until his head ached.

Chapter 10   James Goes To War

Father Mulcahy's weekly meeting with Charlie was going nowhere this morning. He tried to engage him in conversation, but Charlie's eyes were glazed over and his mind years away.

"Charlie, can you believe the rumor about you being one of Hitler's spies during the war? What will they think of next?"

Charlie leaned his head back in the wheelchair and closed his eyes. He knew about war. His memory was branded with the images that never faded. He drifted back to the day he enlisted.

***

Beads of perspiration rolled down James's forehead, stinging his eyes. Today was the 19th day of June and the fourth day of an early season heat wave. It was also one month from the day his sentence was handed down, peppered heavily with the unspoken stipulation that he join the war effort and leave town, which he did without hesitation.

The weather wasn't the only thing making James sweat. He was standing in front of an Army sergeant, filling out his enlistment papers to go to war halfway around the world. This wasn't exactly what he had in mind when he was planning to leave home. That seemed so long ago now. All he ever knew were Gloucester and the sea. The men on his father's side of the family were fishermen from Nova Scotia, but he was too young to remember them with the exception his paternal grandmother, whom they visited the summer he turned six. He recalled some of the stories his father used to tell him and his siblings around the fire before he got too drunk and ruined the night.

After his dad's death, James's teen years took a rebellious direction. His mother chalked it up to James seeing his father die in an accident on the water, so she doted on him, so much so that even James had to agree he was spoiled by her, at least he was until the freeloader husband came along. But now, Alfred Lorentzen was also dead and the first leg of James's life—the formative years, as his mother called them—was behind him. He was saddled with mixed emotions, but he was moving on. On his own.

James's revelry was rudely pushed back into reality when he felt a shove in the small of his back and stumbled forward a bit. "Move up, soldier. Pay attention." James snapped, dropped everything and took a swing at the man behind him, but his attempt was abruptly stopped by a vice grip on his forearm.

"I'd turn around and mind your business, son, or you're out of here. We don't want any hotheads. Got it?"

The man had the dead eyes of a predator and they were focused on James. He recognized that look. He'd seen it before on a day he'd never forget. While out hand lining tuna, he was engaged for hours in a fight to land a bluefin tuna of considerable size when a huge shadow, right below the surface, rolled up on its side to get a long, cold look at James. It was the largest shark he had ever seen. He watched as the shark bit through his line before biting his prized catch in half.

The tension on his arm released, but he kept his eyes on the man as he bent down to pick up his belongings and turned quietly toward the front of the line. The shark glared at him as he continued to walk the line, sizing up the boys who came here in droves to sign up. His job was to make them become men simply at the signing of their names on enlistment papers.

James felt a slight nudge on his arm. The young boy behind him looked to be no more than sixteen years old. His long straw-colored hair framed a freckled face and water-blue eyes that jumped side to side with excitement.

"Hey," the boy said, "this is great, isn't it?"

James's face soured. "Oh, yeah? What's so great about it?"

"We're going to get to shoot those bastards."

James suddenly grinned at the young man's enthusiasm. "Ok, farm boy, you may have a point. How old are you anyway?"

A conspiratorial, toothy grin spread across his face. He leaned toward James and whispered, "I'm going to tell them I'm eighteen."

Good luck with that, James thought as he nodded in understanding, but he didn't agree. He wouldn't be here if he had a choice.

The line was long, but orderly. There was a different line for each of the items on the application check list. No one was talking, which was strange, because there had to be sixty or so men from all walks of life in the hall. Maybe a hundred. He was up next and as the man in front of him stepped away from the table, he saw an older woman look up at him and give him a perfunctory smile. Her long skinny neck reminded him of a crane he had seen down on the shoreline, pecking away diligently at the wet sand, devouring small crustaceans and mollusks. Her features were sharp, with a pointed thin nose and small peering eyes. With a stern look, she slapped a form and a pen down on the table in front of her and started her well-rehearsed spiel.

"I'm going to ask you a few questions and then I need you to sign this." She rattled them off in the raspy, monotonous voice of someone who recited the same blurb thousands of times and could easily do it in their sleep.

Her eyes scanned him as she asked rhetorical questions, answering them herself aloud, as she filled in the form.

"Color of hair? Black."

"Color of eyes? Brown." She flipped the card over.

"Ok, now, date of birth, please?" Questions snapped out of her mouth, firing one after another.

"March 19, 1896," he told her.

"Any distinguishing marks on your body?"

His mouth tightened and when he didn't respond right away, she must have felt the need to explain. "This is used for body identification, in case your dog tags are lost."

He tried to swallow before he answered, but his tongue felt swollen and his mouth was dry like sawdust. She noticed he was nervous, so she helpfully prodded him by reciting the same script she had to many boys before James. "Your mother must be so proud." She grinned, her teeth small and sharp, like a bluefish.

He managed a slightly mordant smile, "Yes, madam, she's proud I'm here." *She's glad I'm anywhere but home with her,* he thought.

"So?" she waited, keeping her impatience in check by the tapping her pencil on the desk.

"Yes?" James's voice cracked.

"Do…you…have…any identifying marks? Tattoos, scars?" Her impatience broke through as she slowly enunciated each word.

"Oh. No, none."

She filled in the answer on the last line, then with a dramatic flair she swept her arm up in the air and across the table like a crane taking flight, and handed him the form. Without looking up at him, she said, "Proceed to Room 7. Next!"

Room 7 was a sight to behold. The room was set up with various medical stations, all out in the open, with no screens for privacy. In front of each station were long lines of naked flesh. Each man carried his bundle of discarded clothes, wrapped with a cord. Some held the bundle lower than others to keep their last shred of dignity from being stripped away. All eyes were straight ahead on the back of the head in front of them.

An orderly waved James over to the first station and ordered him to strip. His clothes were taken, folded and wrapped with a cord in an efficient bundle and set aside on a chair. A doctor approached James, or at least he thought he was one because of the white coat he was wearing. James watched warily as the doctor pushed up his sleeves.

"Open your mouth wide, soldier," he ordered. James did as he was told and stood nervously as the doctor whipped the tongue depressor roughly side to side and up and down in his mouth. Then he took his thumb and pressed under James's eyes, shining a light in each one. He moved around behind James and ordered him to bend over.

James hesitated, looked around and launched a protest. "But…"

The doctor got in James's face. "Butt? You think you're funny? I am not amused, mister. This is not a joke, this is an order. Bend!"

For the first time in James's life he felt embarrassed, but he did as he was told. The doctor finished with him and the orderly shoved his bundle of clothes in his hands and prodded him forward.

The orderly yelled, "Move up to the end of the next station line. Close the gaps. Nuts to butts, men! Nuts to butts."

At the next station, a man stood behind a table and scrutinized James. Up and down his eyes went, sizing him up and then after looking at James's file, he scribbled something on a piece of paper and handed it to James.

"Get your gear in that line over there," he growled. "Then report to Room 8."

James picked up his sack and started to turn when he heard the sergeant say something to the recruiter and his assistant standing beside him.

"If anyone can straighten this little prick out, the Army can." A honking, sarcastic snort erupted from the sergeant's nose as he threw the file down on the table.

The recruiter agreed, "I know, selective service, my ass. This kid is lucky to be getting a reprieve." A stogie flapped up and down between his lips as he spoke.

The assistant, a pimply kid, newly enlisted himself asked, "What do you mean, Sarge?"

"What I mean is, this Lawson kid avoided going to the slammer on a manslaughter charge. Guess they figured he'll be a good one to have on the front lines. Yup, a real killer instinct, this one has."

***

In April of 1917, President Wilson asked Congress for a declaration of war, and James received his orders to ship overseas. His company was scheduled to sail on the *Saxonia* on September 25th. He stood on the dock in awe of the ship, waiting for the command to board her.

She's a beauty, he thought as he admired the graceful lines of the vessel.

Growing up on the coast, he had seen a lot of ships in his young years, but she was something to behold. The *Saxonia* weighed in around fourteen tons, but it wasn't so much her size that he loved. It was the unusually tall stack positioned amidships and surrounded by four beautiful masts that was her most distinctive feature. The *Saxonia* stood out from the rest and he stood nervously waiting to embark on her and on a new chapter in his life. He felt proud to sail on her and with voices raised singing Cohan's "Over There", James arrived in France on October 19, 1917.

War mobilization extended across the country. The large concentration of young men in close proximity in military training camps helped the pandemic of the great flu to flourish, and when troops were shipped overseas, the sickness went with them, adding to the misery.

These were dark years and fear weighed heavily in everyone's hearts. James was not sure of himself for the first time in his life and he wasn't alone. It seemed the young men who were the tough bravados in their old neighborhood gangs on their home turf hung with the same here. Like everyone else, they were trying to navigate their way through this war, but this wouldn't work for James because he was a loner.

The war was being fought in the trenches, and soldiers suffered everything from the wet and bone-chilling cold to trench foot and lice. James hunkered down against the side of the muddy trench and listened to the sucking sound of fellow soldiers' boots sinking into the thick quicksand-like mud. Often their boots stuck so steadfastly in the muck, they needed help to be pulled out. Now, they waited uneasily, their nerves tugged taut to the breaking point. It had been eerily quiet for many hours, a record the men knew would not hold.

***

James looked at the soldier across from him and broke the silence. "Hey, Macklin, you got a smoke?"

Macklin's cherub cheeks exuded his happy-go-lucky personality in the big Irish face.

"Indeed I do, friend. Sure wish I could offer you nice smooth bourbon with it," he wistfully drawled the words out as he shook his head in regret. The soldier opened the flap of his haversack and shuffled through the inside, pulled out a half-smoked stub, lit it and handed it to James.

James inhaled deeply and slowly let the air in his lungs slip out, relishing every second. He could feel the tension ease out of him, carried away on the smoke, at least for the moment. He nodded his thanks and after a few minutes he asked, "Where are you from, Macklin?"

Macklin grinned, "Lexington, Kentucky, son, where we have beautiful horses and fast women."

James laughed, "Well, I have to add that to my list of places to go someday."

"You sure do! We've got the finest horseflesh in the states. Our stables rival any in County Kildare, my family's homeland. Look me up, that is if we make it out of this hell hole. I don't have to ask you where you're from. You've got to be from Boston."

"Yup, north of Boston. Gloucester, Massachusetts to be exact. Guess you could tell from my accent."

"That's right. If you come out my way, the horses wouldn't have the slightest notion what you're talking about." He reached into his heavy coat, pulled out a crumbled picture and handed it to James.

James took the photo. "What's this? Your girl?"

"Yes sirree, best girl in the world, the love of my life, that's Lucy."

James looked at it. "It's a horse!"

"Sure is, best horse in the world too. She does what she's told. Loyal, smart, beautiful and I don't have to wonder what she's thinking. They'll never betray you."

James thought about that statement. "You might have a point, Macklin. Women may not be worth the trouble."

James liked Macklin for two reasons: he knew the right time to shut up and he never asked James about his family. Oh, he did once, but he must have had a knack for reading people, because he never asked again. Macklin could talk, though, and for the next few weeks James lived vicariously through Macklin's stories of his large family back in the sprawling bluegrass of Kentucky.

James figured if the war couldn't make him forget Gloucester, Macklin's stories would, so he let them transport him away. Away from the war, away from his past.

He often thought about where he would go after the war, if he were ever lucky enough to make it out of here. Days had turned into weeks, and weeks into months of trudging back and forth across Eastern Europe. Knowing that he would not be welcomed home again, James thought the big city would be the place to go, and he chose Boston.

His mother, Annie, had testified in his defense, but their relationship was never the same afterwards. After all, he had killed her husband, not to mention he was an embarrassment to his family in the town. James also had his own suspicions regarding his mother agenda and he had to learn to deal with them.

One day, he even thought he saw a twinge of fear on her face. *My God, she was afraid of him.* He had looked at her again, knew he was right and it angered him. He felt his blood boil. At that moment, he hated her as much as he loved her. Even after the trial was over, people never stopped staring at him. They did stop talking to him. They were aloof and work was nearly impossible to get. No one wanted him working on their trawler or on the docks, but that would never happen anyway because the judge had made it clear he was to leave Gloucester.

"Hey Lawson," Macklin broke him out of his dark memories. "Did you hear we're headed out?" His arms swung back and forth swatting the flies away. "Damn flies, I'll never eat rice again after all these disgusting maggots."

"Where are we going?"

"They're not saying, except it's a small town in France."

James thought about that, jumped up and grabbed Macklin by both arms. "Mack, moving on to France could be a good thing. Coming full circle, back to where we started. Maybe this will end."

And end it would. His division battled forward through heavy winds and torrential rain for five days. They navigated through woods without lights to guide them, forming a human chain by holding the haversack of their fellow soldier ahead of them. At times, the mud on some roads was knee deep and barely passable. The men pushed and pulled the artillery inch by inch through the countryside until they were close to exhaustion.

Once they reached their destination, they hunkered down to make camp, digging the six by three foot trenches that allowed them to stay below the enemy's line of fire. Standing up was a sure death sentence.

"What I'd give for a nice piece of fresh Atlantic cod right now." James bent over the duckboard to prepare dinner in the trench. "Instead, all we've got on the menu is a tin of Bully beef and rock-hard biscuits."

Macklin stooped over and waddled like a duck sloshing through the muddy water with a can of condensed milk to pour on the biscuits. "Here, pour this over them biscuits. That'll soften …" James never heard the end of the sentence. That was when the shell hit.

It hit a couple of hundred yards away, but the shrapnel cut through Macklin's flesh worse than any shark attack James had ever seen. The night sky lit up in a series of explosive flashes and he saw Macklin was still standing, his mouth opened in shock.

"Get down, get down!"

At first James thought he was okay, but massive amounts of blood bubbled up over Macklin's lower lip spilling down the front of him, and his body suddenly dropped to the ground like a lead fishing weight.

The earth shook as James crawled through the muddied water to pull Macklin's head up so he wouldn't sink. He propped him up against the dirt wall. The sounds were deafening, pain shot through his ears and mud, dirt and rocks showered over them.

"Macklin!" James yelled, but his voice was lost among the screaming men. His face was so close to Macklin's he could smell his sweet, sticky blood, but Macklin never heard him. He wondered if Macklin's blood smelled of Kentucky bluegrass, and then James wondered if he was going mad. He didn't know how long he stayed down beside Macklin's body, intent on surviving. He didn't want to be here. He wanted to pick his own battles and this was not one of them. The shelling went through the night and finally stopped at dawn's first light.

The silence was just as unnerving. James opened his eyes and saw the carnage. Then the inevitable appeared. Scavengers. The four legged kind. He heard the vermin before he saw them. Scratching and squeaking. Corpse rats! They were swarming everywhere, scampering in, out and over the dead. It was too much to take in. There were dozens of dead bodies near James alone and the disease-carrying critters were gluttonous in their sinister feasting, so much so that they fattened up until they were the size of the common house cat, right before his eyes. A couple of rats chewed on Macklin's boot leather and within minutes there were so many writhing and moving that James swore Macklin's body was coming to life again.

James used his rifle butt to knock them off Macklin's face. It took a minute to realize he would lose this battle, so he reached inside Macklin's uniform and retrieved Lucy's picture. He held it for a second before reverently placing it in the bottom of his haversack. James climbed out of the trench and never looked back.

***

The 26th division was in Saint-Mihiel in northeastern France, and on the morning of September 13, 1918, they were an integral part of the offensive, coming in from the west to join with the 1st Division from the east. The United States and France lost seven thousand men at the Battle of Saint-Mihiel before victory. James didn't know it at the time, but the war was almost over. They just couldn't see it through all the death and misery.

When the men of the 26th received the official word the war was over, the men celebrated and the wine flowed. It would take a few months to wrap up loose ends before going home. Preparation meant their first bath, delousing and burning the only set of clothes they had worn day and night during the war.

For James, the wait to step on home soil turned out to be a lot longer than some soldiers. Five months later, on February 23, 1919, he was still in Europe waiting to be shipped back to the States, when the dreaded flu pandemic caught up with him.

He was admitted to a military hospital where he experienced firsthand that there was another kind of war being fought in Europe. For every bullet that killed a US soldier, the Spanish influenza took another. James was so close to going home and now a damn cold was trying to kill him? But once again, he was one of the lucky ones. He recovered and was discharged home to the states on a transport carrier that arrived in Boston on April 4, 1919.

Chapter 11 Myles 1957

Myles Bingham sat alone nursing his third Manhattan. He had gone for a drink after work with other magazine staffers, who had long since gone home to their families. Once they left the bar, Myles's thoughts turned to Charlie, the unknown soldier.

This must be how Charlie feels all the time. Alone. Myles wondered what he would do if he were facing a vague existence and his mortality. It's not like he had a family either. His career was not conducive to being tied down with a home life. He shivered. The thought of ending up old and alone frightened him to his core.

Nothing about Charlie made sense and, as a reporter, Myles knew to shake off his pity party and get down to investigating.

The priest wouldn't be a help to him. Charlie must have something to hide if he requires all his conversations to take place during confession. Father Mulcahy's hands were tied by his vows, but something he said stuck with Myles, on a personal note. The priest said Charlie's two possible reasons for starting to talk were age and redemption.

The government had given up the search, but he had to be someone's family, a brother, a father, an uncle. Something. Everybody makes someone happy, disappoints people, leaves a mark somewhere on somebody. He needed a direction to start in, so he jotted down some notes on his cocktail napkin, folded it in half and put it in his shirt pocket.

He watched Warren, the bartender, drying the wine glasses, holding each one by the stem up to the light, checking for water spots and vigorously rubbing the glass.

Warren was an excellent bartender who knew his customers. Myles liked to be treated with an air of importance and left to his thoughts. He knew how to read people, kind of like Myles, who could smell a story.

Myles leaned forward and pushed his glass away. Warren's attention to detail picked up immediately on this imperceptible movement and headed Myles's way.

"Can I get you anything else, Mr. Bingham?"

"No, thank you. I'm going to call it a night, but first, I have a question."

Warren put the glass and rag down and put both hands, palms down, on the bar. Listening was part of his job and he took it seriously.

"Of course, sir, ask away."

"You see all kinds of people in your line of work. I'm sure you hear their woes when they come in to drown their sorrows." Warren was nodding as if he were listening to an invisible beat.

"Yes, sir, all part of the job. You need to be a confidant."

"Like a priest, for example." Myles leaned back on the barstool.

The bartender grinned, "Well, sir, I agree, although I've never been mistaken for a man of the cloth."

"What would you think if you met a man who didn't seem to speak to anyone and everyone assumes he has amnesia, yet he speaks daily to a priest, but only under the sacrament of confession?

Warren frowned and then spoke. "Well, I would have to believe he's hiding something. Everyone knows priests are bound by their vows not to divulge confessions."

Myles was quiet as he pondered Warren's answer. After a moment Warren continued, "And whatever he's hiding is big."

"Why do you say that?"

"Because I was brought up Catholic and confession is not possible for all our faults, but it is required for grave and mortal sins."

"I didn't know that. Thank you, Warren." Myles stood up and paid his tab along with a handsome tip.

Warren looked at the tip. "Yes, sir, thank you. But sir, do you think he is?"

"Is what?" Myles asked.

"Hiding something?"

Myles met Warren's eyes. "Yes, I have no doubt."

He walked home, hoping the night air would clear his head. Before retiring to bed, Myles looked at the notes he had written on the napkin.

If no one is looking for you, it's possible they may believe you're dead – check newspapers

Check newspaper for the weeks in '45 prior to when he showed up at hospital

Wounds not consistent with war wounds or prior medical treatment – not POW?

No one on ship recognized him – not military?

Age – possibility he's a mariner

Missing finger – check shipyard accidents
Canvass harborside bars with a picture

Tomorrow, he would start his investigative with old-fashioned footwork. His first stop would be the Fore River Shipyard in Quincy, a coastal suburb, located down on the south shore, outside Boston.

***

Myles called a manager at the Quincy shipyard and asked for authorization to view the injury reports. They had been introduced at one of the paper's VIP cocktail events. The next morning he was at the gate as the whistle blew announcing the start of the work day. He made his way to the main office and spoke to the secretary who gave him directions the records keeper, two buildings down.

A middle-aged man with black horn-rimmed glasses looked up from his desk. "How can I help you?"

"The name's Myles Bingham. Are you the records clerk?"

"Oh, yes, Mr. Bingham. The boss told me you were coming. What do you need?"

"I want to look at your records of yard accidents prior to February 1945."

The clerk's head titled and his eyes narrowed, "Look, I don't mean any disrespect, especially to the friend of the boss, but are you crazy?"

"No, is there a problem with that request?"

The clerk shook his head and stood up. He motioned for Myles to follow him through the door behind his desk that led to another room and when he turned on the light. Myles answered his own question. There was a problem. Rows upon rows of boxes filled the narrow room. Each row contained thousands of files.

"Hope you've got a lot of time. Are you looking for any particular injury or death? Burns from welding, crushing trauma from heavy equipment?" Myles noted the sarcasm in the man's voice and felt irritation build in his stomach.

"I'm looking for a finger amputation."

A snigger escaped the clerk. "So my boss told me you have no name for this man, you're not even sure the guy you're looking for was working here and you're looking for a finger amputation? Good luck."

"Well, you have to start somewhere."

"Well, I don't want to dampen your enthusiasm, but I'd suggest you start somewhere else."

"Why's that?"

"Mister, go look in the yard. Just about every yardbird here is missing a digit or two."

Myles realized the record keeper was right. It was a waste of time to start here. He thanked the clerk. On the walk back to the car, he counted three out of seven men missing a finger, or part of one.

The next day Myles started at the newspaper morgue. A lot of people thought research to be tedious and depressing work, especially in a windowless, dusty, mite-infested room with mountains of old newspapers, but he loved it. The smell of the ink, the old stories and the style in which they were written were like a drug to him. He could research for days in a state of euphoria.

The office occupied the basement of the city newspaper building. The sign on the door, embossed white letters on a black background, read "Archives Librarian." He signed in on the clipboard on the counter as the librarian came around the corner.

"Good morning, Mr. Bingham. What brings you to the morgue today?"

"Top of the morning, Alice. Don't you look lovely today?"

Alice Pearson blushed and raised her hand in a coy gesture to her cheek. As she did, Myles caught a whiff of mothballs from her blue wool sweater. He prided himself in being a master manipulator and knew flattery would go a long way with the middle-aged spinster. In the past she let him stay after closing, brought him hot tea and even did the unmentionable offense. She let him bring research materials home overnight. A desperate measure for a desperate woman.

"Thank you, kind sir."

Pleasantries over, Myles explained what he wanted.

An assistant brought him to the location where the 1945 newspapers were stored and he was pleased to find the papers had been transferred to microfilm for preservation.

He pulled over a stool and sat down in front of a cabinet with small, rectangular drawers and got to work right away looking for the index labeled the week prior to February, 1945.

Myles's boss was limiting the time he could spend on writing this article on Charlie, but Myles couldn't let the mystery go. He would resign himself to the fact he might have to do this on his own time, but right now the plan is to find incidents, in and around Boston, Charlie may have been injured in.

After locating the index fiche Myles moved to the oak, straight slat-back chair in front of the microfiche machine and went right to work. His only interruption was Miss Pearson bringing him a cup of coffee. She stood beside his chair looking down at him. When he smiled at her she reciprocated and slowly opened the top button on her starched high collared blouse. He was mesmerized as she continued opening two more and extract a small flask from her bosom.

As grateful as he was for her thoughtfulness, on two counts, he had to pass the opportunity. He was not about to let a dame get in his way of finishing a story.

Three hours later, he found an interesting article on the second page of the Feb. 8th paper.

Neighbors Awakened by Late Night Explosion

Last night neighbors reported hearing an explosion in the vicinity of a Scollay Square men's clothing shop. Upon investigation police found an old storage container that belonged to the neighboring construction company had blown up. They believed it contained a small cache of forgotten dynamite. Further investigation in the daylight revealed a large amount of blood pooled in the dirt in the lot bordering the alley. The owner of the clothing shop had no comment. It has been rumored both shops have a connection to the Beneditto crime syndicate. Word on the street is that the mob is embarrassed after being robbed by some small time crooks, but that has not been substantiated.

I'm barking up the wrong tree. If Charlie was involved in a local robbery and was shot, by the Beneditto family for instance, they would have whacked him. Dr. Templeton said Charlie had shrapnel wounds, not bullet holes. Maybe shrapnel wounds from an explosion?

Charlie was older and could have been in the Merchant Marine. If Charlie wasn't a wounded soldier and was wounded somewhere in the local area, how would he get brought in by the military, to a military hospital? Myles started doubting his search which was turning into a vicious circle of questions. Frustration overtook Myles and he threw his notepad on the floor.

Sweat dripped off his forehead and he stood up to stretch before proceeding to view the next film and the next after that. Finally, an article in April of '45 caught his eye because of the headline.

Owner of Newly Acquired Property Makes Disturbing Discovery

Roland Hoffman recently bought property at 15 Morton Terrace, Boston, which included a grim discovery in the basement. Questionable bloodied items indicated evidence of squatters (a recent growing problem in the neighborhood) or an old crime scene. Items found included a cot, a shredded shirt and jacket covered in blood, used bandages and a three-quarters empty bottle of *Cutty Sark*.

Myles stopped on the last two words. *Cutty Sark?* "Cutty Sark," he said again, this time out loud. *Could this be connected?* He needed to look into this. At the very least he needed get in touch with this Roland Hoffman. He didn't know what Mr. Hoffman could tell him, or if he could be found, but Myles needed to know he followed up on all possible leads no matter how mundane. He had a reputation to preserve and it consisted of digging deep for indisputable, black and white facts. He continued reading the rest of the article.

Police were called in to check the findings, but they announced the items were old. Mr. Hoffman acquired the building from the city after being abandoned by the prior property owners approximately seven years ago.

Myles headed out to city hall to look up contact information for Roland Hoffman. He copied down his residence and business addresses and checked the time. Two o'clock on a Thursday should still find him at the office so he headed downtown to Hoffman Insurance Agency. and asked the receptionist if he could speak to Roland.

She went into the corner office, announced his name and occupation and he was promptly waved right in.

A portly, balding salesman in his late fifties came out from behind his desk and extended his hand for a friendly greeting. Myles cringed at the thought that Hoffman might think he was there to buy an insurance policy.

"Have a seat, Mr. Bingham," he said in a booming voice. "What can I do for you today? Are you looking for a policy?"

"Sorry to disappoint you, sir. I'm here to ask you about a piece of real estate you acquired quite a few years back, in April, 1945 to be exact. The building at 15 Morton Terrace."

"Oh, yes, but I sold that a while ago. Good little investment it was. It was abandoned, got it cheap from the city. You know what they say."

Myles suppressed a sigh. "No, what do they say?"

"Buy low, sell high, son," he roared laughing. "'Real estate is the way to go,' my dad told me. I was fortunate to be able to acquire properties early on."

"Right, but I'm more interested in the discovery you made in the basement. I came across it in a news article."

"Discovery?"

"Yes, the article stated you found abandoned items. Some blood-stained, and the police were called in to check them out."

"Oh, that old stuff. I had to call the police, didn't want a possible crime scene coming back on me, you know. Damn scene spooked me out. Why do you want to know? That's old news."

"I was going through old newspapers looking for a story lead."

Hoffman laughed, "You writing the 'Great American Novel'? Or something?"

Myles's face stayed flat. "Or something," he muttered. He knew this was going to be a waste of time.

Hoffman studied Myles's face and then cleared his throat. Myles didn't think the big man was at a loss for words frequently.

Hoffman returned to his desk and plopped heavily in his chair. "So, what can I do for you?"

"If you could go over what was in the basement, I would appreciate it."

"Well, like the newspaper said…"

Myles interrupted, "I like to hear facts from the horse's mouth, so to speak. Some newspapers seem to gloss over things."

"Ok, well, let me think. The entrance was a bulkhead so you had to duck on the bottom step so you didn't hit your head, but once inside, you could stand up straight. Of course, there were no windows so it was dark and quite musty, with the dirt floor and all. I needed a good look at the structural beams, so I brought in a lot of light and, lo and behold, I found an old cot, some clothing all bloodied up, an empty bottle of booze—Scotch I think—some blood-stained bandages that were thrown in the corner, along with a bucket with dried excrement in it. Oh, there was a tool bench with a pile of old tools on top. Looked like a damned POW camp."

"Did the police find any blood on the tools?"

"No, not that I heard about. Whoever was down there may have used a monkey wrench though, because that was on the floor, if I remember correctly. I guess it could have been used to hit someone."

"Anything else?"

Hoffman sat back in the chair and looked up at the ceiling. "Let's see. Oh, there were a couple of Moxie crates in the middle of the room."

"Not in the corner or piled up?"

"No, come to think of it, there were three of them, like placed in a circle."

Myles thought about that. *Could that be for three men and maybe a fourth one wounded on the cot?* It was a long shot to think there could be a connection. They had no idea when the stuff showed up in the basement.

"Did the police take the items with them?"

"Naw, are you kidding? I threw them out myself."

"Any identifying marks on the clothes? Anything distinctive?"

"No. Wait…there was something. It fell out of the blanket on that old cot." Hoffman got up and turned around to the credenza behind him. He opened a drawer and pulled something out. He handed it across the desk to Myles. "I don't know why I kept it. I buy a lot of property, you know, and people tend to leave things behind. I guess you could call me a sucker for memories. My wife said I can't throw anything away. Guess I thought this meant something to somebody at one time."

Myles looked at the object that was handed to him. It was an old photograph. Faded, but he could still see the picture. It was a picture of a beautiful horse. He turned it over and saw "Lucy" written on the back beside the year 1917. Rust-tinted fingerprint smudges were on the front and back of one side.

"Is that blood?"

Hoffman's cheeks flushed. He shrugged his shoulders and mumbled, "Ah. I believe it is. You see, the way I figure is this. If someone was hurt and still holding on to the picture, it must have meant something. My wife thinks I'm a big softy because I couldn't throw it in the trash."

He stood and handed it back to Hoffman. "Thank you for your time, Mr. Hoffman."

"No problem. So, what do you think?"

"About what?"

"Did you learn anything? Find a story, whatever you guys do."

"Not a thing. Guess it was just a lot of junk squatters left, like the paper stated. Good day, Mr. Hoffman."

After scouring the microfilm, he found nothing else in the days prior to Charlie showing up at the hospital, so he called it a day. Back at the office Myles sat down and put his feet up on the desk, when his co-worker came over.

"Hey, Cardi's looking for you. He said to tell you to head to his office when you come in."

"What for?"

"How would I know? Am I a mind reader or something?"

Myles knew his boss wanted to pull the plug on his story and he would need to do some fast talking. Cardi looked up as Myles approached the open door to his office. The editor-in-chief always kept it open. He said it pays to keep his finger on the pulse of news room.

"Bingham, get in here and give me an update."

Myles wanted to keep this brief so he didn't sit. "Still following up leads, boss."

"This is eating up too much time, Bingham. So what you're telling me is nothing is panning out."

"I'm not at a dead end yet. I was thinking since the US and UK couldn't identify him, he may be German.'

"What? Are you saying German military?"

"It's as much a possibility as anything else."

The editor's face turned a deep red. "Do you know what the public will do if they think this country's been coddling a Nazi with kid gloves in one of our fine hospitals?" His boss was standing now, leaning on fists that were planted on his desk.

"Boss, calm down. It's a theory, that's all."

"Well, look into that theory first and, as much as it might be a good story, you better hope it's not true. Disprove it."

Myles turned to leave, throwing his parting words over his shoulder. "I believe I know a way to do that."

"Good, because I want this wrapped up by the end of the week, Bingham."

It was useless to argue with his editor or anyone worthy of being an editor for that matter. They were, as a rule, unbendable, so he left the newsroom and headed to Beacon Marine to see Father Mulcahy. As he walked through the lobby, Myles saw Dr. Templeton cross the intersecting corridor ahead of him. He hurried to catch up to the man.

"Dr. Templeton, excuse me, Dr. Templeton." He walked faster to close the gap. *Damn his long legs,* he thought, *they've got some speed to them. The doc must be used to these long pipeline corridors.* "Dr. Templeton, may I have a word with you?"

The doc turned his head and slowed down enough for Myles to catch up. "Oh, Mr. Bingham, how is your story coming?"

Myles struggled to keep up with the long stride. "I have a question about Charlie's shrapnel wounds when he was admitted."

As Templeton walked, he removed his glasses and proceeded to clean them. Myles thought the man never wasted time, always doing two things at once.

"It was a long time ago, but go ahead, ask."

"You said the wounds were infected. How long do you think it took them to get that way?"

"Well, it was obvious his wounds hadn't been treated immediately and it depends on the conditions he was exposed to, but I'd have to say maybe three days or more."

"But Charlie came in on a hospital ship that had the resources to treat him, and it took longer than that to cross the Atlantic from England. If he had been on that ship, those wounds would have been cleaned and dressed in a professional manner."

"Yes, Mr. Bingham, that would be a true statement, but as I have said before, no one had the time to ask these questions, never mind formulate them."

"And were there were no records on him from the ship?"

"No, only the four pieces of information on a piece of paper in his pocket. Name, age, religion and hometown. We assumed records had been lost. There were rumblings that he may have been released from a prisoner of war camp."

"You look skeptical."

"Yes, I was. The timing was off. We had enough men brought into this hospital back then to know who had been a POW or not. You know, back in those days there was a government investigator here that asked Charlie questions. He hit a dead end, but that only fostered more rumors."

"Such as?"

"Some people thought Charlie could have been part of 'Operation Greif' during the Battle of the Bulge. Are you familiar with it?"

Myles eyes widened, "Of course I am. Another one of Hitler's brainstorming tactics. There's doubt the plan worked the way he intended."

The doctor continued, "The timeframe in question fit. Charlie was admitted in early 1945 and the Battle of the Bulge took place in December, 1944. The investigator thought Charlie may have been a Nazi soldier. Hitler was known to put older men who spoke English in the uniforms of dead American or British soldiers. They would then slip behind enemy lines to spy and sabotage where they could. Some infiltrators bombed bridges. This investigator proposed that Charlie may have been one of these men and he was wounded, brought to Southampton, England and put on the USS Lejeune with the rest of the wounded to return stateside under the guise of an American."

"Makes an interesting story, but what do you think?"

"Still doesn't fit the timeline for the wounds."

"Doc, you don't believe Charlie was on the ship, do you?"

"I don't get paid to speculate, Mr. Bingham. He's my patient and I haven't given much thought to anything else."

"Okay, forget the story. Between you and me, what do you think?"

"Okay, I think he has a lot of secrets, no clue what they are, nor do I care, but it was a curious thing when the investigator found the identical four pieces of information we found written on scrap paper in his pocket, also handwritten on the last line of the ship's manifest."

"So what's so strange about that? Myles asked.

"Besides being the last entry in the log and the only written one? The whole manifest was typed. Good day, Mr. Bingham. I have rounds to do."

***

Why was his name handwritten in the ship's manifest on the bottom of a typewritten page to match the same information on the paper in his pocket? Was he a legitimate add-on or was it fraudulently added as a cover-up?

Myles spent the next hour questioning nurses and aides who were assigned to Charlie. Some of the hospital personnel thought Charlie may have been a ship's steward, a seaman whose job was to wake his mates, because he would make morning rounds in his wheelchair, knocking on every door to say good morning.

There were so many questions, no answers and soon there would be no time. Myles ran into the old priest again. Father Mulcahy gave Myles a conspirator's wink and slapped him on the shoulder. "Mr. Bingham, how are you this fine day? Digging up any clues to Charlie's identity?"

"Well," Myles whispered, "Between you and me, I'm beginning to give credibility to the German theory."

The priest's eyes opened so wide Myles thought they looked like the expansive blue sky today, but there was something else in them. Maybe a glint of humor or something Myles couldn't put his finger on.

"Pray tell." Father Mulcahy was amused. "Charlie a Nazi?"

"Possibly." Myles answered.

"I would be most interested in hearing you out, Mr. Bingham, after I visit one more patient. That is, of course, if you need a sounding board to see if your theory holds water."

Myles looked at his watch. "Your office in thirty minutes?"

The old priest was already shuffling off when Myles heard him say, "I'll have the tea steeping."

Half an hour later, Myles sat down beside the priest. He felt comfortable, like they were old friends.

"So tell me about this fantastic idea of yours."

"Not so fantastic, Father. I'm sure you've heard about Operation Greif, when Hitler ordered..."

He didn't finish before Father interrupted. "Of course," the priest nodded, "that deception created paranoia in the ranks." "Yes, it caused immense psychological impact by undermining trust between men. You didn't know if the soldiers you met up with were friend or foe because they dressed in US uniforms and used confiscated Army vehicles and weapons. Under cover in their Western guise, these men sabotaged anything they could. They blew up bridges, turned signs around and caused mayhem."

"Weren't they found and executed?"

Myles nodded, "Some were. One of the lead officers, Skorzeny, I believe that was his name, was tried after the war for violating the laws of war during the Battle of the Bulge. Another officer, Schulz, was tried and executed."

The priest shook his white locks, grief weighing heavily, drawing down the lines on his face. "The laws of war," he repeated. "So there are rules to killing?" His melancholy voice was barely above a whisper.

"Yes, I'm afraid so, Father."

"So why do you think Charlie could have been one of Hitler's spies?

"The timing for one, although Dr. Templeton disputes this theory because of his wounds. Charlie shows up in February, '45. Battle of the Bulge was December, '44. His age, because he's older. The mysterious entry in the manifest that was handwritten when everything else was typed. His repetitive answers stating only the written information. The amnesia no one believes he suffers from. If he is a Nazi, he knows if his cover is blown he would be executed, and being unable to walk, he's stuck in this situation. Might as well make the most of it."

The priest sat back with his hands together, fingertips of one hand gently tapped in rhyme on the tips of the other with each thought that generated in his mind.

"Well, well, Mr. Bingham, that's very good."

"What's good, Father?"

"You seem to have forgotten to mention why you are telling me your theory."

"And why am I?" Myles asked.

"You, my son, are checking out theories and you think by running this one by me you can knock it off your list. You don't believe it yourself, but you came to the only person who may be able to verify it."

"You have a keen sense of people, Father."

"Yes, I do. It's a prerequisite for the job. People are my work. I will tell you this much, Mr. Bingham. I can assure you without compromising my position as a man of the cloth that Charlie is not a Nazi."

Myles stood up to leave. "Good enough for me, Father. It was a pleasure chatting with you and thanks for the tea."

Myles's deadline was still a day away when he was pulled off the investigation by his editor and assigned to another story. He filed his research away in his archives and went on to the next assignment. The quest to find Charlie's identity went the way of the Holy Grail.

Chapter 12   Boston 1919

After the war, many of the mass troops returning home were met with parades and cheers, but this was not the case with all soldiers. James was on one of these ghost-like ships that pulled into Boston without fanfare.

He watched from the upper deck of the USS *Mt. Vernon* as the wounded and infirm were carried off in silence to hospitals and, for some, to a grave future. He leaned over the rail and watched the people scurrying on the dock like ants. Most of the women were nurses and caregivers. He wondered about the others. Were they wives or mothers of the soldiers?

A fellow soldier beside him waved furiously at a woman he spotted below. He yelled her name, "Grace, Grace, I'm here! Up here!"

James felt a pang of jealousy strike through his heart. "Is that your girl?"

"Sure is. Isn't she something?" he grinned with pride. "You got a girl?"

James thought of Macklin's picture of his prized racehorse, Lucy, and patted his pocket where he kept it for safekeeping. "Yeah, she's a tall, chestnut beauty, great legs," he said.

James spotted Grace again right at the moment she located her soldier. She jumped up and down, blowing kisses into the air. James felt awkward and out of place. He was an intruder in a personal moment and he was jealous, because he knew there was no one down on the pier waiting for him. He thought of his own mother's distraction and how she never even waved goodbye. He picked up his haversack and headed for the gangplank to disembark.

Once he stepped on the dock he was lost in the crowd. James reached the end of the pier and turned to take one last look at the ship. With nowhere to go, he headed for the last bar he was in the night before he shipped out, if for no other reason than it was familiar territory.

***

Whiskey was flowing heavily at the smoke-filled Imperial Café in Scollay Square where war-weary soldiers let loose and were rejuvenated by the music and the inviting company of women. For those who didn't have a home to go to, or couldn't make the transition to see their families yet, this place offered a smile, companionship, and fellow soldiers who understood the score. But, it wasn't all friendly camaraderie. There were many fights, most of the men releasing their tension the only way they knew how, by breaking an occasional bottle over the head of the unassuming bloke standing at the bar.

James shouldered his way sideways through the crowd to the opposite end of the bar. The bartender yelled over to him, "What'll it be, soldier?"

"Double whiskey," James shouted back over the noise.

The man standing next to him extended his hand and nodded. "Good man, starting right. There's nothing a good, smooth whiskey can't set straight. I can't stand that beer crap."

James ignored him. The last thing he felt like was small talk. There were things to figure out, like where to live and where to find a job.

The man interrupted again. "Mind if I join you?"

James eyeballed him warily and noticed the man was wearing a suit. He was overdressed for this dive and he was the only other person in the joint, besides the bartender, in civilian clothes. James, now vaguely curious, shrugged, "Suit yourself. It's a free world, at least that's what we were fighting for."

"Bartender," the man shouted as he raised his arm to signal the bartender. "Make that two. On me." He turned back to James. "So, what's your name, soldier?"

"Lawson, yours?"

"Donohue, John Donohue."

The bartender put the drinks on the bar in front of them. Donohue reached in his pocket and threw a thick roll of money on the bar. The bartender grinned, but the skepticism in his raised eyebrow didn't escape James. No one had that kind of cash and if they did, they didn't let it show in a place like this unless they could handle themselves, but Donohue's physical attributes didn't fit this bill.

Donohue pushed the roll with his index finger toward the bartender. "That ought to keep you down at this end of the bar. Keep those whiskeys coming and I'll make your attention to detail pay off."

He continued, "Lawson, the rest of the night is on me. It's the least I can do for someone who fought for my freedom."

"Thanks," James said with a little edge in his voice. He looked Donohue over, not sure about what he saw. He was a small man with prematurely thinning hair combed straight back in long, greasy strands. His eyes were not weasel-like though; on the contrary, they were too large for his face. The man's eyeballs popped out above the blue-black shadows giving the impression that someone was strangling him, cutting off his oxygen.

Donohue reminded James of those creepy Kewpie dolls his mother liked. James thought about his mother and the day she showed him pictures of a new doll advertised in her *Ladies' Home Journal* magazine. *That must have been back in 1909, when I was thirteen,* he thought. He remembered it vividly because this was around the time his father died, and the Kewpie doll reminded him of the last time he saw his father's face, and that was not a memory that he wanted to remember.

Donohue's elbow bumped his arm. "Hey, son, are you with us?"

James shook off the memories. "What?"

Donohue raised his glass in a toast. "For your service." He threw his head back and downed it. James followed suit, embracing the warmth that flowed through him. The alcohol felt good. It would help him forget. Forget his mother, forget Macklin and forget the war. James laughed out loud when he realized he had more of his life to forget than to remember. Suddenly, he didn't care that he was on his own with no job, no place to stay and no woman's warm arms to hold him. The more whiskey he consumed the better he felt, and with every swallow the burn chased away his problems.

His distrust of Donohue had disappeared by the third round of drinks and so did the hours on his first night back stateside.

***

James stirred and found himself looking at the backside of his thin eyelids. They were translucent; he could even make out tiny worm-like capillaries. He willed his eyes to open. It was morning and he wondered if the heat from the sunlight could burn a hole in his eyeballs. It was an effort to open them and even more of an effort to recognize where the hell he was.

He didn't remember much about last night, but according to how he felt when he woke up on hard ground, his limbs stiff, wedged between two overflowing trash barrels, he must have had a hell of a good time. It would have been a night to remember, if only he could. A noise at the end of the alley startled him and the critters who scurried away. *Macklin, no....get off him!*

Someone opened the back door of an establishment to throw rubbish in trash can. James propped himself up against the side of the building. He turned his head first to the right and then the left, realized he was in an alley and that the pain in his eyes wasn't from the sun, but from inside his head. He had a world-class hangover and the smell of garbage violently assaulted his senses.

71

His stomach heaved and retched vomit until everything inside was expelled. Exhausted, he struggled unsteadily to his feet, which were numb from lying so long in one position, and he gathered his belongings.

I need to find a place to stay, James suddenly realized. He also realized that this was the last thing he remembered thinking the night before. So, finding lodging was on the top of his list today. *A drink,* he thought, *will clear my head.* James held onto the side of the building and made his way out to the top of the alley one brick at a time. He staggered into the bar, which was already opened for the early clientele that needed a little hair of the dog that bit them. James shuffled in through the door; his eyes squinted to adjust to the dark before he headed to the men's room to clean up. The bartender eyed him and growled, "Hey, you gonna order a drink or what, buddy? We ain't no rooming house."

"Set me up, whiskey, I'll be right back." He cleaned up the best he could, splashing the cold water on his face and slicking his black hair back. The mirror was filthy and broken, but he could still see his image in it. He had never liked what looked back at him, but he was drawn to mirrors, hopelessly waiting to see someone different. This time, the difference was startling. He had aged. His appearance was dirty and unshaven, which made him look forty years old. But it was not his face, it was his eyes that were old, lifeless like they had been seared with the war's darkest images and they couldn't be blinked away.

James wiped his face on his sleeve and went out to the bar to down his drink. He pulled out his billfold to pay the bartender. *Damn, I've been rolled.* He had enough for one drink and in the place of his last service paycheck was a small, neatly folded piece of paper. He paid for the drink, belted it back and walked out into the sunshine.

James leaned back against the building and waited a minute for the drink to seep in, before he unfolded the piece of paper. His hands shook from the aftereffect of the night's binge drinking.

Finally he read it…Lawson, you're all right, kid. If you need a job, go to Mosey's Diner on Tremont. A friend of mine owns it and he'll take care of you. Don't thank me for the drinks, you already paid me back, ha ha. See you around, Donohue.

Chapter 13   James 1919

Even though the economy was picking up since the war ended, jobs were still hard to come by due to the countless numbers of soldiers returning from overseas. James begrudgingly took Donohue up on his offer of a job as a waiter/busboy at Mosey's Diner on Tremont Street, the small restaurant owned by Michael O'Brien, Donohue's friend. What choice did he have with no money in his pocket?

He had been working at the diner for a month and couldn't figure out why he hadn't seen Donohue since that night at the bar. O'Brien told James that Donohue lived in Rhode Island, not Boston, and he traveled a lot between Providence and New York for business.

James noticed that O'Brien seemed to sell more goods from the back room than meals in the restaurant and he surmised the goods were hotter than the food. It didn't take him long to figure out a knock on the kitchen's back door, leading to the alley, always meant someone was looking to buy something, but he wasn't privy to what they were purchasing.

The diner was small and the people were friendly. Strangely enough, in spite of O'Brien's questionable sideline, many officers of the Boston Police Department frequented Mosey's. In their conversations, James detected an undercurrent of anger and discontent with the police commissioner. The men were seeking better pay and working conditions, and rumors of a possible strike were rapidly gaining popularity.

Plates clattered as the short order cook snatched the next order off the spindle. He slapped the food on the plates and yelled to the waitress.

"Gertie! Your orders are up for Table Six. Four fried beans and eggs."

Gertrude Wilding, better known as Gertie, waddled to the window and picked up two of the four breakfast plates. She placed one in the crook of her arm, the other in her hand. Her free arm she used to steady her old legs by leaning on the back of every chair on the way over to serve the officers. As James watched her, he felt a pang of sadness for the old lady. Gertie had worked there since O'Brien's father had opened the business upon arriving from Ireland. Gertie's feet were stuffed like sausages into black, thick-heeled shoes. Her long skirt didn't fully cover her swollen ankles, and bluish veins that could be seen through her nylons. She reminded him of his grandmother on his father's side. Not that he knew much about his grandmother, but he knew she worked long hours of manual labor well into old age.

On impulse, he put his broom down and hurried forward to help her deliver the remaining two orders. Her mouth opened, about to protest, but didn't. Instead, the old woman's tired eyes sparkled a bit and softened.

"Thank you, James," she mumbled as he followed her lead to the table where four policemen sat. She indicated to James where the orders should be placed. The policemen asked for more coffee and, without hesitation, James told Gertie he'd take care of it. She nodded, shuffled herself around in the opposite direction and limped off to perch on a stool behind the counter.

James took his time pouring the coffee, slowing hovering around the table. He was interested in what the policemen were discussing. The heavier cop puffed his chest out as he spoke to the others. "By the love of sweet Jesus, how are we to support our families? There's been no wage increase in a dog's age."

The younger one said, "We're working the minimum of seventy hours a week. Support them, you said? I don't even know who they are anymore. If I'm home at all, I'm sleeping. My family never sees me." They all grumbled, nodding their heads in agreement.

James listened to them commiserate about their low wages and work conditions. As he filled the third coffee cup, the cop looked up and said, "I trust that I'll find no rat droppings in there." James froze, not sure what to say, until the cop looked at the others and added, "Unlike the little turds floating in the station house coffee." The men snorted sarcastically.

The oldest cop shook his head in disgust. "A big fat rat ran across my foot the other day. Bigger than a cat, it was. It's bad enough we have to deal with this sickness that has gripped the town, but now we also have to work out of a slum building teeming with vermin. I say we go to that meeting, support our brothers and do something about our working conditions. Who's with me?" he shouted in an attempt to gain support. He stood and pounded the table with both of his fists as if to drive his question into their heads.

The men looked at each other briefly and three hands shot into the air and gave a rally cry in unison. "Aye, aye, aye." They got louder, which didn't matter much to other customers because there weren't any. Since the sickness hit, the townspeople pretty much stayed isolated and away from public places. James walked away from the table, placed the empty coffee pot on the counter and went back to sweeping.

A week later, on the morning of September 9th when James reported to work, Gertie pulled him aside in the kitchen. "So, James, did you hear the scuttlebutt about the police? They are going to be looking for young men."

For a second, James thought he was in trouble. *Are they on to me? Does O'Brien suspect I was skimming the till?* Then he remembered the policemen's daily disgruntled conversations and answered her, "No, what about them?"

"They did it! They're going on strike. What's this town going to do now? First the war and the sickness and now there will be trouble in the streets, mark my words." Gertie's arthritic finger pointed to the morning paper on the baker's table. He glanced over at the headlines.

SEPTEMBER 9, 1919 BOSTON POST

Police vote to strike tonight. Walkout at 5:45 p.m. roll call. Ballots cast at enthusiastic meetings following Commissioner's verdict of guilty in trial of 19 officers on charges of violating rules by joining a union. The Governor, the Mayor and the committee are in conference today over the crisis.

James knew Gertie was right about trouble in the streets, but at the same time he thought this would benefit him. It would be easy to pull some breaking and entering jobs while the heat is off. This job didn't pay much, but in the next moment Gertie came up with a better idea.

"James, you fought in the big war and those are the very men they want to replace the police force with in order to keep the peace in this town."

"You mean me?" he said incredulously, "Me? Become a cop? That's a laugh."

"You're a World War veteran, boy. They'll pick you up, no questions asked." She was good at reading people. Gertie knew James had a side to him that was not on the up and up. People had to survive and who was she to judge? She'd had a wild past in her younger days. During all the years she waited on customers, she had met all kinds, but there was something about the boy she liked. He had charisma, she thought. If only she were younger. A bad boy with charm, interesting and fun, but that kind had never done right by her.

James was hesitating until she physically pushed him and ordered him to go down to the station right away. "I'll tell the boss you're sick, so if it doesn't work out you can always come back here," she said. He still didn't move.

"Move, boy! You mark my words, James. If this strike happens tonight, there'll be hell to pay in the streets. They'll hire you as fast as you can put a uniform on. Go, boy, this is your chance. It could be a golden opportunity."

He smiled, leaned down and gave her a peck on the cheek. The old woman blushed as he noticed her tears. For an instant, James wondered if she was playing back long gone memories of blossoming womanhood.

Many Boston nights were marred with violence, proving Gertie right. Making good on his word, the commissioner hired replacements for the men on strike and quickly put them on the streets. This meant limited training, but Gertie's information proved solid and WWI veterans were first choice candidates. They already had the know-how. James applied a few hours prior to the strike and soon became a Boston police officer.

Eventually the town settled down and James was assigned his own territory. It didn't take long for James to learn that he could use his uniform to his advantage. He ducked into bars on his beat to indulge in drink while he intimidated the owners, telling each one how they needed his protection. *What a cushy job,* he thought.

A month into his new assignment he crossed the street and headed for the bar a block up on the left, planning to introduce himself to the owner. The night was heavy with fog, which limited visibility. As he approached a bar in Scollay Square, James saw a man on the sidewalk, leaning up against a streetlight. The figure lit a cigarette and in the glow of the light his profile looked familiar. It was the weasel he met his first night in Boston after returning from the war. The one who left him in an alley with an empty billfold. James watched John Donohue lean back and blow smoke rings into the air.

That bastard, he thought, I'll teach him to screw with me.

James walked up to him, stopped, gave him the once-over. Towering over Donohue, he said, "We have some unfinished business."

"Well, well, look what we have here. I heard you traded in your busboy apron for a uniform. Lawson was the name, wasn't it?"

"Where have you been, Donohue? I think we have some things to discuss, like my *money?*"

Seemingly unperturbed by the aggression in James's voice, Donohue reached out and flipped the lapel on James's uniform. "Hey, I left you enough for a little morning libation. I knew you'd need it. Last time I saw you, you were in the gutter."

"Yeah, thanks for that. If it had been cold that night, I would have frozen to death."

"That's a little dramatic, isn't it, Lawson? I'll agree it was a bit cold for a summer's night. Hey, I see you're coming up in the world. A copper? If I had to take a guess, I wouldn't think the job would suit the likes of you."

James's head bobbed in agreement, "I can be persuaded to work both ends, but back to that night…"

Donohue scoffed, not letting James finish his sentence. "Ahh, I thought you had potential. I'm usually pretty good at sizing people up. But, as you say, back to the night in question. The truth is I didn't think you needed looking after. Last I saw, you had a buxom blond on your lap," he winked.

"I had my own demons to take care of, if you know what I mean." Donohue let loose a raspy laugh that led to a coughing fit.

"People are talking. Saying those things will kill ya." James pointed at the cigarette and then pulled one out and lit up. He shrugged his shoulders. "But, everyone's going to die someday."

"That's the spirit, kid."

James had to admit he was curious about Donohue. "So, what rock have you been hiding under?"

"I was traveling around, but I heard my friend O'Brien hooked you up. Did the job work out for you?"

James thought this was Donohue's way of saying that they were square with each other so James would never mention Donohue rolling him again. "Yeah, thanks. It served its time."

He continued, "So what's O'Brien's real gig at his diner? The back door was busier than the front."

"You're the copper. That's for me to know and you to find out. Word on the street is you've got your own gig going on."

James changed the subject. "So, Donohue, where have you been traveling?"

"I had some jobs going on down in Providence. Pretty lucrative ones, I might add."

James eyeballed him. Donohue was wearing a dapper business suit, an expensive one at that. "Must be good work considering those glad rags you're wearing."

"Hey, how about a drink? I'll tell you all about it." Donohue asked, "When are you off duty and out of that flea-infested, double-breasted monkey suit impersonating a uniform?"

James thought for a split second before giving a what-the-hell shrug.

"What does that matter?" He twirled his nightstick. "Let's go renew our friendship."

Donohue patted him on the back. "And also our new partnership, I believe?" He looked at James waiting for an answer. James nodded an unspoken affirmation.

***

Donohue was a successful flimflam man. He possessed an uncanny way of getting people to trust him. James was the perfect partner to bring in to work his newest con.

"Where are we going?" James asked as he leaned against the box truck, smoking a cigarette.

"Warehouse over in Pawtucket. You know what you have to do with this baby?" Donohue pointed to the truck.

"Yeah, piece of cake, pull around to the back with her, have the dolly ready. When our contact opens the back door, load up the truck with the goods and get the hell out. I'll meet you up in Attleboro in that park on the river."

"Right, okay."

Donohue thought for a second like he was trying to remember something, and then opened the driver's side door and pulled out a clipboard. "I've got the manifest with the product numbers for the shipment that came in two hours ago." James nodded, flicked the cigarette to the ground and crushed it with the toe of his boot.

Donohue continued rehearsing the plan. "All I've got to do is put the corresponding product numbers from the manifest on the phony merchandise in my truck, which I'll do now. I'll unload the fake pallet in the back corner of the warehouse. It'll be a week before they catch on and get wise that the boxes are filled with rocks, but by that time we'll have the real goods delivered to our buyers.

James nodded to Donohue. "Okay, I'm ready. You?"

Donohue snuffed out his cigarette in the dirt. "Let's roll."

Three hours later, the job was done and, to James's amazement, not hard to pull off. James was sitting on the river bank at the designated meeting place when he heard Donohue's truck coming up the road long before he spotted it.

Clouds of dust billowed up from the dirt road and floated back on the ground as Donohue pulled up beside James's truck. Donohue stepped down onto the running board with a wide grin on his face.

"We did it, James, my boy."

James laughed, "Like taking candy from a baby. Where do we go with the goods?"

"Not we, James. Me. I've already got a buyer lined up in New York. You and I will trade trucks. I'll be meeting them at the state line in Vermont."

"Where's this truck going?" James pointed to the one Donohue drove in.

"Take it up to Vinnie's garage in Somerville. He'll know what to do, he'll be expecting you.

James nodded, "You didn't tell me what's in that shipment we just stole."

Donohue swung himself up into the driver's seat, slammed the door shut and leaned out the window. "No, I didn't. You're getting paid well for your part, James. Do you really care?"

James knew Donohue had a sweet business going and he wanted a piece of it so bad he could taste it. This was easier than breaking into joints. He nodded. "Guess you're right. See you in a few days."

The job turned out to be lucrative even after they split the proceeds with the inside man. James thought it was so successful it deserved to be thoroughly celebrated, and that's what he did until the wee hours of the morning. Good to his word, Donohue returned by the end of the week. It was payday. He handed James his cut and they headed to Dooley's Bar for the evening.

Chapter 14   James Meets Esther

On his second visit, Myles sat beside Charlie in the common room. He thought the change of rooms might help, but Myles continued his one-sided conversation.

"So Charlie, have you ever been married?"

No answer.

Charlie turned his back on Myles and wheeled himself to the window. Outside, the snow swirled in the wind and mounded in triangular shapes in the corners of the panes. He raised his hand and flattened it against the cold glass. The soft whiteness of the flakes reminded him of Esther's porcelain face.

More than anything, Myles wanted to unlock the old man's brain, but it wouldn't be today. Charlie was gone again.

***

Light snow swirled in the wind the next morning as James walked his beat reeling unsteadily in the quiet misery of a world-class hangover. During the night an icy fall frost covered the town, and the cold felt like a dozen icicles stabbing his head.

He walked up Centre Street and came across a young woman overloaded with bundles. James saw she was struggling not to drop them, but before he could assist, a young boy ran out of the alleyway. The boy ran past the young woman so fast he turned her around in a circle. The boy had grabbed her purse straps, but was pulled up short because she was holding tight, clutching the straps fast to her bosom with no intention of letting go.

James yelled at the boy as he ran toward them. The boy looked up, surprise on his face and James saw the waif's dirt-streaked cheeks and thin rags.

"You little street urchin," he shouted.

The boy let go of the straps so abruptly, the young woman fell backwards to the ground, the contents of her purse spilling out. James started to go after him, but stopped to see if she was hurt.

"Are you all right?" He bent down, extending both hands to help her up. She steadied herself on his arm to brush the snow off her clothes.

"Yes, I am. Thank you." Her voice trembled as she checked herself over. She smoothed her dress and ran her delicate fingers through her hair.

"You're pretty tough to keep a hold on that bag," he smiled. "I'm impressed."

The young woman looked at him, unsure, until she noticed the police uniform. A warm smile came across her face. Her head tilted toward him and he instantly liked what he saw. Her pale face was framed with soft, ash brown curls surrounding watery blue-green eyes. James was mesmerized. She broke his gaze to pick up her purse.

"Can I help you with your bags?" James asked, forgetting all about the ragamuffin thief who was far away by now.

"I could use the help. Thank you, you're very kind, sir."

"Where are you headed?" He looked at her while he waited for her to answer. She had lowered her head and looked a bit mysterious, her face partially hidden under her cloche hat. Or maybe she's shy, but what he could see of her face he liked. James forgot about his hangover as he marveled over the beautiful woman. She had the fairest, softest skin he had ever seen. Smooth like alabaster.

"Up to Ashley Street," Esther answered with noticeable hesitation.

"I'll walk you home," he told her decisively.

She interested him, her face so feminine and delicate, but her chin squared with a strong determination and he knew, right then and there, he wanted to know her better.

"I'm James Lawson. What's your name?"

"Esther Gadda," she mumbled.

"Esther, I like that name." He noticed she blushed and turned away.

As they walked she relaxed, and soon they were deep in conversation. He learned she lived with her two sisters and her parents, who had emigrated from a small island called Dönso in the archipelago near Göteborg, Sweden. James asked the questions and let her do the talking for two reasons: he liked to listen to her voice and he wasn't a fan of talking about himself.

Time passed quickly and before they knew it they were standing in front of her house on Ashley Street. She nervously looked up at a second floor window of the three-decker. He followed her eyes and noticed someone standing behind the curtain looking down at them.

"We're being watched," he said suspiciously. "Who is that?"

She smiled softly, "My father. He's overprotective of me and my sisters."

"You're of age, aren't you?" James asked.

Esther blushed, "Yes, I am."

James towered over Esther. She faced him, looked up at him and said, "Thank you so much. I never would have made it this far. I'd like to pay you for your trouble."

He was being forward when he said, "You could let me take you out. That would be payment enough."

The blush on her face blossomed as she whispered, "I'd like that, but…well, I don't know you."

He tilted his head to the side, his brown eyes pleading, "Baby, you never will, if you don't go out with me."

Esther nervously laughed aloud. "Do you mean a date? My parents are not advocates of this social interaction."

James's eyebrows rose, not sure if he heard her right. "Social inter-what?" He noticed Esther was embarrassed by his mocking tone when a scalding flush climbed up her neck to her cheeks. "I'm sorry. I didn't mean to disrespect their views," he said as he looked up at the window again.

"They're so old-fashioned," Esther added, her voice filled with irritation, which showed her disagreement with her parents' rigidity. "I mean, they are fine with a man spending time courting me in the parlor, with one or both of them chaperoning, of course."

James wasn't taking "no" for an answer. "Well, how about it? Let's break the mold," he prodded, his smile exuding a confident charm that he knew could easily persuade the ladies.

She looked at him and suddenly burst out in a defiant voice, "Yes, I will. I will go out with you!"

He took his hat off and grinned. "All right, that's better. How about tomorrow night? Get all dolled up in your glad rags because I'm going to take you out and we're going to paint this town red."

***

James met Donohue at their favorite watering hole. Donohue informed James he'd lined up a job for the next night.

"So you know what you have to do?"

James didn't answer. He was gazing at space beyond Donohue.

"Hey, James, did you hear what I said?"

"Tomorrow night? No way, I've got a date lined up with a babe."

Donohue leaned back and looked at James, surprise on his face. "You're kidding?"

"No, I'm not kidding. I met her today."

"Where? Down at the Howard? Is she one of those new flappers?"

"Naw, she's a good girl, pretty too, with the softest looking skin. Reminds me of peaches and cream."

Donohue rolled his eyes. "Sounds like you got it bad, Lawson, but I hate to tell you, a night with the likes of *her* kind, *a good girl*, is probably going to be a 'flat tire,' kind of like dating your mother. You know what I mean?"

"Hey, watch your mouth! Do you think the only dame I can get is a floozy?"

"Are you calling your mother a floozy?"

James stood up fast, knocking the bar stool over. Donohue put a hand on James's chest. "Whoa, James. I didn't mean anything by it. Look, you go have a good time tomorrow. I've got someone I trust who can do the job with me for one night. We'll meet up after your *date*," he chuckled.

James sat back down and signaled the bartender. "Two more whiskeys over here." He ran his fingers through his hair. "Look, Donohue, I'm sorry. I'm trying to get something normal around me. My life's been shit the past couple of years."

"I know what you mean, kid, but sometimes that's your destiny and you got to go with the plan."

James snorted, "When did you become a blooming philosopher?"

Donohue's face grew serious as he asked James a question, "So tell me, does she at least have good gams?" The two of them laughed a loud *whoop* and clicked glasses high in the air.

"Well, does she?" Donohue asked again.

James grinned, "It sure looked like it."

***

The institution of Prohibition in the country was the scuttlebutt of patrons in gin joints all over Boston. The 18th Amendment was added to the Constitution in January, 1919, to take effect January 17, 1920.

James's new circle of friends included many saloon keepers, and James was already well prepared to profit from them when the police were ready to enforce the new law.

"This Prohibition thing is nuts," James said. "What does the government think they're doing? Where's our freedom?"

Donohue slapped his hand on James's back. "Don't worry, James. Where there's change, there's opportunity."

"That I know and I'm prepared, but I don't have to like it."

"Well then, bottoms up. It is the last time we'll be drinking. Legally that is." Above the rowdy noise of rebellious complaints, they clicked their glasses.

Prohibition blew into Boston with the force of a hurricane. It was instant pandemonium. Throngs of lawmen, along with religious do-gooders, filled the streets looking more like rioters than legal enforcers. They opened up the storm sewers and poured barrel after barrel of alcohol into the dark swirling rivers that ran beneath the streets of the city. A heavy smell of fermentation enveloped the masses in a heady cloud creating a deadly cocktail of raw emotions.

***

A Boston policeman's job was demanding with long hours and little time off, but despite the time constraints, the relationship between James and Esther continued flourishing throughout the winter and into the spring and summer. In August, the city was suffering a brutal heat wave. People slept in the parks and on rooftops hoping to catch a breeze. Tempers flared and eventually succumbed to lethargy.

"Esther, honey, I'm burning up. Let's spend the evening at Revere Beach. We'll have a romantic stroll on the boulevard and you can pack one of your famous picnic baskets."

"That's a wonderful idea, James. I'll get ready."

They boarded the narrow gauge, fighting the sweaty crowds of irritable people who all had the same idea to escape the stifling city air. Men rolled up their sleeves and women fanned themselves furiously with their hats. Upon exiting the train station, James and Esther walked, hand in hand, east toward the boardwalk. It was dusk and the boulevard lights were joining the stars above, glistening and twinkling like diamonds. Heavy humidity covered the park in a magical veil creating a dream-like appearance. Occasional ocean breezes gave brief periods of relief.

A loud rumbling from the Jack Rabbit roller coaster car whooshed by them. Screams from the thrill riders sent goose bumps up Esther's arm. James used this as an excuse to put his arm around her and hold her close as they walked. Esther leaned in toward James, feeling the strength of his muscular forearm tighten around her waist as he guided her through the crowd to the beach.

They weaved in and out of the patchwork quilt of blankets on the sand. James scouted out a spot to put theirs and they each took an end to spread it out. James helped Esther down on the blanket and then put the picnic basket between them. Esther opened the cover and laid the spread out. She smoothed her dress and placed a napkin on her lap.

James's eyes opened wide as she loaded his plate with cold chicken, lettuce sandwiches, herring, and her canned bread and butter pickles and, last but not least, he caught a glimpse of her Swedish rice pudding still in the basket.

Yep, he thought, *she's a good cook*. Esther might make a good wife. They ate ravenously and laughed lightly. James had never experienced this feeling before. He could not label it. Was this contentment? Love? James stood up and extended his hand to Esther. "Come on. Let's go on the rides."

She protested as he pulled her up, "James, you shouldn't spend all your money on the rides. With a policeman's wages, I don't know how you have so much extra pay to fritter away."

James's face clouded over. His pay wasn't substantial at all; most cops barely made it by, even with the long, overtime hours. It was his extracurricular activities that afforded him to spend as he liked, but he didn't need anyone else to notice this fact, especially Esther. Hopefully she didn't suspect how he got the money.

He dropped her arm and she fell back onto the blanket. "Let me worry about that. I'll do what I like," he growled.

Taken aback by his abrasive manner, she looked away and whispered, "I'll pack everything up."

"Leave it, we'll come back and get the stuff later." He pulled her roughly to her feet and across the beach to the seawall stairs.

Once on the boardwalk, Esther was mesmerized by the lights and excitement and she soon forgot James's display of anger. Organ music drew Esther toward the Hippodrome with the carousel's brightly colored horses. She begged James to ride the ornately carved chariot harnessed to two stallions adorned with royal plume headdresses. He placed his hands gently on her waist and lifted her up into the carriage. She felt like a queen. The music played faster and the carousel went around and around until the real world fell away.

The best view of Revere Beach was from the top of the Ferris wheel. Whatever was left of Esther's reserved demeanor disappeared in the night's air. The cool ocean breeze rushed through her hair as they rode the wheel high into the night's sky, electrifying her with excitement. They were at the top when they noticed a melee below. A mob of people gathered at the edge of the park, close to the entrance.

"James, what's happening down there? I hope no one is hurt." Right before their eyes the crowd below swelled, doubling and then tripling, swallowing up the ground below.

James kept his eyes on the ground. From the bird's-eye view, he mapped out a plan to get to a park exit. "It looks like some kind of a riot or something. All I know is that we have to get down off this thing and out of here before they surround this ride."

The car descended to the ground and the Ferris wheel slowed. Their car was still swinging when James lifted the bar, scooped his arm around Esther and made a run for it. They ducked bottles being propelled through the air and shattering all around them as they hurried out to the "Great White Way," the cement boardwalk which ran the length of the park.

The unrest was escalating and spilling out onto the boardwalk. They pushed through a tide of angry men. Once they were safely on the beach, they gathered their belongings and walked quickly to the train station. When they reached the station, they sat for a moment to catch their breath. Others escaping the riot were also waiting for the narrow gauge to travel back to Boston. No one knew exactly what happened on this steamy night when tempers seemed to boil over. Finally, one man approached the tracks and told everyone that the mob had moved to the police station and was causing all kinds of destruction. He told them the rioters had even taken the arcade's shooting rifles from their tethers and were firing at the station house.

Once they were on the train, Esther relaxed, but the crowded car and the stifling heat made them forget the reprieve of the beach breezes. It was late by the time they reached Esther's porch. They sat silently on the front steps and gazed at the stars. Esther put her hand on his and thanked James for getting them safely home.

James thought this was a good time to sneak a kiss as a reward, and did so. She let him. He didn't tell her that he would have preferred to stay in Revere in the middle of it all and would have relished a good brawl.

***

Tommy's Tin Whistle was one of Donohue's so-called clients. The dive drew a good crowd no matter the time of day, and this morning was no exception. At nine o'clock, Donohue sat at the bar with a stubby pencil in one hand and a whiskey in the other. He and James had arranged to meet here to go over Donohue's book that listed jobs, pick-up dates and amounts.

James showed up on time, ordered a beer and threw his leg over a stool. "It was a wild time on the north shore the other night. Did you hear about it?"

"Yeah, you mean the all-out riot up on Revere Beach? Of course, I heard. It's all over the papers. They said the troops from Fort Banks in Winthrop were called out."

"They weren't the only ones. They called in the Chelsea police and the Boston Navy Yard." James slapped Donohue's shoulder. "Bunch of seafarers were roughhousing the landlubbers like you, Donohue."

"Did they call your station to go?"

"No, but I finally had a day off and needed to get away from this oppressive heat, so Esther and I took the narrow gauge to the beach to cool off for the evening. All hell broke loose. You should have seen it, Donohue. What a brawl."

"Did you get in there and deck a few?"

"Naw, I didn't want Esther to be upset. She thinks I'm a gentleman."

Donohue choked on his whiskey. "She's got that wrong."

They both had a good laugh and got down to business. Donohue placed a small, black leather notebook in front of James. "In this booklet are the amounts you need to collect from each one. This way everyone is fat, dumb and happy." Donohue explained, "Clients feel safe and our pockets are nicely padded."

Their operation ran smoothly until the day they ran into "The Wall." Their protection shakedowns were stepping on gangster turf and they both knew this was dangerous territory and not worth paying the price with their life.

"The Wall" was Nick Seremetis, a local mob enforcer. At 6 feet 4 inches tall and five feet wide, his bulk filled the doorway, barring any one from entering. He turned sideways to pass through the frame and stood inside the door of the bar, turning his massive, beefy head side to side while surveying the clientele. The din quieted as if someone lowered the volume on a radio. The tension rose as heads turned to see who "The Wall" was looking for. Most customers gave an audible sigh of relief when his eyes settled on James and Donohue. He lumbered over and stood directly behind them, crossing his arms. James ignored him, took a draw on his beer, chased it with a shot of whiskey, turned and asked Donohue, "Dunny, are you expecting an army of one?"

Tommy Coyle, bartender-owner of the joint, swaggered over to them at the end of the counter with a half-assed apologetic smile on his face. Tommy concentrated on cleaning the bar in front of them, wiping it back and forth, over and over, not looking at them. He kept his head down as he addressed Donohue and James. "Looks like I won't need you boys watching over things anymore." Then he looked beyond them at "The Wall" and hurried away.

James shouted out to him, "Hey Tommy, what the…" He never got the rest of the words out of his mouth. No one expected the speed that exploded from this mountain of flesh. James received a right-fisted kidney punch to his ribs from behind that knocked the breath out of him. Nick Seremetis swung

Donohue and James around, grabbed both of them by the front of their shirts and told them in no uncertain terms, "You boys consider yourselves unemployed in the neighborhood. Got it? My boss is expanding his business ventures and he likes what you got going here and when he likes something, he sends me to acquire it for him. Are we straight?"

Donohue and James glanced at each other and nodded that they understood. Whoever this guy's boss was, he had sufficient muscle behind him and they were only a couple of small-time crooks. Donohue put his hands in the air as he slid off the bar stool. "Hey, we're just trying to make a living. We don't want any trouble. It's all yours, buddy."

James stood, and as they started to walk out, his arm swept Donohue's beer off the bar to distract the big guy. In the second it took to drench "The Wall" and before the mug hit the floor, James thrust his boot-clad foot up between the big guy's legs, dropping "The Wall" to the floor like a rock. They left him twisting like a contortionist, moaning in pain.

Tommy didn't look too happy as he ran over to them. "Hey, get out of here. They're going to come down hard on me. These guys are not people to fool with."

"You're in for it now, James," Donohue snapped. "They won't let that go."

James laughed, "Naw, it won't be a problem. Only problem we've got is no income now. 'The Wall' will lose his reputation if anyone knows he got taken down, and his boss won't be happy."

"Got to admit that was pretty good work, James. Let's go have a drink at Dooley's and figure out our next plan of action." They sauntered out, without a care in the world.

They were not happy about losing business, but they couldn't go up against the city's notorious crime boss. It was time to re-invent their career.

"James, my boy, no worries. I've given this a lot of thought and came up with two pieces of criteria that are a must in our plan."

"What's that?" James asked.

"Well, we need to keep on the move, kind of like your 'hit and run' house break-ins you were doing, and we need a mark who carries money on him. It has to be a sure thing. Don't want to waste our time."

"Ok, are you going to tell me or keep me guessing?" James drawled the question out sarcastically, getting tired of waiting to hear his idea.

"Cabbies, we going to take down taxi cab drivers."

"Oh, that's cold, Dunny, real cold, but brilliant!" James's face broke out in a grin. "And you know why I think it's brilliant?"

"Why?"

"Because they have their own little turf war going on right now. It's like a war zone with those guys. The station doesn't want anything to do with it. The police figure the cabbies will work it out among themselves or kill each other trying," laughed James.

Wasting no time, they developed a plan to hit cab drivers and agreed to meet the next night to implement it.

Tuesday was a relatively quiet night due to torrential rain. James and Donohue huddled in a doorway of a building on the corner of Tremont and Dartmouth Streets, hats low on the brow so their faces were hidden as they waited for the first cab. They didn't have to wait long.

Donohue, the smaller frame and less intimidating of the two, stepped out into the rain to stand curbside and flag down the cabbie. The cab pulled up beside him and he jumped in the back seat and pushed over so James could hop in behind him.

"Night's not fit for man or beast. Where to, gentlemen?" the cabbie inquired.

"Down to Atlantic Ave.," Donohue mumbled. They drove in silence for a couple of minutes and then Donohue pulled out a gun and held it to the base of the cabbie's skull.

"Hey, hey, take it easy," the cabbie choked. "What do you want?"

James reached his hand over the seat and rubbed his index finger and thumb together up in front of the cabbie's nose, indicating they wanted his money. The gesture wasn't lost on the cabbie. "All right, calm down. This isn't the first time I've been robbed and hopefully it won't be the last. Get my meaning? I'll give you the cabbage, just don't kill me."

James slapped the driver's cheek. "Shut up and hand it over."

The driver indicated he was going to reach in his pocket. James waved his hand, signaling him to go ahead and watched carefully as he pulled his night's fares out of his pocket and deposited the money right into James's waiting palm.

"That's all the cabbage I've got, I swear."

"Pull over," Donohue instructed the man.

The cabbie wasted no time and pulled the taxi over to an abrupt stop. The drenching rain was pelting the roof of the cab, the symphony drowning out all other sounds. Donohue instructed him to get out of the cab. The driver hesitated. Donohue growled, "Now! Get on the sidewalk, face up against the building and don't turn around."

The driver didn't wait to be told again. James got out of the back seat, quickly stepped around the back of the cab and slid in behind the steering wheel. Donohue stayed in the back and they simply drove away.

"Where are we going to dump this heap?" James asked.

"Drive, James," Donohue laughed as he pretended he was addressing his personal chauffeur. It took only one backwards look from James to tell Donohue that he wasn't in the mood for joking around.

"All right, all right, head to Forest Hills Cemetery. There's two hundred and fifty acres there. We'll ditch this hay burner in the middle of it."

Donohue sank low in the back seat, put his hat over his eyes and told James to wake him when they got there.

James entered the cemetery under the elaborate stone arch, weaving slowly in and out of the many narrow roads lined by rows upon rows of gray gravestones. He pulled over in a remote area that was not visible from any of the abutting neighborhood streets. They got out of the car and started walking briskly in the rain, which had lightened up a bit. They came to a pond in the center of the roundabout where the cemetery roads intersected. James threw the cab's keys into the water.

Once they deserted the cab, he wanted to get the hell out of there, but the walking wasn't easy in the pitch black of night with the wet and uneven terrain. The low overcast prevented any light from the moon from guiding them, and every once in a while James would jump when he suddenly found himself beside a large looming stone figure of an angel or a saint.

"This place gives me the creeps," he told Donohue.

"What are you jittery about? Everyone's dead."

"All these damn statues give me the creeps. It feels like a thousand eyes watching us. I don't like it."

Donohue stopped and pulled a flask out of his overcoat. "I've got just the thing to make things warm and cozy," he said. He unscrewed the cap, took a swig and offered it to James.

"Here, this will calm your nerves and keep your demons at bay."

James took it and guzzled half of it down before handing it back to him.

Donohue spread his arms out in a theatrical gesture and turned slowly around in a circle. "You know, James, you're in the company of great personalities."

Forest Hills Cemetery, located in the Forest Hills section of Jamaica Plain, was designed in 1848 and serves as the final resting place of many famous citizens, but James was not impressed with its history or the elaborate marble statues and mausoleums.

"I hope you're not talking about yourself, are you, Donohue?"

"No, not me, James, my boy, but we'll all be here someday. Don't worry, I'll come and visit. You know, put flowers on your grave or something."

"Yeah, right, like I got someone to put flowers on my grave? If I know you, you'll probably water the flowers by pissing on them."

"How'd you learn all that crap anyway?"

"When I first came to the States, I learned I had the great gift of talking. I can talk a dog off a meat wagon, so I spoke to everyone and, believe me, I learned a lot. The other gift is listening. You learn their strengths and weaknesses, so you can use them to your advantage."

James shook his head, "Now you're a philosopher and a teacher?"

"I could have been a teacher. Test me."

Ok, who's buried in here?"

"William Dawes is buried here, for one. A great American patriot. Sacco and Vanzetti were cremated here, but they were shipped back to Italy. Another great..." James was getting tired of hearing this prattle and cut him short.

"Donohue, look, I don't care who's feeding the grass as fertilizer, as long as it isn't me. Now let's get the hell out of here."

A clinking sound to the right of where they were standing startled them. Donohue whipped his gun out and yelled. "Who's there?"

As their eyes adjusted to the dark, they could barely make out a figure sitting under the shelter of a tree. "I asked, who's there?" Donohue yelled.

"Wanna drinky, gentlemen?" An old man attempted to stand up, but kept falling down. Finally on the third attempt, as they watched, he stood and held a bottle out to them with a shaky arm. To the left of the drunk was an open grave, most likely awaiting an occupant's arrival the next morning.

"It's a drunk," Donohue pointed the revolver, "This will scare him off."

James's nerves were already on edge and this little interaction was not what he needed. James turned to Donohue and pushed down on the gun barrel. "Put that thing away. I've got a better idea." Before Donohue could protest, James reached forward and in one smooth swoop he grabbed the liquor bottle out of the drunk's hand and pushed him backwards, down into the wet, open grave. James took a swig from the bottle, expecting whiskey, but getting a mouthful of wine. He immediately spat it out.

"Damn cat piss, he's a wino." Then he threw the bottle down in the hole with its owner.

A voice came from the grave. "H-h-hey, y-rrre aww-right, b-buddy," the drunk slurred.

James laughed and walked away after telling Donohue, "Leave him be."

They headed for the nearest whiskey to fend off the chill from the rain.

"How much lettuce did we get?" Donohue asked.

James pulled the wad from his pocket and counted it quickly before throwing money on the bar for the drinks.

"Twenty-eight." He thumbed off half and gave it to Donohue.

"Well, that went smooth enough. We could do a couple of these a week. Beats working, doesn't it, James?"

James saluted with his whiskey. "Beats walking that damn beat every day."

Robbing cabbies turned out to be lucrative and not without a little humor. Late one night as James and Donohue stood on Broadway in the South End, they saw a cab approach the corner. They planned to jump in and surprise the driver when he slowed down.

As James flung open the back door, the driver, a young man in his twenties jumped and slammed on the brakes, "Hey, what do you guys think you're doing?"

"Shagging a cab ride, what do you think?"

"But..."

"No buts, shut your trap and take us over to Forest Hills," James ordered him.

"Hey mister, I don't know what you're thinking, but I'm not a cabbie," he chuckled. "It must be the hat, I'm a gasoline attendant. Just closed the station up over in Somerville and I'm headed home."

Donohue started laughing and James shook his head. "What the hell!"

The young man smiled and politely said, "Hey, I'm going that way so I'll be glad to give you gents a ride if you want. It's late and there have been some robberies around here. Streets are getting dangerous lately."

James nodded. "Yeah, we know. What's this world coming to? "

Donohue leaned on the back of the front seat close to the driver's ear. "Yeah, we'd appreciate the ride. Look, drop us at the end of Broadway."

The man grinned, "Sure thing, mister. Glad to help."

They got out of the automobile, stood on the curb and watched the gas attendant drive away with his money still safely tucked in his pants pocket.

James turned to Donohue, "So, you do have a heart, Donohue."

Donohue shrugged, "I need a drink."

***

Esther should have known better. As she was the oldest girl, people always said she was grounded, ingrained with good old common sense inherited from her parents, but she was thrown off guard when it came to James. His brown eyes smoked with an intensity that intoxicated her. She knew from the start that he was the wrong beau for her, but the magnetic attraction was incredibly strong and she could not make a rational decision regarding him. She felt weak in the knees if he stood close to her.

Her sisters knew she was infatuated with James and told her not to do anything rash. They told her there were more suitable men out in the world and invited her to go with them to parties. Esther politely refused, insisting she was the oldest and wanted to act accordingly. Father wouldn't want her to be an embarrassment to the family, so she put her youth behind her and carried on with her household responsibilities to help her parents while waiting patiently for the next step in their relationship, which she secretly hoped to be marriage.

When her sisters returned late in the evening, the three of them would gather in the front room and sip on a brandy nightcap while they told Esther tales of their escapades around the town.

There had been only a few nights of "painting the town," as James called it, and that was in the first months of their courtship. As the days turned into weeks, most of their time was spent walking in the park, relaxing on the beach, or sitting on the front porch. Looking back on it now, Esther realized that

James, like any lonely young man, to put it bluntly, was looking for a port in a storm, a place to hang his hat, while he went about his business.

They were the right age, they could produce a handsome family and Esther had the family house to live in. She knew somewhere inside that James was looking for a practical, good girl, but that was only one layer of a complicated man. He would not be satisfied with a good wife waiting for him at home. But, in a determined move for a normal, family life, while she was still young enough to produce children, she pushed forward, ignoring all the warning signals.

Esther's father displayed his dislike for James immediately, but despite his protests, Esther and James's dating led to marriage.

James moved into Esther's family's house the day they became man and wife. Her father kept his objections to himself, not wanting to upset his daughter, but one night early on, in passing James on the front stoop, he let him know he was watching him. James didn't answer his father-in-law. Instead he shot him a cocky smile and whistled as he walked through the front door.

James didn't want to live up to his part in the marriage, but he wanted it there when he returned home at the end of the day. If he did return home, that is. It wasn't long before Esther found out James had two sides to him. Her sisters, Evelyn and Clara, would eventually refer to him as a "street angel, house devil."

Eventually Esther's family made a point of staying away from him and gave the newlyweds their space, which wasn't hard to do in the large three-decker. Esther was a homebody who loved to nurture and cook while her sisters traveled many times overseas to visit family in Sweden. It didn't take long for Esther to admit to herself that they had been right. James's charm vanished as fast as he did after dinner. Esther was left to clean up, alone again. At least before, she had her family around, but they were making themselves scarce for her benefit, so how could she tell them how miserable she was?

Not long after the New Year rolled over to 1921, Esther discovered she was pregnant. She was thrilled and foolishly thought James would feel the same way. James accepted the news in silence, but this was better than the shouting and carrying on when something set him off. James thought of the baby as Esther's child, Esther's responsibility. This was what she wanted and if it kept her quiet, so be it.

On August 15, 1921, Esther's mother, Josephina, performed the midwife tasks she had learned from her mother in Sweden and delivered her own grandchild. The beautiful little girl looked like her father. Her complexion was dark and her head was crowned with a mop of wavy, black hair. Esther felt a deep-seated pride in her family's ancestral roots and named the baby Doris, which means "bountiful" and "of the sea."

During this time, James and Donohue had forged an even tighter partnership, one that James kept hidden away from his family life. Everyone knew Donohue was not always on the up and up, because despite having no visible means of employment, he never lacked for money in these bad times.

When James was home, which was rare, the tension was unbearable. Even though he was the catalyst, he hated being at the house any longer than it took to eat dinner. Family life transported James back to his mother's house. He didn't want to remember the past and tried hard to forget it. Yet every time he walked through that door he started to sweat. He felt trapped, restless.

Esther learned early on not to rile him. He was not an easy man to live with, but he was her husband and she was determined to be a good wife. She came from sturdy Scandinavian stock and could stick this out. Yes, she could do this.

Chapter 15　　　James 1923

Lacking respect for any authority, James continued to take advantage of his police uniform. Eventually the indiscretions caught up with him and in the spring of 1923, James was summoned to his commander's office at the Joy Street station. His fellow officers filled the air simultaneously with low foreboding whistles. He never felt camaraderie with his fellow officers. He was still a loner. James glowered at them as he walked across the station's squeaky floorboards to a heavy oak door adorned with an impressive wood and brass plaque. He knocked.

A booming voice gruffly answered, "Enter." James opened the door, approached Captain Hallett and saluted him. The commanding officer looked hard at James as he stood at attention. He walked out in front of his desk and around James to close the door, then turned back and sat at his desk. In silence the Captain lit a cigar and blew rings of smoke into the air.

After what James thought was an eternity. Captain Hallett breathed a heavy sigh and finally spoke. "Lawson," he growled, "I've heard a lot of bad reports about you, and do you know what I think?"

Not realizing it was a rhetorical question, James attempted to answer and was stopped by his commanding officer's hand. "Like I was saying, do you know what I think? I think the rumors I've heard about you are only the tip of the iceberg. You give the police a bad name and, therefore, I have no other choice but to do what I am about to do." He stood and reached across the desk and tore the badge off James's chest. James flinched at the movement, but stayed rooted to the spot and his defiant attitude.

"James Lawson, you are hereby stripped of your uniform, dismissed from the force for behavior unbecoming an officer and for performing duties while intoxicated. Now get your ass out of my sight."

James was unfazed by the ordeal and after turning in his uniform, he headed out to find Donohue. There were better ways to make some dough.

Donohue asked him the obvious. "Hey, why aren't you slaving away like the other fine boys in blue today?"

James flagged the bartender for a drink before he answered, "They canned me."

"What are you going to do now? You have another kid on the way."

"I know, I know, but that's the benefit of living with Esther's family. They're not going to let us starve." He tilted his head back and threw the whiskey down his throat in one shot, simultaneously pounding the bar with his hand indicating he wanted another round. Outwardly he didn't seem to care, but inside, he dreaded telling Esther he lost his job.

"I could use a right-hand man I can trust on some of my larger jobs," Donohue said.

James didn't hesitate. He already knew the implications. He clicked his glass against Donohue's. "Count me in."

Donohue became James's mentor, teaching him the ins and outs of being a confidence man. He told James that the first time he saw him, he knew that he would be a quick study. On a few occasions, James would question the game plan.

"Dunny, come on, who's stupid enough to fall for this con?"

Donohue would laugh and say, "James, remember what the man under the big top said. 'There's a sucker born every minute.'" Sure enough, the next job and the next after that one would prove this to be true time and again.

Boston had a larger criminal element to go after than two small-timers like James and Donohue. The decade was riddled with crimes that would go down in infamy, like the Sacco-Vanzetti case. Al Capone would get his infamous start in Boston, as an apprentice to Johnny Torrio prior to relocating to Chicago, and currently Beantown was the hotbed of the up and coming Beneditto mob family. Organized crime was flourishing, burning up the town, and Prohibition was the fuel feeding the fire.

***

Three days and two nights passed before James stumbled up the front stairs to his father-in-law's three-decker house. He was reeling from the moonshine served at the juice joint he and Donohue frequented. His head was throbbing and pinpoint spots of red hindered his vision. All he wanted was to go to bed.

The door creaked, announcing her husband's return. Esther heard it, removed her apron and hurried down the hall to greet her husband.

"James, I was so worried about you." She whispered so the family wouldn't hear. "Where have you been? You've been gone for days."

She touched his arm, instantly regretting her gesture when she saw the look on his face, and she pulled her hand back. He shoved her. She stumbled forward, crashing into the coat rack. Shaken, Esther backed against the hallway wall to steady herself. She stood trembling as he climbed the stairs to the bedroom, weaving side to side between the banister and the wall.

James slept the sleep of the dead and when he woke, he lay there staring at the ceiling. He listened for any sounds in the house and realized how artificially quiet it was. His life was a mess and he wanted to disappear. Isn't that what you do? Start over. Out with the old, in with the new. That's what his mother did to him. This is the life lesson she taught him.

He struggled to sit on the edge of the bed for a moment to clear his head, and then he put his pants on and trudged downstairs. He found Esther in the front room cleaning the triple windows in the alcove. Her back was toward him and she must have sensed he was there because she jumped around looking like a scared jackrabbit.

Rage flickered when he recognized the fright in Esther's eyes. A vivid memory of his mother's face after the trial flashed in his mind.

"James, you frightened me. What's wrong? Are you all right?"

"I'm hungry," he stated, in a tone that sounded more like a demand than an off-the-cuff statement.

She picked up the rag she had dropped on the floor, smoothed her apron and hurried out to the kitchen. He sat quietly staring out the window, watching the pigeons on the roof of the neighbor's three-decker. They perched on the gutters and cooed in harmony all the way through James's dinner.

He devoured the food she served him without so much as a smile. Only after he ate the last bite on his plate did he ask about Doris's whereabouts.

"Mum and Father took her visiting over the Johanssons' house so she could play with their grandson."

James pushed his plate away and looked at Esther. "Sit," he ordered her. Obedient, she pulled out the chair from the kitchen table and sat.

"Esther, I've lost my job. I'm no longer one of Boston's finest," he said sarcastically.

She stared at him. He ignored her, not offering any explanations. He could tell she was biting her tongue. She wanted to ask, but said nothing. This made him even madder. He would relish an argument with this woman; what he couldn't stand was the bloody silence. Everyone tiptoeing around him. His skin flushed hot with anger and as he stood he knocked the chair over backwards. When Esther reached to pick it up, he grabbed her forearm and pushed his pregnant wife out of the way. Like a frightened doe she stayed on the floor, listening to his footsteps recede down the hall.

Spring passed and the summer was hot and uncomfortable, especially for Esther who was due to deliver once again during the dog days of August. James came and went as he pleased, disappearing for days at a time with Donohue and another friend of his who drove a taxi cab. She suspected he was up to no good, but kept quiet. She was a private person and didn't want her family to know the abuse she suffered at his hand. He made sure, when he pushed her around, he didn't hit her where the marks would be visible. Every now and then, he would leave money on the night stand for groceries. She thought he most likely did this out of guilt, but it wasn't enough. As soon as this baby was born, she would need to find a job.

On August 18th, Josephina once again delivered her grandchild. This time it was a boy, whom Esther named James Robert, but she preferred to call him Bob.

James's knowledge of how to bring up children was extremely limited. The two things he was sure of were that childrearing was the woman's job and that children were to be seen but not heard. This was his father's way when he and his siblings were brought up. However, he did remember his brother and sister were tolerated easily by his father, unlike James who accepted his role as the "black sheep" and lived up to all its hardships like a brooding martyr.

So the day that Esther lay in bed with their newborn son in her arms, James expected her to watch three-year-old Doris and have dinner on the table before he went out to meet Donohue for the night. And she did just that. Not out of marital responsibility, but out of fear.

As the years passed, Esther's life was all about establishing routines that wouldn't anger her husband. One night, Esther heard her husband yelling slurred words on the front steps and there was no mistake that he was drunk, again. She ushered the children toward the front hall, intending to send them upstairs to play so they wouldn't bother him. But she was too late. He opened the door, half falling over the threshold and banging the door violently against the hall wall. The children ran up the stairs to their rooms.

"James," she attempted, "your dinner is..." He stopped her from finishing by clamping his hand over her mouth, binding her lips together. Taken by surprise, Esther stumbled backwards and slammed against the wall.

"Shhhhhh, woman. I need quiet, not all your chatter. You sound like my mother. 'James this' and 'James that'."

Their eyes locked on each other; the brown puppy dog eyes that had once attracted her to him were no longer discernible. Now they were dark and feral like his heart and Esther was afraid.

"Ungrateful nags, that's what you women are. Do you know what I did for my mother? Do you?" The louder he got the harder he squeezed her lips until his fingers gouged into her cheeks and he shook her head from side to side. Suddenly James roughly removed his hand, went upstairs and passed out.

***

Doris sat on the footstool, her back to her mother, so Esther could brush her hair of thick dark waves. *She looks so much like her father*, Esther thought.

It was Sunday morning and they were getting ready to walk to church as a family, with the exception of James.

"Sit still, Doris, so we can be on with it. Grandma and Granddad are waiting."

"But, Ma, why doesn't Daddy go to church with us?'

"I don't have the answer to that question, honey, but Lord knows he needs it."

Doris turned and pouted. "You mean he needs it because he's so mean to us? Why's he so mean all the time?"

Esther was at a loss for words. She'd had tried so hard to protect her children from his anger, but as her own mother often said, *Children are wise little beings. Maybe we could learn from them.*

The door opened and Esther's younger child, Bob, flew through the room, his small arms spread wide, dipping from side to side simulating an airplane. The moment to talk to her daughter was gone and the relief showed on her face as she and Doris laughed at Bob's antics.

Some things are better off unspoken, she thought.

"Come on children, we'll be late for church." She quickly ushered them out the door, but Doris's unanswered question weighed heavily on Esther's mind. There are things that cannot stay hidden forever.

This turned out to be true when one day, months later, James's secret life of crime came to light publicly, much to the embarrassment of Esther and her family.

Chapter 16   Con Men James and Donohue

Donohue stepped off the curb and hailed the cab. Once again, he and James climbed in the back seat and Donohue instructed the driver to head south to Wrentham.

Taking his time, the driver removed a stub of a stogie from his lips with nicotine-stained fingers, rolled down his window and spit a large clump of phlegm out, hitting a lamppost with the accuracy of a star ballplayer. He rolled the window back up and turned to look at his passengers. "It'll cost you," he said.

The back seat of the cab had a twelve-inch draw to the floor and pushed James's knees up in an awkward position. They hadn't even left town and he was already irritated. He snapped at the cabbie, "Drive."

Wrentham was a small town, population around 4500, located approximately halfway between Boston and Providence. James and Donohue had picked this location because secluded wooded areas surrounded the town and they intended not to pay the fare. The cabbie was going to pay them.

They approached an area called Wrentham Woods. Donohue and James exchanged a quick glance. James nodded. Donohue leaned forward in the seat. "Hey cabbie, pull over up there."

"There? Where do you mean?" the driver exclaimed, "There's nothing here."

"Pull over. I have to take a leak." The driver nodded and drove another hundred feet before he located a gravel road up ahead on the right. He pulled the cab over onto the shoulder beyond the intersection.

Donohue opened the door, hurried out of the back seat and walked around the back of the cab. When James saw him come up along the left side of the door, he sprang forward wrapping his left arm around the cabbie's neck and stuck the gun he held in his right hand against his temple. The cabbie's body stiffened and he made some unintelligible sound which James could feel vibrating on his forearm. He tightened his hold on the cabbie's neck until the man's Adam's apple couldn't move.

"Nice and easy now, buddy. What's your name?" James asked as he released the pressure on the driver's neck. The cabbie pointed with his yellow, calloused finger at his license hanging on the visor. James looked and answered his own question.

"William, it is. Okay, William Lyons, get out slowly. My partner will help you."

Donohue was standing outside the cabbie's door now. He opened it and, without warning, pulled the cabbie out and threw him to the ground. Donohue kicked the cabbie so hard, he rolled him over onto his stomach. "Stand up," he ordered.

The cabbie was shaking so much he had difficulty getting onto his knees. His jowls shook, reminding James of a fleshy turkey wattle as his mouth blubbered out unintelligible words.

James stood over the groveling man, watching him struggle, before lifting his foot and slamming it down into the middle of William Lyons's back. He reached his hand down and grabbed the back of the man's coat, pulling him to his feet and spinning him around to face him. The top of the cabbie's head came to James's nose. The cabbie raised his eyes to look at James.

"What…what do you want?"

"Give me your money," James instructed the man.

He stuttered, "I don't…I don't have much."

"Did I ask you how much you have? Empty your pockets now," James ordered. William Lyons looked from James to Donohue, reached into his pocket and pulled out a wad of cash. James grabbed it out of his hands, counted it and shoved it in his jacket. He grabbed the cabbie's shirt and cold-cocked him.

The moment the man hit the ground, Donohue jumped on top of him, yelling as he pummeled the man's face with both fists. "You liar!"

James leaned up against the bright yellow cab, lit a cigarette and watched the show.

After a couple of minutes, James pulled Donohue off the man and steadied him until he calmed down. "Come on, let's walk into town to get a drink. We'll pick up another cab ride afterwards."

Donohue wiped the sweat off his forehead with the back of his hand and brushed dust off his clothes. He said nothing as he followed James's lead down the road. James looked back at William Lyons as the twilight shadows overtook the sides of the country road. The man resembled a rag doll lying beside the glaring yellow cab.

A farmer pulling his harvest wagon behind his tractor happened across the injured cabbie and brought him to the town doctor, who in turn notified the police. Underestimating the prowess of the small town's police chief, Donohue and James were tracked down before they finished their third whiskey. They were identified as the perpetrators by the cabbie and arrested. They were sentenced to a year in prison on the assault charge and one month on the fare evasion. James immediately appealed the thirteen-month sentence without success.

***

Panic overtook James when the cell door locked. Suddenly he was twenty years old again, suffocating in a Gloucester cell. He paced until exhaustion took over, then curled up on the bunk and fell into a deep sleep. He woke abruptly, covered in sweat, when a guard rattled his baton against the bars. "Get up, Lawson! Welcome to the Charles Street Jail."

The city jail was cold in the winter, suffocating in the summer, and James was thankful there wouldn't be more than one season of each. At times, he thought his stay there rivaled the time he spent in the broken-down station house while he was on the police force. Pigeons roosted in the rafters, their excrement covering the floors, providing fodder for the rats. Charles Street was well-known for its unsanitary, overcrowded conditions. He had to laugh, thinking both ends of the justice system worked in the same squalor. A cop and a crook living in all the same shit.

When darkness fell, the prison came alive with sounds of scurrying and gnawing. Sleep was nearly impossible, as he doubled his watch for the four-legged as well as the two-legged vermin. He would start to drift off only to feel rats crawling over his body as they began their nightly quest for food. Eventually sleep would come, along with nightmares of Macklin riding his horse, Lucy, through the trenches to escape the hordes of rats. As Macklin reaches down to pull James out of the mud, James sees the rider's head is a faceless, writhing mass of maggots. In time, he began to admire the rodents. This was what life was about – survival of the fittest.

Chapter 17 James and Esther

Esther put her cheek close to the stark-white linen sheets that were gently flapping in the wind. The yard was as small as the old house was large and covered with rows of clothesline, but it was high on the rocky hillside that overlooked Boston and one could smell the ocean breeze when the wind blew from the east. The billowing sheets reminded her of the large sailing vessels in Boston Harbor venturing out beyond Graves Light and into the world. Her sisters traveled on these ships and she loved to hear stories of their adventures, but she did not envy them. It was something she would never do. She was content to be a homebody.

Esther took a deep cleansing breath, letting the crisp, clean smell engulf her. Then she exhaled slowly as her muscles released the tension that had been building since James returned home. She knew it was silly, but this was one of her favorite pastimes. She desperately wished life were as simple as wringing her dirty laundry in the washer and having it come out brand spanking new. But it wasn't, and it was time to fold the wash and go in the house to face him. These were never pleasant times when James returned home after a lengthy disappearing act or, in this case, incarceration.

After serving his time, James came home to his family. He seemed to resent anything she had to say. His little girl, Doris, was now six years old and he was virtually a stranger to her. James showed no interest in getting to know his children. That was women's work. He continued his daily drinking, returning home to take his frustrations out on his wife.

One afternoon, he pinned Esther up against the wall. Before he raised his hand, he felt a pain on the outside of his knee. Doris had kicked him and was winding up for another one, desperately trying to protect her mother. He yelled and released his grip on Esther. In that moment she gathered her two children and flew out the front door, down the stairs and around the side of the house to the coal cellar. The children knew this routine as well as a school fire drill.

Once they were safely downstairs, Esther sat on the edge of the coal bin and wrapped her arms around her children in a comforting hug. Doris's little hand pushed her away. "Mama, look, at the hop toad hole," she whispered.

Esther looked at the coal chute and then at the narrow windows on either side of the coal door. Doris would play with the frogs that got caught in the well and named the windows 'hop toad holes.' The glass was covered with soot and it was difficult to see out, but there was no mistake. She could make out her husband's shoes close to the window well.

She placed her right index finger over her lips and leaned down close to her children's' ears.

"Let's play a game and see who can be quiet," she said as she reached into her apron pocket and pulled out a small skein of yarn.

Little Bob loved this game. He was only three and thankfully didn't understand the situation, but Doris did. Esther watched as her daughter took the yarn and sat her brother, his face covered in soot, on the floor in front of her. Then Doris wove the yarn skillfully in and out of her little fingers, playing cat's cradle and Jacob's ladder as Bob watched, mesmerized.

Esther knew James wouldn't look for them for long. He was drunk and would stumble about until he either passed out or decided to leave.

Sure enough, she heard the front door slam and the floorboards above them creak as he walked from the front of the house to the back door and back again. She still waited until she heard him climbing the stairs to the bedroom. They stayed hiding out there, breathing in the black coal dust until she was sure he was asleep.

The worm had turned and James was the type of man he told everyone his stepfather, Alfred Lorentzen, was. A wife beater.

***

Ironically, through the help of a friend, James obtained employment driving for a Boston cab company and, for a while, things in his life seemed to almost be normal, until January 28, 1929.

James was driving on Tremont Street near Massachusetts Avenue in the South End when he struck a pedestrian. The man was semi-conscious when he was taken to City Hospital. He sustained a fractured skull and internal injuries, and his outcome was grim.

Upon questioning, the man kept repeating his name and address, which was, "H. S. Jones, 65 years old, Parker Street, Roxbury" over and over again.

The police tried to establish the identity of the man who now was in critical condition, but he passed away and they never found any relatives. The fact that James had run this man down and he was now deceased didn't bother James, but he did dwell on the fact that the man wasn't identified. James thought how nice it must be to not have any ties and no one who knows you. James would love to be invisible. Think of what he could get away with.

Not long after the unfortunate pedestrian's death, home life on Ashley Street became unbearable for everyone and James made a decision to desert his wife and children without a word. He simply never returned home.

He obtained a room in a boarding house and on occasion traveled back north to Gloucester. He didn't know why he made these trips. It was an endless cycle of watching his mother from a distance, tying one on at the nearest bar and then getting a fine for drunk driving, or ending up in jail for disorderly conduct. The Gloucester Police Department knew Lawson and it was well documented that trouble always came with him when he returned to town.

***

Months passed, and one day Esther accepted that James was not coming home, ever. No one had come to the door to inform the family he was in jail like the last time. There was no information on his whereabouts.

An elderly family friend, Mrs. Mears, lived down the street and agreed to hire Esther as a housecleaner. She would finally have an income. Esther could start after arrangements were made for Doris and Bob's care while she worked.

Esther stood on the first floor and looked up to watch her son's paper airplane dip back and forth as it slowly descended from the second floor balcony.

"Ma, when's Dad coming home?"

She was conflicted by her feelings as she looked up at her little boy's face and wondered how she was going to answer that question. Her sister, Evelyn, stood in the doorway. She had overheard Bob, came and stood beside Esther, and put her arm around Esther's shoulder. They laughed as Bob slid down the stairs on his bottom and chased away the cat that had been swatting his paper plane.

Esther smiled. "He loves planes. Did he tell you what he wants to be when he grows up?"

"Yes, he did, but right now you have to think about what's right here."

We're here for you Esther. James is not coming back. Not that his presence contributed. It'll be okay."

Esther stiffened, "I know. Mrs. Mears said I could start as her housekeeper Saturday. Would you mind watching the children?"

"Of course I don't mind. We're family. We'll all work it out," Evelyn answered before reassuring her with a hug.

Esther worked on her hands and knees, scrubbing floors and performing other cleaning duties at Mrs. Mears's house. She would come home and help her parents, clean and cook, and take care of her children. It was a hard life, but she could breathe a sigh of relief now that James was gone from their lives.

In 1932, Esther filed for and was granted a divorce, something unspoken in the day. The grounds were three years of utter desertion. She kept her eyes on the newspapers, but never mentioned his name again to her family.

Chapter 18   Murder on the Tracks

Donohue handed James his cut from their last scam. "The last hurrah was late last night when the goods were picked up. This job gave us a nifty take. So, what's the story, Jimmy boy?"

"Whatddya mean?"

"Your bride and your little ones. You haven't seen them lately. You haven't gone home at all."

James downed the contents of his glass. He beckoned the bartender for a refill before he answered.

"Yeah, well, that chapter is closed."

Donohue's head bobbed in agreement. "Good for you, no man needs baggage tying him down." He tapped his chest. "Look at me. Free as a bird. Don't need some skirt nagging me, even left my own mother at twelve. I stowed away on a freighter to come to this great land of opportunity."

"Seriously, Donohue? You had a mother? I thought you were hatched."

"Hey, you should talk, James. You never talk about where you came from. Your Mum and Da."

"What's to tell? He died when I was thirteen and she, well, she remarried."

"So you went in the war when she remarried?"

James's face darkened, "No, not right away. Not until I killed him first."

When James left Esther and his children, he never looked back on family life. He simply decided it cramped his lifestyle and it was time to move on. The last few years he and Donohue were inseparable, pulling off small-time robberies and cons between Boston and Providence to sustain their lifestyle.

On January 2, 1934, James and Donohue were sitting at the diner down on Tremont Street when a mutual acquaintance of theirs, John W. McManmon, a taxi driver from Jamaica Plain, walked into the restaurant looking for them. He joined them at their table, hunching forward, indicating he had something to tell them in private.

James acknowledged him in a low voice. "What's up?"

McManmon put a finger up to wait. He waved the waitress over and ordered a drink. Before she came back, he told them he had a way to get all of them a good score.

"Look, I've got a drunk out in the cab and he's carrying a heavy roll," he whispered.

Donohue laughed, "And where did you say you were going when you pulled over and stopped here?"

"He's so drunk he doesn't know what the hell is going on. I don't even think he heard me when I told him I had to stop and take a piss."

"What's a heavy roll? How much?" James asked.

The waitress returned with a Scotch for McManmon. He slowly swirled the liquor around in the glass and took a swig, waiting for her to move out of earshot. Once she was far enough away, he told them, "The guy told me he was carrying his entire savings." McManmon shook his head.

Donohue looked out the window at the cab. "What a dope."

"You got that right. So I asked him how much lettuce he's got and he pulls out a bankroll of seven hundred smackers. Says he's headed out of town after celebrating or something."

James and Donohue looked at each other and both let out a low whistle. Neither one said anything. They worked so well together, one could finish the other's sentence. They tipped their heads back, finished their drinks and got up. McManmon looked startled, but then he followed suit, bumbling out behind the two of them to his waiting cab.

McManmon was right about one thing, James thought. McManmon's fare was blind drunk. Before he knew what was happening, James and Donohue had sandwiched him in the back seat. The drunk looked back and forth at them; drool dribbled down his chin. Slurring his words, he asked, "Hey, whattssss yo' guys doing?" They didn't answer him.

Donohue pointed to McManmon, who was standing on the curb. "Drive," he instructed.

McManmon climbed in the driver's seat, put on his scally cap, then turned around and asked, "Where to?"

James didn't hesitate. "Take Dover Street to Albany, then over to Randolph Street."

The drunk attempted to protest, but only garbled words came out of his mouth before his eyes rolled back in his head. He gave no resistance. A heavy sigh escaped his lips before he closed his eyes and his head sank back on the seat.

McManmon pulled the cab away from the curb and no one spoke until they got to an abandoned lot close to a bridge above the railroad tracks, where James told him to pull over. The three of them got out of the cab. James pulled the drunk out and threw him to the ground. Donohue bent over, rolled the man's pockets and came up with the bankroll. He grinned and held it for a minute before he handed it over to James.

They could have left then, but James knew when Donohue handed over the money, he wanted some action with this drunk. Donohue was small, but he was a mean son of a bitch with local talent acquired through necessity when he was a youth on the streets of Cork. As a young man, he made his way in the fight rings of New York City. It was the Irish scrapper in him.

Donohue kicked the man, who unceremoniously attempted to get up. When he got to his feet, Donohue hit him so hard he swung around and fell into James. Quickly, James shoved the cash in his pocket before he grabbed the man by his shirt with one hand and put his other fist in his face. Blood splattered as the man's nose flattened against his face.

McManmon got in on the action and the three of them passed the drunk around, giving him a good beating. Winded after their frenzy, they looked down at their victim on the ground while they caught their breath. McManmon retrieved the man's duffle bag from his cab and threw it on top of him, then turned and asked James for his cut.

James laughed, "Your cut? What are you talking about?" Still laughing, James turned to walk away when McManmon sucker-punched him. When Donohue joined in the brawl, McManmon made a run for his cab. A hand grabbed his shirt as he reached the driver's side door. He held onto the door handle to avoid being pulled back to the ground, but lost his foothold when it broke. James beat McManmon to a pulp, dragged him out to the street and threw him in the gutter. The two of them got in McManmon's cab and drove away.

***

James was driving and knew they had to get rid of the cab. He drove to Dwight and Tremont Streets, pulled the cab over to the curb and they got out. James pocketed the keys and they walked over to one of their regular haunts to have a drink and divvy the money up.

An acquaintance of Donohue's by the name of Smitty and a woman named Janice Mazzio spotted them and joined them at their table.

"Who's the babe?" James asked, eyeing the tall, buxom blonde with shapely legs who towered over Smitty.

Smitty shrugged his shoulders and looked at Janice as he answered. "She's a buddy's wife. Keeping her company, ya know, while he's in the hospital."

"He's in the hospital? And you say you're doing him a favor by taking care of her? Right!" James snorted.

"What do you care?" Smitty retorted. "You guys interested in going to a party?"

James eyed Janice and smiled. She reciprocated, sporting a sly smile below fluttering eyelashes. "Yeah, sure."

Donohue shook his head. "Naw, I'm beat. I'm going to find a hotel and flop. I have to head back to Providence tomorrow."

The four of them walked to Castle Square where Donohue said good night and went his own way.

***

The weather had turned overnight and the next morning the skies were overcast, threatening precipitation. James walked briskly down Tremont Street, his hands shoved down deep in his pockets and a fisherman's cap low on his brow. Recently, he had picked up a part-time job at a restaurant a couple of doors down from the bar, where he bused tables. If he was strapped for cash, he would pocket leftovers from the tables he cleared. But before work, he fortified his day with his regular breakfast, black coffee and a shot of whiskey. This took place on the last stool at Dooley's bar.

The coffee was still steaming when Donohue walked in and straddled the stool next to James. "Did you see the *Globe* this morning?" Donohue asked.

"No." James answered in a short tone.

"You're in a foul mood this morning. What did you do last night, James?"

"What are you jawing about, Donohue? And why are you here? Weren't you going back to Providence?"

"I'm going but thought I should check in with you about last night. What'd you do, James?"

"I tied one on. What do you think? And you know, you're giving me a worse headache, so show me a little consideration, will ya?"

Donohue ignored him and hailed the bartender. "Well, I think you're going to need to read something before you start your day. Hey, Dooley, bring today's newspaper before you get my beer."

"What did your last maid die of?" Dooley snapped at Donohue as he reached his large tattooed arm under the counter and came back up with the *Boston Globe*. The bartender slapped it down in front of Donohue. Without another word, he limped off to pull the draft.

Donohue didn't say anything to James. He tipped his beer to his mouth and took a long swig before swallowing. He nonchalantly pushed the paper in front of James and tapped his finger a quarter of the down the front page.

"What?" James growled.

"Just read the bloody thing."

James snapped the paper up and looked at the article. He felt Donohue's eyes on him as he read the first line and drew in a deep breath.

"Bartender, pour me a double. Now."

109

Boston Globe
January 3
Shortly before 7 this morning, a man walking near the railroad tracks under the Exeter and Huntington Bridge found the mangled body of John McManmon, taxi driver. Both of the man's legs had been amputated by the train. Police are investigating.

James was quiet, and looked like he was contemplating a problem. He rolled the paper up, pushed the coffee away and downed a shot of whiskey.

He looked at Donohue and asked, "We're square, right?"

"Right." Donohue nodded in agreement.

"Our stories are straight? They're going to ask you, you know."

"Who are they? The coppers? Why would they?" Donohue asked, "Anyway, I don't have anything to hide."

"Dunny, I was a damn cop, you know that. We were both seen with McManmon last night. They'll come. There'll be no doubt about it."

Donohue thought for a second and then agreed. "Okay, you're probably right. Let's go over things outside."

Donohue and James entered the narrow alley between the bar and the adjacent building. They sat on wooden crates and each lit a cigarette before talking. The smoke helped disguise the stench of the urine-soaked ground.

Donohue looked hard at James. "So what happened after I left you the other night?"

"What do you mean, what happened? Smitty, the dame and I went to that party. Are you saying I had something to do with this?" He waved the paper in the air.

"Well, I left. I flopped at the Union House. How'd I know you were going to go back and waste him after we already kicked his ass?"

James's face darkened, "You're crossing the line, Donohue. I never went back to where we left McManmon."

"You pocketed his keys, James. If you didn't go back to the tracks, then who killed him?"

***

At first, police thought McManmon jumped from the bridge to the Boston-Albany railroad tracks below. The evidence pointed to a possible suicide. The investigator spoke with the cab driver's wife and learned he had been depressed over his health, which she thought could be a reason for taking his own life. Not being able to work on a regular basis led to money problems for the McManmon family and to his worries over not being able to meet his obligations.

McManmon's taxi was owned by Fred Kirchgassner of the South End, and he had a different theory. He told the police the cabbies in the Park Square area were fighting over fares and he thought McManmon's trouble stemmed from an altercation over fares and territory.

Despite these theories, James was right about the trail leading the police to him and Donohue. Before the end of the day, on January 4, 1934, he and Donohue were taken into custody for questioning and each held on $5,000 bail.

Chapter 19   Boston Police

Inspector John McCarthy walked into his office and frowned at the unorganized piles of paperwork hiding every inch of the surface of his desk. Most of the files on top were active cases and the ones sprawled all over the floor needed to be filed away as closed or cold cases. He threw his hat into the air at the coat rack, attempting to get a "ringer," as he called it, and sat down heavily on the chair behind his desk. McCarthy sighed. "Overwhelmed" didn't cover it. Crime was escalating, manpower was lean and the paperwork was insurmountable.

His friend, Detective Manny Carlotta, stood in the doorway. He looked at the hat on the floor, picked it up and placed it cockeyed on the post. "You missed, John."

"Yeah." McCarthy vigorously rubbed his ruddy face with both hands.

Carlotta pulled up a chair and promptly threw his feet up on the edge of the desk. "What's the matter? You look like shit."

"I've got an itch I can't scratch. You know that cab driver case?"

"The suicide on the Huntington tracks?"

"That's the one. I'm not convinced that was a suicide."

"Hey, the wife thought so. Said hubby was depressed over money."

"I'm not buying it yet. I keep playing it over and over in my head and I think it smells. There are too many things unanswered, like how did the cab's door handle get broken? And those guys we held for questioning? They weren't angels. No sir. Their stories smelled worse than Boston Harbor being dredged at low tide."

"Maybe the door handle was already broken and he just left it hanging there," Carlotta said.

"No, it was confirmed with Kirchgassner, the owner of the cab company. It was in good shape before McManmon took it out."

"Did McManmon have a record?"

"The records show McManmon had been involved in a hit-and-run of an Anatas Pappas, a fruit peddler back on Tremont Street in 1927. Let's see." McCarthy sorted through the papers. "He wasn't the driver, but he was in the car with two others and had been drinking all night. The report says they ditched the car. When an officer found it, McManmon approached the parking lot. When asked if it was his car, he didn't answer and shuffled his feet. Eventually he confessed and gave up the other two. Served some time, but nothing else on record."

Manny's face lit up. "So, John, it looks like our vic had a guilty conscience. Think about this. What if he had one about a recent crime and threatened to talk and those guys took him out?"

"Yup, that would be murder. It's possible, and I can't see the suicide angle. If he didn't off himself after the fruit peddler was run over, why do it now?"

Carlotta nodded, "Okay, so what are you going to do about it?"

"I'm going to keep digging, Manny. Keep my eyes and ears open until I can nail the bastards. Did you know Lawson, the ex-cop, already had a criminal history?"

"Yeah? What's his rap?"

"I found out he buried his stepfather six feet under back in '16 up in Gloucester."

"No kidding?" Now Carlotta's interest was piqued and he leaned closer to John's desk. "You know, I think I remember that one. Let's see, the case was about eighteen years ago. I was new on the force. Used a monkey wrench, I think."

The inspector nodded, "Yep, that's the one. It was a big enough story that it hit the *Boston Globe.*"

"Did he serve any time for it?"

"No, they downgraded it to manslaughter on account of the mother's testimony. He was defending her, pled guilty and he was released on probation."

"Well, as you know, John, murder can become a nasty habit."

John's eyes were fixed on the eight-by-ten crime scene photo in his hand. "Yeah," he mumbled, "It's kind of like putting your pants on every morning for some guys."

Chapter 20   Esther

Outside the open kitchen window, pigeons cooed in unison with the creaking of Esther's rocking chair. Early morning was her favorite time of day before the children were up for school. Life seemed uncomplicated and quiet. She savored a cup of tea and daydreamed without interruptions.

Esther's sisters, Clara and Evelyn, came in to the kitchen, devoid of the usual back and forth bantering and chatter. Clara approached Esther and handed her the morning newspaper.

She took it, but didn't look at it. Instead, she studied their faces for a moment, as if seeing bad news in print would be worse.

"What is it? Bad news?"

Clara put her hands on her hip and with a smug smile said, "Not exactly, it's *old* news, as in your *old* husband. Maybe now that bastard will be put away where he belongs." She nodded to the paper, indicating to Esther to read it.

Esther was puzzled until she looked at the front page and froze. She turned to the inside page where the article on McManmon's death was continued. When she finished, she stood and, with great resolve, folded the paper, went outside and threw it in the garbage pail.

Chapter 21   Investigation

In newspaper interviews, Captain Perley Skillings stated that Lawson, former policeman, had previous trouble with McManmon and he has refused to answer any questions. Despite this, Lawson was expected to be released the next morning. They had no concrete evidence to hold him, especially when a Back Bay policeman had come forward to clear the former cop of any connection with the death. This policeman testified he had seen McManmon in a Back Bay restaurant. James had bought him a drink and he saw no trouble between them. Two women, restaurant patrons, could corroborate this story.

The police determined that McManmon left the restaurant after having a drink and went for a walk. Then, once on the bridge, he leaped over as a train was passing by.

Inspector McCarthy threw the report down in disgust. Detective Carlotta had been his friend long enough to read his mood, and was smart enough not to say anything. He opted to go to the break room for two cups of strong black coffee. It was evident this was going to be a long night.

Carlotta returned with two ceramic mugs, sloshing hot coffee over his hands as he put them on the desk. Swearing, he took his handkerchief out of his back pocket and dried himself. He turned to McCarthy. "So, what's the report say?"

McCarthy pushed the report across the desk to Manny. "It says, beware of being run over by a train."

"What?"

McCarthy wiped the papers off the desk in a swift sweep of his forearm. "Because *all* the evidence gets mangled. *That's* what it says."

"What can we do? One of our own is vouching for him."

"Yeah, right."

Months passed with nothing new in the investigation until May, when an anonymous tip came in to Inspector John McCarthy that there was a person responsible for McManmon's death. The tip led to Providence, where Sergeant Manuel Suzan went, bringing back John Donohue. Special Agents William Lindahl and William Gallagher brought in Frank (Smitty) Smith who, after being questioned by the inspector, was booked as a suspicious person.

Donohue made a statement to the Providence and Boston police that McManmon had tipped them off about his fare carrying a large amount of money. He admitted he and James rolled a "drunk." McManmon expected a cut and when James refused, they fought. James beat the victim and left him in the street. They took his cab and abandoned it at Dwight and Tremont Streets. After splitting the money, they ran into Frank Smith and a woman named Janice. They were going to Castle Square, but he left when they decided to go to a party. He stated that he registered in a South End hotel and then the next day he went to Providence. He then took the night boat to New York and sometime later returned home to Providence.

Inspector McCarthy sat on the edge of the interrogation table and looked down at Donohue. "So, you admit to the robbery, but didn't lay hands on the guy?"

"I wouldn't dirty my hands on the likes of him." Donohue pulled out a cigarette and balanced it on the edge of his lower lip. "Got a light?"

"I might. Got anything else for me?"

"Yeah, I have one more thing. Lawson pocketed the keys to the cab. According to my friends, after I left, Lawson took off and didn't show up at their party until hours later."

After hearing Donohue's story, Inspector McCarthy ordered that Lawson be taken into custody. Detective George Smith and Sergeant Leonard Banks found James in his hangout on Tremont Street and brought him down to the station. Now Inspector McCarthy knew he had to search the records for the Warren Avenue and Back Bay stations.

"Manny, there's got to be a report on the alleged beating and robbery if it occurred. Find it."

Manny hit pay dirt at the Dudley Street station. A report was filed that Joseph Begin, a 64-year-old man from Auburn, Maine, had been robbed of $700. According to the log he was found at the intersection of Warren and Dudley Streets, Roxbury, after walking a mile and a half after the robbery.

Lawson and Donohue were charged with the robbery and held for $20,000 bail each for a hearing set for May 28th. They made arrangements to contact Joseph Begin and have him be present for a lineup.

According to witnesses from that night, there was a mystery woman seen with Lawson, and the inspector was determined to locate her for questioning. Frank Smith identified her as Janice Mazzio from Beacon Street

Mazzio was eventually found and arrested at a Waltham hospital as she sat at her sick husband's bedside. The woman allegedly entertained James and Donohue in her apartment on the night in question, and because she refused to answer any questions, she too was arrested as a person of suspicion. In an unfortunate turn of events, while Janice Mazzio was being detained, her husband, Dominic Mazzio, passed away in the hospital.

In the next forty-eight hours, the medical examiner declared that McManmon met his death while trying to board a moving train and Joseph Begin could not identify robbers in the police lineup. He had been too inebriated to remember much of anything. Even though the police were not satisfied with the answers in their investigation, once again, the two men were released. There was nothing substantial to hold them on.

Having escaped another murder charge unscathed, James went back to his everyday existence, but from that day forward James and John "The Rat" Donohue—as James dubbed him— parted ways, ending their crime sprees.

Chapter 22   James and Rose

James had to change his life. He found new territory to hang out in. He walked into the Eastside Lounge and met Rose. She was small and fun-loving, with dark skin and black curly hair, and he was immediately drawn to her energetic and flirty personality. Being small didn't hinder her being a bartender, a profession uncommon for a woman. Even the most burly, macho man cowered with respect for her when they were drinking on her turf.

"What'll you have, soldier?" Dark, exotic eyelashes fluttered over cocoa-colored eyes.

"That was a lifetime ago. How'd you know I used to be a soldier?"

The bartender looked at him like he was the village idiot. She pursed her red lips and in doing so her dimples were so pronounced, he fell for her right there and then.

"Who wasn't a soldier, baby? Not to mention those tattoos on your arms."

She reached over the bar. Her fingers lightly traced the rose on his forearm and they locked eyes. For a moment James thought about the tattoos. He and another guy had gotten those years ago in Scollay Square before they shipped out overseas. On one forearm was a heart with an anchor over it. On the other was a rose with the word "MOM" under it.

His musing was interrupted when she announced, "How fitting. My name is Rose. What can I get you to drink?"

"I'll have a whiskey. Can I get you one?"

She cocked her head, still sizing him up. Finally she said, "I don't drink on the job, but I'm off in ten minutes and I'll take you up on that."

Something inside James shuddered. He hadn't felt alive in a long time. "Good, I knew I'd like this joint."

James had been a bit surprised to see a woman bartender, but the longer he watched the more he understood it was great for business. Every pair of eyes at the bar was on her and this didn't bother her a bit. In fact, James thought she thrived on it.

She performed her job with a fluid ease, confident that she had respect and admiration from even the lowest form of masculinity seated in the bar. And she did.

The door to the kitchen swung open and an older man backed out carrying a crate of glasses. He put the crate down and shuffled over to Rose. She ceremoniously passed the bar towel to him, laying it over his left shoulder. They spoke briefly in a foreign language James didn't recognize before she leaned forward, stood up on her tiptoes and kissed the man on the cheek.

James watched Rose in the mirror as she bent over to retrieve her pocketbook from the lower shelf. Sensing his gaze, she straightened up in one slow, seductive and graceful move. She turned to her reflection and took her time to primp before joining him on the other side of the bar. She put her hand on his arm, but didn't sit beside him. "I'll have a gin, straight up," she told him and motioned that she would be at a table in the back.

James paid for the drinks and brought them to the table, aware that the old man behind the bar was watching him like a hawk. He sat down across from Rose and stared at her.

She cocked her head and smiled. "Do you always stare down your prey?"

"If you're my prey, I'm in for quite a delicacy. I've never met anyone like you. And a female bartender to boot. What happens if one of these hooligans bothers you?"

Rose rolled her eyes and waved her hand through the air as if dismissing an unwanted visitor. "Oh, they'd find themselves on the bottom of the harbor." She stated this in such a matter-of-fact tone of her voice that James didn't doubt for a second that this would be true.

"Usually I wait tables. Tending bar is taboo in some gin joints, but this is a family business. I've got five uncles, all with sons scattered around the globe. I'm the only girl. I help my uncles out a couple of nights a week. We take care of our own. You know, help where I can and I don't care what other people think."

Her voice dripped with a kind of defiance with which he was familiar. He liked her rebellious attitude and found himself attracted to this refreshingly beautiful woman, who was obviously a few years younger than he. Seventeen years younger, to be exact.

James grinned. "Well, then we have something in common. I don't care what anyone thinks either, so we should get along just fine." Their eyes held fast as their glasses clinked in a toast.

**

These were the Great Depression years and employment opportunities were few and far between. James had to compete with the younger people of both sexes knocking on doors, standing in line. Things were easier when he and Donohue could score an easy mark, but after the McManmon affair he sent Donohue packing with a nice shiner. He knew enough to lie low for a period of time. He wanted a change in territory, a new start, which was why he walked into Rose's bar.

Rose was a willful, young woman, but she was raised in a strict and traditional family. She always had a thing for older men and found herself mesmerized by James, whom she thought vaguely resembled a new movie star, Errol Flynn. He had that same troubled and slightly dangerous air about him, a handsome, bad boy.

They were inseparable from the first night. James would sit on the last bar stool until Rose's shift ended and then they would usually end up at someone's house party until the wee hours of the morning.

A couple of months into their relationship, Rose slipped a piece of paper across the bar to James. Written on it was a man's name, along with the address of the Fore River Shipyard in Quincy.

"What's this?" James asked her.

"That's my uncle's name. He's the oldest of the brothers and I spoke to him about a job for you, James."

Immediately anger and embarrassment boiled up in him, but he kept it under control and didn't say anything. She could read the disapproval on his face, and yet she loved him, so she put her hand on his shoulder and gently prodded him.

"James, you need a job. He's kind of a 'big cheese' at the yard. He said if you're interested in working at the shipyard, he'll hire you. You can't go on like you have been much longer. Flopping wherever we end up at night after a party. Taking a room for a night here and there. What kind of life is that?"

She was right. Men would kill for a job at the shipyard and here it was being handed to him. He heard they paid well and he would be around the water again. How bad could that be? Rose stood in front of him and any residue of anger slowly dissipated as he looked at her small, pert frame adorned with those red, pouty lips.

He sighed heavily, "Okay, Rose, I'll go see him tomorrow." He leaned over the bar and kissed her lips.

***

James met with Rose's Uncle Alouche, a small, swarthy, Lebanese man in his early sixties, and immediately disliked him. They squared off across Alouche's office. When her uncle finally spoke, there was no color-coating his real reason for offering employment to James. Like his brothers, he was protective of his niece.

"My Rose, she needs a good man who can carry his weight. I need a worker. You keep your part of the deal and I'll keep mine. I take care of my family and my Rose. She may be a force to deal with, but she is a favorite of mine and I will be watching over her."

James laughed. "Are you threatening me, old man?"

Alouche raised a calloused finger and pointed it at James. "My eye will be on you."

The man's look made James think twice. There was something unsettling in the silence and James nervously shifted his body weight. It was the familiar look of a predator.

Suddenly Alouche spoke. "You want the job, you report at 7 sharp on Monday morning. You don't want it? Well, then, *boy*, you find yourself another girlfriend."

Upon Uncle Alouche's pronunciation of the word *boy*, James stiffened and stood up quickly, holding his eyes steadfastly on Rose's uncle until he heard a noise behind him. Two large men were positioned on either side of the door frame. James took another look at the man behind the desk. "I'll see you tomorrow, *Uncle Alouche*." He turned around and swaggered slowly to the door. The entire time he felt three sets of eyes boring a hole in his back.

Monday morning, James reported to the crew office and got briefed on his new job. After the first week, James became aware of how much he had missed working around the waterfront. He loved being near the ocean again, the sounds of the gulls, the halyards knocking against each other in the wind. And then there were the huge hulls of metal being riveted together to float. Shipbuilding was a miraculous feat and James finally felt he was a part of something.

Rose and James were the hot item couple around town and on October 22, 1935, they took a road trip north to Derry, New Hampshire and got married. They settled on Milford Street in Boston and, once again, James attempted normalcy in his life. He liked the shipyard and befriended coworkers and mariners, with whom he continued his drinking nights.

Rose helped out at the family's bar until late March of '36 when she discovered they were going to have a baby. She sat on the edge of their bed, waiting impatiently for James to open his eyes to tell him the good news. A minute seemed eternal. As she watched him breathe, her legs swayed side to side, in sync with the rhythmic beat of his chest. He woke, saw her and playfully pulled her down on the bed.

Rose giggled and squirmed in his arms. "James, James, wait. I have some good news to tell you."

He ignored her, gently rolled her so they were face to face, and kissed her. He went to kiss her again, but her hand came up between their lips and she made eye contact with him.

"James, we're going to have a baby."

There was quiet as the words sank in and then the news hit him like a ton of bricks had fallen on his head. He sat up so abruptly, Rose was pushed to one side.

"What's wrong?" she cried. "Aren't you happy about the baby? Honey, talk to me. Don't close me out." Pleading words spilled out of Rose in a futile attempt to engage James. The silence was deafening. Not another word passed between them. James got out of bed, got dressed and left the house. Rose sobbed until there were no more tears left inside of her. She felt so empty, except for the flutter of a tiny heartbeat.

Chapter 23   Rose and Catherine

The shipyard was currently working on two cruisers to be delivered to the Navy, the *Quincy* and the *Vincennes*. The yard was down to a skeleton crew compared to the number of employees they had employed to finish the government contracts at the beginning of the Depression. But James had heard rumors that more contracts were coming. Evil winds were blowing around the world and having served in the World War, James sensed trouble brewing, which meant more ships would be built.

Since the news of the pregnancy, Rose and James had grown distant. Rose was heavy with child and spent most of her time alone, isolated in their apartment. Her family worried about her after learning from Uncle Alouche that James drank with the men every night after work, but he never harmed her, at least not physically.

James thought back to his first marriage to Esther and how things changed when children came along. He wanted no part of bringing up children. James could have done well himself as an only child. He was meant to be a loner and didn't want this. He liked his life neat and clean, like the jobs he pulled. Easy marks, no strings.

November came, regardless of what James wanted, and Rose delivered a beautiful little girl. James was home and to Rose's surprise he stayed home for a few days and watched over her and the baby. No one was more surprised at this than James himself. At forty-two years old, he entertained fleeting moments of normalcy between his wild days of "living on the edge" on the streets, but once again this was short-lived.

A month later on a windy, rain-swept day, Rose put her baby girl down in the bassinet for a nap. She relished having a couple of minutes to herself to enjoy a cup of hot tea. James was never around and, when he was, he didn't help her with the baby. Sometimes, she thought he was even afraid of her. As she put the kettle on the stove, there was a knock at the door.

Who on earth could that be? she thought, hoping it was not one of James's friends looking for money, or worse, a bill collector. Money was tight and if it were not for her uncles slipping her money for the baby, Rose didn't know what she would do.

Rose opened the door a crack and looked out.

"Who is it?" she cautiously asked.

Through the small opening, she saw a well dressed, attractive woman with chestnut brown hair neatly pinned up under a hat with a short veil.

"Hello? I'm looking for James… James Lawson," the visitor responded.

Rose, now more than curious, opened the door a little wider to obtain a good look at the woman.

"Who are you?" Rose's voice was tinged with jealousy. She didn't mean for it to sound the way it did. Her heart rate accelerated with anxiety when she thought this could be someone James was out carousing around the town with, although she guessed this woman was older than James's liking.

The woman seemed to read her mind and smiled reassuringly. "I'm James's sister, Catherine. And you are…?"

"Sister?" Rose flung the door open with such force it hit the hall wall.

Rose's shock was obvious to her visitor. She released her breath, opened the door and motioned the woman to come in. She closed the door and walked down the hall to the kitchen. James's sister followed her. Rose pulled out a kitchen chair and motioned the woman to sit.

Rose was speechless as she sat across from James's sister. Steam hissed and spit on the stove, progressively becoming a steady whistle. She recovered and stammered, "I'm sorry. Where are my manners? My name is Rose. I'm James's wife. I was about to have a cup of tea. Would you join me?"

The woman's eyebrow rose slightly as she reached up and unpinned her hat and placed it on the edge of the table. "I'd love one, thank you."

Catherine watched Rose prepare the tea and then softly broke the ice. "I take it you didn't know James had a sister. You probably don't know much about him at all," she added in a matter-of-fact statement.

Rose found it odd she was not offended by Catherine's statement. Most women would consider a comment that they don't know their husband well to be an insult. But deep inside, Rose knew this was true and felt deeply embarrassed. Rose placed the two cups of tea on the small, wooden table. She sat down and slid the creamer and sugar bowl over until they were in front of her guest. She couldn't speak right away. She felt a lump in her throat and swallowed a sip of tea to smooth her nerves. *Damn him,* she thought. *He's reduced me to the type of woman I hate.*

"Of course I know my husband, he…," Rose's voice faltered, "No, you're right. I don't. I don't even know when James will be back. A deep flush scalded her cheeks as she turned away. "He's been gone a couple of days."

Catherine nodded and Rose noticed a knowing look of resignation in her eyes.

"So when did you two marry?"

"October, last year." Rose sat up proudly and announced, "You have a niece. Her name is Helen. She's sleeping now. You'd be surprised how much she looks like James."

Catherine smiled warmly, "I'm looking forward to meeting her."

Rose felt stupid, spitting out choppy sentences like she was born and bred in the back woods, but she was at a loss for words. There were a few minutes of small talk before Rose asked, "Please tell me. What was James's life growing up like? I know so little and he is not forthcoming with family information." She gazed into her teacup, avoiding eye contact. "Or any information for that matter." She hoped she wasn't crossing the line by asking questions that were too personal.

James's sister leaned back momentarily and Rose wondered if she was trying to decide how much she should share with her. Rose would never know that she was not the woman Catherine expected to open the door. Catherine had kept tabs on her brother over the years. She heard he had married a woman named Esther and had two children. Apparently he had moved on to another family and Catherine felt she should not mention this fact. Why hurt the poor woman? She's got enough to deal with being her brother's wife.

Catherine straightened in the chair and looked Rose square in the eyes. "Ok, I'll tell you about James's childhood. I'll tell you everything up to the time James left Gloucester."

Rose sat back and took a deep breath, anxious to hear James's story. Catherine took a sip of tea and cleared her throat. They each sensed they had to be in the right space for this conversation.

"There are three of us. We have a brother, Peter. James wasn't the baby of the family, Peter is, but James was so clingy. Mother doted on James's neediness and our father was jealous. Right from the beginning it seemed James butted heads with Father."

Rose thought about their baby girl. These people were her family and for her sake she needed to know who they were. "Your family was from Gloucester?"

"Yes, my father was on a trawler crew, as were most of the men up on the North Shore. James was different though."

"In what way?"

"He loved the ocean and the boats, but hated the fish. I use to think he was lazy, but looking back, I think James believed the work was beneath him, although he did work on the docks. My mother indulged him too much, I suppose. James always looked for the easy way, or for things to be handed him."

Rose thought about this and agreed James was still like that. She told

Catherine how she had to push him into taking the job her uncle had offered. Sometimes, she wonders where he gets his money, but she is too afraid of the answer to ask him. This fact she kept to herself.

"Father brutally criticized James, and James learned to keep his face blank and his mouth shut at an early age. I think this took a toll on him. By the time he got to his early teens, he had trouble with authority figures and he was always on the defensive."

There was so much Rose did not know about her husband. "Did he have friends?"

"James had one or two friends, but he was mostly a loner. He didn't talk much, but he cherished the time he had at home with Mother when Father was out to sea or drinking in a bar."

Catherine reached over and patted Rose's hand. "I don't think James has changed. I don't think he can. He started getting in trouble at eight years old. Father didn't know how to handle him, so between the bad behavior and the jealousy, Father's only answer was to beat it out of him."

Rose took a sharp breath inward. "He beat him?"

"Yes, he whipped him nightly, whether he did anything wrong or not. He said it was for good measure and would cover any wrongdoings he didn't know about."

"But, that's horrible."

"I know, but we were all powerless to stop it. Father's word was law or it was until..." Catherine stopped talking, picked up a spoon and swirled it in a slow circle in her teacup.

"What happened to your father? Is he still living?"

Catherine looked down at her lap for a moment and then slowly raised her eyes to meet Rose's eyes. "No, he died in an *accident* when James was thirteen."

Something unspoken hung in the air, like a storm cloud building pressure in Rose's sinus cavity. Her head started throbbing. Rose's voice was low, "Oh, what kind of accident?" she gasped, "How did he die?"

Catherine picked up her teacup, her two hands wrapped tightly around it as if she were attempting to warm herself against a chill. She took a sip and took her time before answering Rose's question.

"Father and James went out at dawn on a small boat to pull our lobster traps." Catherine was quiet for a moment, her eyes glazed as if she were in some far-off place. "I vividly remember that day. The ocean was like a lake. Smooth as glass, you know? James said Father threw a trap overboard after he re-baited it and his foot got caught in the line. He went overboard, pulled under by the weight of the trap. He drowned before James could cut him loose."

Rose dared not say anything. Heaviness pulled in her chest as she tried to swallow the bile that was building in her throat. She had noticed Catherine's initial hesitation and understood she implied there was more to the story surrounding their father's *accidental* death.

"So, by the time James was sixteen, my brother, Peter, and I had moved out, living our own lives. At that point, it was only James and Mother at home, and before long my mother met someone. His name was Alfred Lorentzen and eventually they married. From the start, it was bad. I know Mother thought it would get better in time, but it didn't and it ended in tragedy."

"How? What happened?" Rose immediately felt stupid, sounding like a parrot repeating the same words.

"One day in March, 1916, James was twenty years old. He came home and said he found Alfred beating our mother. He was afraid he was going to kill her, so he grabbed a work wrench and struck him down. Alfred died from that blow a couple of days later."

"He was trying to save his mother, surely the authorities understood that." Rose pleaded. The tone of her voice was shaky and did not back up the words with any conviction even in her own mind.

"They arrested him for manslaughter and then changed it to murder when they indicted him, so the case was turned over to the court. At first Mother was implicated as well because she had hidden the wrench in the closet after saying she threw it away in a mindless attempt to somehow protect James, but it caused more suspicion. When the trial was over, things were different."

"How so?" Rose asked.

"James saw fear in Mother's eyes and he hated it. Mother feared being alone the rest of her life, fear of being shunned by friends and neighbors, maybe even fear of her own son. He had lost his job when they jailed him and now no one would hire him. After he pled guilty and because of my mother's bruises, the defense negotiated probation and the judge strongly suggested signing up for the war effort. If he hadn't, James would have been basically run out of Gloucester by the townsfolk."

"Why are you here now?" Rose whispered. This news was about to push her over the pivot point. She didn't need to know this. Or did she? For the first time in her life, she felt vulnerable.

"I kept tabs on my brother, during World War I and afterwards. I don't know why, maybe because he is family. Now I'm here to tell him our mother has passed away."

"Oh, I'm so sorry."

"Thank you, but it was a blessing for her. She would have suffered if she had lingered." Catherine got up from the table. "I've taken up too much of your time. Thank you for your hospitality."

"Thank you for filling me in about my husband's life." Rose bit her lower lip as she thought how pathetic that sounded.

Catherine stopped at the door to pin her hat on. She turned and looked at Rose, as if she were about to say something, but nixed the statement with an almost imperceptible shake of her head. Instead she said, "Yes, well, you're welcome, dear. It's not a pretty story or one our family is proud of, but it would be better to have all the facts, in case you need to make a decision in the future for yourself and your child."

Rose opened the door and Catherine stepped out onto the stoop. She didn't bother asking Catherine if she wanted to see the baby because she knew they would never see her again.

"Catherine, wait! Should I tell James you'll be back, or where he can reach you?" Rose inquired.

"No, tell him Mother didn't suffer, she went in her sleep. Goodbye, Rose."

She had instantly liked Catherine and somehow felt like she was losing an ally, something she could use right now.

Catherine started down the stairs and suddenly stopped and turned back to Rose. "Tell James that his name was the last word she uttered before falling to sleep."

Rose's eyes widened, "Did she ask for James?"

Catherine eyes narrowed, "Before our mother fell into a deep sleep on her last night on this earth, in her restlessness she moaned repeatedly, 'Why did you do this again, James?'"

Rose felt weak. She watched Catherine descend the steps and disappear from view as the sidewalk turned onto the cross street. Rose stood on the stoop, arms folded across her shivering body, until she heard her baby cry. She took one more look up and down the street, turned around, went inside and shut the door.

Later that evening, after Rose put the baby down for the night, she sat in the parlor with the lights dim, trying to absorb the information she had learned today. She went over and over Catherine's story of James's father and stepfather. Their deaths, the accusations...it was all too much.

She jumped when she heard a key in the door, shocked to see James this early in the night, or at all for that matter. Rose dreaded telling him Catherine's message. He approached her and kissed her on the cheek.

"You're still awake, Rosie. Is something gnawing on you?"

"James, I have something to tell you."

"Ah, with a tone in your voice like that, I'll need a drink. I remember the last time you said that to me." He sneered and pulled a flask out of his back pocket. He took a large swig before falling back into his easy chair.

"You had a visitor today, James."

"Anyone looking for me can't be good." His voice was callous, as he lay his head back on the chair and gazed at the ceiling.

When she didn't say anything right away, he became irritated. "I'm tired, Rosie," he said sternly, "Out with it."

"Your sister, Catherine, was here."

James reacted like a puppet whose puppet master had jerked his strings in a seizure-like motion, snapping him to attention. He lurched forward, his ears were ringing and he felt the heat of the whiskey burn in his belly.

"Catherine?" Her name was all he managed to say in a hollow whisper. Rose reached for his hand and held tight.

"She came to tell you that your mother passed away."

James stared at her and Rose couldn't read him. His face was blank. His eyes gave away nothing.

She continued. "Catherine said to tell you, she didn't suffer. She died in her sleep." Now she saw James's face change slightly, right before he bellowed a coldhearted laugh. His head jerked back and his shoulders heaved as he laughed and wept at the same time. James stood up, tears streaming down his face, howling with laughter as he walked out of the apartment, slamming the door. From the bedroom, the baby wailed.

***

Over the next few years, things seemed to go as well as could be expected. Rose and her daughter spent most of their time with her family, while James carried on as usual, going to work and then to the bar.

James held his family at arm's length emotionally, but for a couple of years he did provide for them. The little girl loved to see him come home and James did think this was amusing once in a while, but when he was hung over or in a foul mood due to money problems, he would tell Rose to keep her out of sight.

Money was tight and one night the temptation to acquire funds easily was too strong to refuse, and James slipped back to his old ways.

Chapter 24   Lefty

At one of James's watering holes, he became tight with a couple of mariners by the names of Dominic Spinelli and Scotty Koval. They had a lot in common, being of seafaring blood. Also, many men in the Merchant Marine were older. They had no family to tie them down and they chose to travel the world, port by port on supply and transport ships assisting US troops. James envied them their freedom and lived vicariously through stories of the countries they visited and the women they met.

The seedy bars on the waterfront attracted the worst of the criminal element. Down by the docks, the most dangerous rats walked on two legs. It was in these dens of iniquity that he befriended thieves and murderers. They liked him because James, for all he was not, did possess a magnetic personality, and a con with charisma was a winning combination on the streets.

Crime was escalating and many of the buildings in Scollay Square had hidden tunnels and rooms that had been used as part of the Underground Railroad to hide escaped slaves. Now these spaces were being used for hookups by the criminal element.

James was becoming known as a "hit and run" expert, meaning he would partner up with someone he trusted. The partner would be his lookout as James picked a target in a quiet location and then assault and roll them for cash. The lookout was a necessity because the roof lights on the tops of police cars started to disappear in order to comply with blackout orders during the war. After he hit the mark, he would meet his lookout in a predetermined hiding place, most of the time in one of the many deserted buildings, where they would divvy up the loot.

The lookout would be Dominic Spinelli's job if he was in town. Dominic was on the serious side where Scotty was the opposite. He was a practical joker and at times he got under James's skin. Scotty was only serious when it came to food, something he was never without. His mouth and his doughy jowls were always in constant motion. He chewed with his mouth open, reminding James of a bloated puffer fish.

James's favorite cohort in crime was Lefty, a tall Irishman who could play a mean tune on the squeezebox. He was serious about the jobs they pulled and, having been a former boxer, he was quick on his feet. The only problem was he made up ballads to sing that told of his criminal escapades. When all the cops in Boston loved Irish music because they were Irish themselves, James was worried someone would put the songs together with the deeds. Once he explained his concerns, Lefty burst out laughing.

"Ya, right there, James. Those songs I'll sing as lullabies from now on to put me to sleep and keep the law-abiding ballads for the public's ears."

Lefty had a wife and nine kids to support, so he needed all the income he could get. He was the type of guy every social class liked. This included the Irish who dominated Boston. Lefty used this to his advantage and procured his day job at the city mortuary after doing a favor for one of the politicians. He assisted with autopsies, dug graves, filled out death certificates, and did general mechanic and cleanup work. As morbid as it could be, he loved it.

James laughed when he heard about Lefty's job. "Hey, Lefty, is it true dead men don't talk?"

Lefty gave a little squeeze on the box, bowed and said, "Sir, I can play and sing my songs all I want and my audience never gives me any grief, unlike you. Also, it gets me some quiet. My place has nine little ones running around and ya can't hear ya self think."

***

In 1943, James was working on a Baltimore class heavy cruiser, the USS *Canberra*. The yard was breaking its production records. The hours and work were grueling for the thirty-two thousand employees and not without danger.

Uncle Alouche had been killed in a work-related accident during an inspection, leaving James with no one to cover his constant tardiness following his long nights of drinking and pilfering. One month after Alouche's death, James was called into the foreman's office.

James walked in and removed his hard hat. "You wanted to talk with me?"

"Lawson, I'm going to warn you only once. If you show up late because of your drinking or any other reason again, you're out of here."

"Boss, I…"

"Do you understand or not? There are long lines of able-bodied men, younger than you waiting outside the gates to be a 'yard bird.' Shape up or get out."

"Yes, sir."

"Get the hell out in the yard and get back to work.

The foreman didn't waste any time sizing up his crew. His focus was on safety and he had spotted James's habits right away. Despite his better judgment he would keep him on for the time being. The man had a skill and when James worked, his work was exceptional. On the other hand the foreman knew the *Canberra* was already scheduled to be commissioned in October. The ship was so close to being ready and when the ship is done, so is Lawson.

***

In October, James was fired from the shipyard. After hearing James lost his job, Rose knew she would have to make some changes. Rose told him she learned from one of her uncles there were good jobs available out on the west coast and that she had decided to go to California. She and their little girl could stay with relatives until she acquired a job in one of the airplane factories out there. A new start in sunny California didn't sound bad. James agreed and, to her dismay, he told her he would soon follow.

Rose wasn't sure she wanted him to join her, but said nothing. She was surprised he was allowing her and Helen to go. She had grown tired of being fearful of angering James and she wanted a better life for her daughter. He had sucked her life dry and she needed desperately to feel alive again. Secretly, she prayed this was goodbye as she packed the suitcases and made the final arrangements to take the train cross country.

Two months later, James left Boston to join her, but found Rose had changed. She had found her voice again. Suddenly, she was like the confident and fun-loving Rose he knew when they first met, but this time she wanted nothing to do with him. They fought constantly and he threatened her, not because he wanted a life with her, but because he didn't want anyone else to. After barely spending any time with his daughter previously, he started to manipulate her to get through to Rose. The situation frightened Rose enough to make a choice and stand her ground.

They were staying with Rose's aunt and uncle and it wasn't long before James was asked to leave. But, the truth was, by the time this happened, James had been looking for an excuse to leave. Life with the new Rose was trying because he realized he wouldn't win her back and this was the perfect opening for James to go back east. He could push off his family again, live free of responsibility and say it was Rose's idea. James took the train back, got a room, a waiter's job, located his old cronies and attempted to regenerate his old life.

**

Crimes in Boston had evolved in the streets, and Scollay Square and the surrounding areas were deteriorating. He looked up his old friend, Lefty, and found him playing his squeezebox at Dooley's.

"James, you're back. How the hell are ya?" Lefty barreled over and pulled up a chair to join him.

"Yeah, I'm back. You know, that 'grass is always greener' thing isn't true."

Lefty agreed, "Ya right there, it tends to turn brown if someone pisses on it too much."

"That's what I missed about you, Lefty. Your words of wisdom."

"Well, here's another bit of wisdom. Things always happen for a reason and when you walked through that door tonight, I knew the timing was good."

"What are you going on about?"

"I'm eyeing a job, James, a good one at that, laddie."

"Ok, tell me, but over a whiskey."

Lefty clued him in about a high-stakes poker game that took place every Friday night, allegedly in a hidden room in the back of a men's haberdashery.

"How high are the stakes?" James inquired knowing full well it had to be a real good take if Lefty wanted to knock it over.

"High enough to tide us over for a long time, but there's a wee little catch."

"What's the catch?"

"The players are all connected."

"What? You mean the mob? Are you crazy? We'll be on a slab in your morgue if we pull a hit on the family. No way, no, no." James took out a cigarette, shaking his head so much he almost couldn't light it.

"James, I think we can do this."

"No, I've had dealings with the mob in the past. Too close for comfort. We don't need that kind of trouble. Besides I'm getting too old for this life. Been thinking lately about going straight."

Lefty lowered his voice. "Look, James, one of my brood is sick. My youngest kiddie needs some special doctor or something. I can't do this alone."

James looked at his friend and, for once in his life, he thought he must be going a little soft, because when Lefty mentioned his kid, a brief image of his own offspring flashed through his mind. The ones he cast away without a thought. He realized he wanted to help him and he could use the cabbage.

Lefty was the only one he had in his life that he could call a friend. His mind drifted for a second and he thought about Donohue and how he had been so quick to rat him out.

"Look Lefty, let me think about it. I'll let you know."

"Ahh, Jimmy, my boy, I know a con man as good as you would find it

133

hard to resist a big score. Thank you James, I owe you and I'll never forget it."
Lefty got up and did a little jig as he played a tune on his squeezebox.

"I said I'd let you know." *Crazy Irishman*, he thought. James signaled the
bartender. "Another whiskey and one for my friend."

Two days later, James met Lefty to stake out the poker game. They agreed
they would take the time to find out who showed up, what kind of security they
had and the best escape route. Only then would James tell Lefty to count him
in on the job.

***

Bridey McConville was not a woman to say no to. She was a robust Irish
woman, dressed in the multi-pocketed apron, which afforded her the means to
carry everything she might need at a moment's notice for her children.
Something to write with, a scrap of paper to write on, a bandage, a small piece
of scarce chocolate to dry a tear and a wooden paddle for discipline. Bridey's
household was her domain and she ruled with an iron fist. Even in the time of
man's dominance in the home, no man could hold a candle to her and Lefty
loved her dearly. When he stepped through that door at night, even with the
power she wielded, she bent over backwards waiting on him hand and foot.
She was a good woman.

Lefty warned James about her when he insisted on bringing him home for
dinner. James protested, but Lefty would hear none of it. He said Bridey already
knew Lefty asked him to come for a pot of stew and she would come out and
get him, even if she had to pull him in by his earlobe. James wouldn't be the
first grown man to get this treatment.

James reverted to an awkward boy in Bridey's kitchen. She had a way of
making him feel vulnerable and he thought maybe she could see through his
façade. The smell of the stew in the McConvilles' kitchen tweaked such
wonderful memories and sensations of a time in his youth before his troubles
began. James flushed, embarrassed that the pleasure on his face would give
him away.

Dinner time was an experience at the McConvilles' house. The kitchen
looked like a dining hall of a prep school. Kids of all ages, bubbling over with
questions, were laughing and talking about their day as they set the table. Bridey
made her way up and down both sides of the old wooden table ladling her
aromatic ambrosia into large bowls. James sat on Lefty's left across from
Bridey, who always sat on Lefty's right in the chair closest to the stove. The
children's chatter died down as they devoured their dinner. James felt a tap on
his shoulder and turned to see the "runt," as Lefty called her, staring at him.

"Hello," she said.

Erin sported a huge grin on her freckled face. She was carrying a wicker
basket filled with warm homemade bread. "Hi yourself," James replied.

134

"Want some bread? Mama makes the best bread and it's a good way to sop up your gravy," she offered.

He smiled awkwardly and was surprised at his thoughts. *How old would my kids be now?* Memories flipped through his mind like pictures from an old photo album.

When he didn't answer right away, she leaned closer and cupped her chubby little hand to his ear. "Psst, do you want to know Mama's secret ingredient?"

"Yes, I would like to know. What is it?"

"Beer," she giggled, "Mama doesn't know I know."

"Thank you, I'll have a slice and I'll keep your secret safe." He understood how she could melt Lefty's heart. She smiled a toothless grin and handed him the largest piece of bread, still warm from the oven. Then she continued around the table to her brother and sisters, playfully sticking her tongue out at the one called Declan.

The stew was the best dinner James had eaten in many, many years. At first he felt uncomfortable around Bridey, but after a while he relaxed and they found themselves talking and laughing the night away.

The children cleaned up and did the dishes as the three adults sat in the parlor. James was taken aback by Lefty's family. They were happy and they all pitched in to help each other. He never knew the closeness of having a family like this one. He remembered Macklin talking about his family with the same pride in his voice as Lefty. James knew it was his fault that he didn't have this. He was the outcast.

When Lefty went down in the cellar to refill the whiskey jug, Bridey got up and excused herself. "I have darning to do and it will give you men time to talk. James, you must come to dinner again soon."

Bridey picked up her darning basket and walked to the door. She hesitated and looked at James one more time. Her gray-green eyes peered into his soul with the wisdom only a mother nine times over would have.

"Ya know, James, the love of a family is life's greatest blessing. Ya don't have one, so ya welcome here."

Embarrassed by the sentiment James mumbled, "Thanks Bridey."

"My husband likes ya and that's good enough for me. You've got the restlessness in you. It's not your fault, but if you don't find a way to tame it the winds will sweep you along in life and you'll never get to smell the sweetness. So don't be a stranger, ya need it. No one should walk this God-given earth alone."

James shuddered as he watched her walk down the hall. He could hear her softly singing an old Irish folk song that sounded vaguely familiar. Then he remembered when he was a little boy, his father sang that song as he pulled his lobster traps.

I am a nomad man of this wondrous green land
Trees are my shelter from God's tears
Paths and crossroads point the way
Always rolling down and away
I am a nomad man of this immense blue sea
The salty depths drown my many regrets
Men and boys all drifters alike know
Winds of change are blowing, trees are bowing
Dark clouds are gathering, a storm is coming
My wandering ways will soon be done

James wasn't the type of man to believe in prophesying, but when he heard Bridey sing the last stanza the hairs stood up on the back of his neck. Change *was* coming and maybe he was feeling his age, but he thought *his* traveling days might soon be over.

Chapter 25   Stakeout

The following Friday night James and Lefty set up their stakeout. The word on the street was that the poker game was being held in a hidden back room of a store on Tremont Row. The square was always busy, and tonight was no different. They passed the Crawford House and stopped at the shoeshine stand. James tossed a nickel to the shoeshine boy and climbed up on the stand to gain a good vantage point of their target's front door. Lefty moved down the sidewalk and slipped into the alley to check out the back of the building. They waited and before long the players were gathering. James watched and counted six men who walked into the shop. Two came out within a reasonable time frame, four of them did not.

When James's shoeshine was done he smoked a couple of cigarettes, keeping an eye on the store. He watched in silence as a curtain was pulled down in the storefront window and the sign was turned around from OPEN to CLOSED.

After a while he walked down the sidewalk in the direction from which he had come. Two blocks up, he crossed the street and walked back down the sidewalk, stopping across from the Crawford House at the Hub Barbeque to meet up with Lefty. They each ordered a sandwich, sat down and ate without saying a word.

Finally, while still chewing, Lefty said, "Two went in the back."

James looked at him, nodded and said, "Four stayed, two left."

They finished their sandwiches and left. This time, James manned the alley and Lefty stood across from the storefront. James slid between a large dumpster which was located at the end of the alley on the left side. He would be here awhile so he made himself comfortable. An eight-foot high brick wall buffered the alley from an empty lot. Behind him was another building and the right side of the alley's end ran behind the stores, parallel to the street, until it hit the first side street. James was counting on the men coming out this door so he could check the head count again when the game broke up. He needed to know if they were packing, aware of their surroundings or too drunk to give a hoot. He suspected the men would keep their wits about them in a high stakes game. No one wanted to lose. James was a survivor and suspicious by nature, and his ability to read people and his environment was fine-tuned after all these years on the streets.

At about 3:30 a.m. all six men came out the back door. He figured they would take a right and go down the alley to the side street, not wanting to use the alley to the main street. They came out quietly, but not over-cautiously and never looked left in his direction. These were the same men they watched go in earlier in the evening, but he and Lefty needed to know who was already in the store when the men entered. He heard someone close the door from the inside. A minute later it opened again and two men stepped out, threw a padlock on the door and sauntered down the alley.

When everyone was out of sight, James climbed out from behind the dumpster. His legs were stiff and a cramp shot through his calf. He stretched and hurried out to the main street, walked down two blocks and waited under a street lamp. About twenty minutes later, he made out Lefty emerging from the shadows.

James pointed his thumb over his shoulder, back in the direction from which he had come. "There were still two inside," James said. "When they left after locking up the back door, they went down the alley to the side street like the others."

"Ok, so now we know there are eight of them." The air was cold and a stiff January wind burned James's face. He pulled his collar up high on his neck, put his hands in his pockets and walked faster.

"How do we know there won't be more? Or less? You know, like a pickup game."

"When the big boys play for high stakes they keep a nice tidy group. They don't want a lot of talking outside the crib. We'll watch for a couple of weeks before we hit them. Make sure."

"You're the pro."

"Lefty, look, I think we have to bring some manpower in on this, so our cut will be lower."

"What? James, I need this money."

"Hey, I'm telling you, to do this right, we need two more guys."

Moonlight covered the edge of the bay and the wind blew unmercifully at their backs as they walked on the shore of Dorchester Neck. Small waves receded on the beach leaving behind frothy debris, whipped by the gusts, on the shoreline.

They walked for a bit before Lefty broke the silence. "James, I want to thank you for doing this job. It means a lot to me. Ya know, this is for Erin, so if you think we have to beef up the manpower, I'm good with it."

Their walking had slowed down when Lefty spoke so James took out a cigarette, and cupped his hand around the match to protect the flame from wind. He inhaled deeply.

"This is it for me, James. I'm going straight after this. One last big take, to help my baby girl." When he spoke, smoke mixed with his breath in the frigid air and hung like an icy cloud in front of him.

James wasn't surprised, "Do what you gotta do, Lefty."

"You're a strange one, James. I haven't figured ya out yet. I know ya got a heart beating in ya, even though ya hide it."

"Don't be too sure of that. My own mother wasn't," James snorted. Lefty chuckled at this remark, until he noticed James wasn't laughing.

"Ya never talk about family, James. Did ya ever want kiddies? I don't know what I'd do without them."

"I think it would surprise you if I told you I had three of them."

Lefty's mouth dropped open. He stopped walking and stood his ground. "What do ya mean? Ya kidding? Right?"

James hesitated a moment. "Yeah, that's right, I'm kidding," he lied. "I gotcha, didn't I?"

Unsure, Lefty tried to analyze the tone of James's voice and then he burst into laughter. "You old sea bag, you got me good." His laughter stopped as quickly as it started and he asked, "So, do you have any regrets about not having any?"

"Only in my dreams, Lefty. Only in my dreams."

"Can't stop dreaming, James. They say a man is old when his regrets take the place of his dreams."

James pulled his collar up around his neck for protection from the cold, or maybe to isolate himself from any more unwanted conversation. His steps quickened.

They kept walking and Lefty didn't speak again until they reached the rooming house where James was staying.

"Okay, you started to say we need help with this job. Do ya have anybody in mind?"

"Yeah, two guys I've worked with before. They're mariners in port on leave. I'll get in touch with them and let you know. For now, we're going to stake out the place every Friday for a few weeks until we're ready. Figure out if there is some sort of a repetitive pattern."

"Ok, you're the boss. Keep the wind at ya back, James."

***

James's eyes took a while to adjust to the darkness inside the Dockside, a little dive down on the waterfront, frequented by seamen. He found the two men he was looking for within minutes. Dominic Spinelli recognized James and yelled over the din to his friend beside him.

"Hey Scotty, look who's here."

Scotty Koval puffed out his ruddy cheeks and whistled. "If it ain't the landlubber himself."

James hated being called a landlubber, but he shook it off. He needed these two mariners for Lefty's job. They had worked with James on other jobs and he trusted them. Besides, being mariners, they never stayed in one port too long, so they were hard to trace since they usually shipped out of town right after pulling a heist.

He slapped them on their backs. "Who are you calling a landlubber? I was working on the high seas when you two were still cutting teeth on your mother's teats."

They laughed, bought James a drink and shared a few manly stories of their conquests of women in far-off exotic corners of the world. Before they ordered another round, James leaned forward. They immediately understood he was calling for a huddle.

"I have a proposition for you." They both nodded silently, confirming their interest. Let's take a walk outside and I'll clue you in."

***

Lefty was an expert lock picker and he could open any lock in record time. Doors, padlocks, even safes were no obstacle for him. On the second stakeout, after their marks left the game and closed up the building, James and Lefty gained entry in order to get the layout of the place.

James placed himself on the corner of the alley leading to the street, back against the wall, so he could watch both directions while Lefty performed his magic with the lock. In twelve seconds the lock was open. Lefty waved a hand out the door signaling James to join him.

Once inside, James took a war-issued flashlight out of his jacket and flashed it on. They were inside what looked like a storeroom, which made sense because they were in the back of the store. The back wall of all the buildings in the alley had no windows. The light went out and James flicked the button again. Shelves lined both walls to the right and left of the back door and on the wall in front of them. That wall separated the storeroom from the front of the store via a solid, four-panel door. He checked the door. It was locked.

The shelves were bowing, weighted down with industrial sized bolts of fabric. An old pattern table used for cutting and measuring took up the middle of the room with one stool placed in front of it. On the table lay various cut out pieces of a wool material and large industrial-sized spools of thread.

James was facing the back door where they had entered and noticed something on the wall to the right of him. On this wall were shelves that were not deep enough for fabric bolts. They were shallow and held many odds and ends as well as a heavy coat of dust. There were scissors, piles of receipts pierced on spindles and little tools he knew nothing about. The shelves were in five-foot sections with a sheath of fabric hung from floor to ceiling between each section. The middle section of the left wall at a right angle to the door held something a little different. A small 8-by-10 picture of a landscape in Italy, possibly Tuscany, in a gilded frame stood alone on this shelf.

The light went out again, he hit the button and called Lefty over and told him to hold the flashlight and shine it on the picture. James reached up and removed the picture from the shelf to look at it.

Lefty looked beyond the picture to the shelf where it had stood gathering dust and looked at James. "Well, mate, would you look at that. How'd ya know?"

James grinned and pulled the small lever that the picture had been hiding and heard a pop. That section of the wall, shelves and all, moved inward away from him as a release mechanism opened a hidden door to an interior room. "I didn't. Dumb luck," he answered.

Lefty beamed, "No, laddie, it was the luck of the Irish."

Lefty followed James through the door and what they saw was enough to take their breath away. The light illuminated the secret room. James whistled. Lefty whispered, "Sweet Jesus."

The room was majestic, fit for Italian royalty. Full burgundy drapes graced the walls that were lined with gold wainscoting. A large eight-sided, round, mahogany poker table was the focal point in the middle of the room, below an ornate glass chandelier. The back wall was a floor-to-ceiling mirror framed by glass shelves, well stocked with the finest liquor. The mahogany bar was inlaid with highly polished marble positioned in front of eight heavy leather-backed stools. The shiny, polished wood floor was three-quarters covered by a thick Persian rug. After their initial shock they searched for another way out of the room and found none.

James whistled again. A long slow whistle of appreciation. "Well, well, I think this will be a worthwhile job. Check out behind the bar to make sure they don't have any hardware hidden there that they can pull out on us."

Lefty did as he was told. "No, nothing here. Hopefully the only pieces will be what they carry in with them."

"Okay," James said, "I've seen all I need to. Let's go plan this thing."

Chapter 26   A Heist Goes Bad

After three consecutive weeks of stakeouts, James and his three friends decided to go for it. They picked the following Friday, which conveniently fell two days before Dominic and Scotty were scheduled to ship out again. As far as Lefty was concerned, this was good because it eliminated two mouths that could talk. James knew this job meant a lot to Lefty, but Lefty had told him he didn't have the same confidence in those two that James carried.

James had found a cellar in an abandoned building on nearby Morton Terrace, accessible by a little-traveled back alley and they made arrangements to meet there on Wednesday night to go over everyone's instructions. James and Lefty arrived early and sat on overturned crates waiting for the other two. Lefty got up and paced nervously, blowing his nose while cursing the musty dampness.

"Stop pacing," James ordered. "You're giving me the jitters."

The creak of the wooden bulkhead made them hold still and listen. "It's us." Dominic's raspy whisper punctured the silence.

"And about time," Lefty muttered.

The two descended the five steps after gently lowering the bulkhead door behind them and stepped carefully toward the direction of Lefty's voice, waiting for their eyes to adjust in the low light.

James pointed to a pile of wooden crates in the corner.

"Pull up a crate and let's get started."

Dominic and Scotty each grabbed a Moxie crate as James strolled over to an old rickety worktable to find a tool he could use to draw a map in the dirt floor. He reached for an iron crowbar, but when he pulled it from the carelessly tossed pile of tools, one fell off the bench narrowly missing his foot. He bent to pick it up and much to his chagrin, noticed it was a monkey wrench. Slowly, in reverse slow-motion, he straightened back up and stood there staring down at it.

Dominic dropped his crate down into the circle and straddled it. The tension was worthy of being cut with a sharp knife and he was irritable.

Irritated, Dominic yelled over to James, "Hey, you going to stand there all night or what?"

But James was years away from that abandoned cellar. Twenty-nine years away to be exact. Once again he was twenty years old, standing in front of his bedroom mirror in the house in Gloucester. It was like he was watching his reflection in a wishing well, he thought, but if that were the case he'd be wishing to start his life over again. The mirror shimmied like ripples of water swirling in a gentle circular movement until a clear and distinct reflection of a familiar face stared back at him. But it wasn't his face. *Dad?*

"James!" Lefty grumbled.

James shook his head and focused his eyes. The dingy dirt floor was coming slowly back to reality. He left the wrench in the dirt where it fell, turned around and joined them.

***

The four men planned well into the night, reviewing each possible scenario over and over it again, until they considered the plan failsafe.

"One more time." James prodded Scotty.

A deep sigh of frustration accompanied a roll of the eyes before Scotty spoke. "Okay, I stay in uniform, get a bottle to swig and pretend I'm drunk. I come up the alley from the side street entrance and when I'm about ten feet from the back door, I slump down against the wall and stay put."

"And?" Lefty growled.

"And what? I watch for five minutes."

"And if you see someone coming from the side street or the main street to the alley, what do you do?"

"I whistle to alert you guys."

"Right." James nodded. "Now Lefty is going to be across the street, positioned to see the front door. I'm going to be across from the back door, over the brick wall, and Dominic is going to be near the dumpster. Lefty is going to make sure our marks are all through the front door and the "closed" sign is put up, before taking his place in the alley. He'll give an owl call when the coast is clear and he's in place."

James made eye contact with everyone to confirm they were still on board. They were, so he continued. "Dominic, besides Scotty, you're the one with the best view of the back door. If Scotty sees that no one is coming down the alley and doesn't whistle, he waits the five minutes and then starts a ruckus to draw them out. Out of the eight, we're thinking two of the men are henchmen

143

guarding the game just inside the back door. We need to get them out of the way and the rest will be like catching fish in a barrel."

"No worries, boss. I can draw them out," Scotty boasted, pounding his chest with confidence.

Lefty agreed about the two guards. "We drew them out a couple of Fridays ago by making noise in the dumpster and chasing out the feral cats. There were two of them, both packing."

James addressed Scotty again. "So, what's the diversion that you're going to create?"

Scotty's smile went ear to ear. "Oh, I'll sing, yell and make a ruckus like the happy drunk I am."

Dominic found this quite funny. "Aye, mate, which should be easy for you, you lush."

"Scotty, make sure you move closer to the wall, back up the alley and into position near me. I'll jump one of them from the top of the wall. They won't expect that."

James continued, "Dominic, when you hear them open the door and they come out to find Scotty, you jump one of them from behind, as I come over the wall. We need an element of surprise, no shooting. Knock them out with your gun butt if you need to. We don't need to wake the neighborhood."

"Right," Dominic agreed as he repeated his part. "I signal Lefty to move toward the door. I rush them from behind, as you jump from above. We make sure they're out cold, gag and tie them and drag them behind the dumpster."

James seemed satisfied with this part. "Okay, we work quietly and work as one. Now, part two, inside. We can't ambush them by breaking into the game room. We're going to be gentlemen. We'll wait for the stockholders to finish their poker game and open the door. Two of us will be in the stock room, that'll be me and Lefty. Scotty, you man the alley corner to the main street, and Dominic, you stay behind the back door in the alley."

James stopped and frowned. "No matter which way it goes, we meet back here. Only come here if it's safe and you don't have a tail. Are we clear on everything so far?"

"Like I said, we don't rush them," James said. "They'll open the door when the game is over. All we need to do is be quiet and patient. We'll have masks over our faces so they can't recognize us."

"Then what?" Scotty had to clear his throat to get the words out. His nerves were raw.

"When we hear someone walk close to the door, Lefty will shine the flashlight at the bottom of the back door. Stay alert for that, Dominic. Lefty and I will rush whoever opens the hidden door back into the room and push them face down on the floor. You stay as a lookout outside. Dominic gets called in to frisk them and help us tie them."

Lefty took his cap off and rubbed his head. "Look, we don't want to kill anyone, we only want the money. We're going to get everyone lying face down on the floor and pull their pieces if they're carrying. After we gag them, we'll hog-tie their feet to their hands, get the money, close the hidden door with the wise guys inside and padlock it with this." He held up a lock. "One key and we'll lose it in the harbor. It's sweet! We'll be long gone before the store opens for business."

Dominic shook his head. Lefty glanced at everyone, "Okay, if there are no questions, we're ready."

Friday came and it was a record-breaking, icy-cold night. Everyone took their positions and nothing in particular seemed any different than the previous Friday nights. The same men entered the haberdashery like clockwork.

When the coast was clear Scotty went into his performance, reeling sideways down the alley swinging a bottle of whiskey. He had taken a few swigs to make his acting debut authentic. The whiskey sweetened his breath and steadied his nerves. From their positions they could all hear Scotty's slurred lyrics cut through the crisp night air.

What shall I do with a drunken Sadie?
Early in the evening.
Lay her down like a perfect lady.
On Saturday night, till the morning light.
What shall I do with her angry husband?
Early in the evening.
Lay him down with all my might.
On Saturday night, till morning light.

Scotty stopped singing and listened. He heard nothing from within the building, so he walked over and put his ear to the door. Then he banged loudly against it and hurried over to the opposite side of the alley, where he quickly slid down against the eight-foot brick wall near the marked area planned.

In the still of the cold night, sounds carried easily and when the lock on the door turned, it sounded like a shot. They all heard it, held their breath and listened. James squatted on the opposite side of the wall on top of a rotted tree stump, ready to spring up on top of the wall and pounce on one of the henchmen. As he strained to keep his legs from cramping, he wondered how long he could go on pulling jobs. He was forty-nine years old and wouldn't be getting any younger. His body was starting to rebel against certain activities and he thought about what Lefty said about this being his last hurrah. Maybe it would be his as well.

The two henchmen were on Scotty in a heartbeat, but James waited. One hovered over Scotty, grabbed his coat and pulled him up to a standing position. The ox had to be strong because lifting Scotty was no easy feat.

All the commotion had given James a chance to pull himself up from the stump and perch on the top of the wall. He had a perfect eagle's eye view of the tops of their heads as long as they didn't look up.

Scotty had to get them facing the other direction and send the signal to James. Scotty winked at them. "Aye, want a drinkie, mates?" That was what James was waiting for. He leaped off the wall onto the shoulders of one of the men. The blow knocked the man to the ground and the gun flew out of his hand and slid across the alley. When the second man turned to see what the scuffle was, Scotty took the bottle and hit him over the head. Dominic swept in from behind. He placed his knee in the small of their backs, gagged and tied them and then dragged them back around the dumpster with Lefty's help. James brushed himself off, picked up the gun and shoved it in his waistband.

Dominic stood by the back door as Lefty and James entered the store room, each manning a side of the hidden room's entrance. Scotty stood lookout at the corner of the alley. And once again they waited.

They kept zeroed in on the hidden room, waiting for any clue that they would soon be coming out. Muffled sounds of men talking and sometimes laughter drifted out to their ears.

An old clock on the tailor's desk ticked the seconds and minutes away. The sound bothered Lefty. It reminded him of his wife, Bridey, admonishing the one of the kids. *Tsk, tsk, tsk, what are ya thinking? Tsk, tsk, tsk, the Lord will be your punishment.*

Forty minutes later they heard a footstep on the other side of the door. They made eye contact, straightened up and pulled masks down over their faces. Lefty quickly shined his flashlight on and off twice toward the crack at the bottom of the outside door to alert Dominic. In that second Lefty thought the Lord will have to wait to punish him. Right now he needed to help himself and his baby girl. Bridey will just have to forgive him.

The hidden door creaked as it opened. James and Lefty were flattened flush against the wall on either side. James signaled Lefty and they rushed the man in the doorway, pushing him backward, down on the plush area rug. Their guns were leveled on the group of men in the room.

A moment across the room caught his eye and James looked beyond the poker table to the tall man behind the bar He was bent to the side with his right arm reaching for the shotgun under the counter. James fired one shot above the man's head, shattering the mirror.

"Drop it! Get your hands up now!" The man put the gun he had in his right hand slowly on bar and raised his hands in the air.

"Everyone get on your stomachs on the floor around the table."

They eyed James coldly and the man they had knocked to the ground growled, "You don't know who you're dealing with."

James laughed. "Don't be stupid, old man. We wouldn't be in here if we didn't know. Now get on the floor." Slowly the man got on his knees, put his arms out ahead of him and rocked like a hobby horse, pivoting end to end on his large belly.

Dominic entered the room. Lefty pulled rope and mouth gags out of his jacket and passed them to him. Dominic worked methodically from left to right gagging each one and, then tying their hands and feet separately at first and then pulling their extremities together like he was lassoing a prized rodeo calf. When the last man was tied, he went and took his post back at the alley door.

As each man was secured, James gathered the cash from their pockets. He pocketed the loot in his pants and backed his way to the door. Lefty was right behind him, ready to stick a rod in the secret door and a padlock outside.

"Come on, get out of there," Lefty yelled being careful not to use any names.

"Okay, okay, I'm out. Lock them in!" James heard Lefty snap the rod in place and they turned to head for the back door. That was the moment all hell broke loose.

A minute before, Dominic was standing by the back door to the alley, but when he looked out he couldn't see Scotty, who should have been visible at the corner of the building.

Suddenly there was an explosive crash from behind them, inside the building. They turned and saw two men had splintered the door between the back room and the storefront and were stepping over the threshold, guns drawn. Lefty heard a *ping, ping, ping* like a heavy rain hitting a tin roof.

They're firing. "Come on, move." Lefty motioned to James as he ran out after Dominic. When he crossed the threshold, he glanced back and saw James behind him.

Once Lefty was out and down the alley, he fired back at them to hold them at bay and noticed James was nowhere to be seen. He thought, maybe when they scattered, James had gone back over the wall, but that would be a feat. There was nothing on the alley side to propel him such a great height. He couldn't worry about that now; he had to make his way to the pre-planned meeting place and hope to hell that everyone makes it back safe.

They separated, sticking to the plan and running in opposite directions, in and out between buildings and through alleyways, in an attempt to throw off their pursuers. Dominic reached the bulkhead of the abandoned cellar first, and Lefty was a couple of minutes behind him.

Dominic looked wide-eyed around the basement and then he looked at Lefty. "Where in the hell did those apes come from?"

"I don't know. Were you followed?" Lefty asked. His chest puffed heavily between words as he tried to catch his breath.

"No, were you?"

"No." Lefty started pacing. The dirt from the cellar floor kicked up in a little cloud around each of his shoes.

Dominic crabbed sideways trying to keep up with him. "What now?" Lefty glared at him. "We wait like we planned."

"What the hell happened? Who were those guys? No one was ever in the front of the store after closing."

Lefty shook his head. "I don't know, all these weeks the store has always been closed and the connecting door locked. I don't know."

***

James was running down the alley dodging from side to side like they taught him to do in the war. His survival instinct took over as he leaped onto a pile of refuse in a lame attempt to propel himself over the brick wall. He felt something rip into his lower back and right shoulder. Shots ricocheted off a large metal container and his back exploded in pinpricks of pain as shrapnel pieces tore through his shirt, piercing deep into his body. Pain exploded in his eardrums before an unnatural silence fell. Hot air enveloped him and a monumental force took him up and over the eight-foot barrier, dropping him forcefully to the ground in a heap on the other side. He only had to look back once at the ball of fire rising above the wall he had scaled before the adrenalin kicked in, blocking the pain. He scrambled to his feet and disappeared into the night.

Reaching the alleyway to the next street, he fell against the brick building. Sweat rolled down his face burning his eyes despite the cold, dry air of the winter's night.

He willed himself to move up the alley as he felt energy seep out of him. *Keep moving....get to the hideout.*

His legs weakened with each step, but he succeeded in getting to the end of the alley when he was grabbed from behind. An arm wrapped around his chest and another clamped over his mouth.

A muffled voice vibrated in his ear. James tried to stay focused but the words were a million miles away and he slipped into semi-consciousness.

***

Something is horribly wrong. Come on, James, where are you? Lefty swallowed hard several times to quell the panic that had a stranglehold on his throat. Scotty finally met up with Lefty and Dominic in the basement of an abandoned house on Court Street.

Lefty paced wildly back and forth, running his fingers through his short hair. "What happened back there Scotty? You were supposed to be watching," he yelled.

Scotty stepped toward him defensively. "They took me by surprise and slugged me."

"Then how'd you get away?" There was an accusing tone in Lefty's voice.

"What are you saying? Those goons left me and ran to the front door of the

148

store when they heard a gunshot. Who the hell was doing the shooting?"

Lefty knew then that they must have heard the shot James pulled off at the guy with the gun behind the bar. Why the hell were they there in the first place? All the nights they staked the place out, no one else had been around.

"Dominic, you were watching near the back door on the alley. Did you see James come out?"

"Hell, no, I took off down the alley when I heard a spray of gunfire. Then I heard some kind of explosion. The only thing I can think of was a bullet hit that large metal construction locker in the alley. Look, I don't need this kind of trouble. I'm shipping out in two days. I'm out of here."

"Dominic, wait!" Lefty yelled, but he was already gone. Lefty and Scotty were discussing what to do next when they heard the old bulkhead squeak and they positioned themselves to jump whoever came down the stairs.

To their surprise, it was Dominic. He was half-carrying and half-dragging James. Lefty hurried over to help. Scotty closed the bulkhead and hurried back to the old Army cot that they put James on. Dominic rolled James on his side and stripped his shredded clothes off of him. "It's too dark, get a flashlight over here," Lefty instructed. Even in the dim light they saw his back was a bloody mess.

Dominic's voice was frantic. "I found him about twenty yards from the door. He collapsed as I reached him."

"We've got to stop the bleeding and bandage him up," Lefty shouted.

"How are we going to do that? There's no bandages, no water. We can't take him to a hospital. They'll be looking for gunshot victims. That explosion we heard will bring everyone in a two-block area out into the street. Those guys are probably hunting us down like dogs now."

"No, they aren't," Lefty said, his eyes not leaving James. "And they won't be, at least not right now if the cops showed up."

Dominic and Scotty looked at him and both said at the same time. "Why not?"

Lefty didn't answer right away. Dominic stepped up to him and took the front of his shirt, crumpling the material tightly in his fist. Dominic clenched his teeth as he asked with unmistakable grit in his voice, "Why not?"

"'Cause, they don't want any trouble. They take care of their own problems."

"Why?" Dominic shouted.

Lefty let out a deep sigh, "They belong to the mob."

Before the sentence was out of his mouth, Lefty was flying through the air. He hit the wall behind him hard and slumped to the floor.

Dominic spat on the ground. "Don't you think that would have been important to tell us?" They rushed him and Lefty, with his hand up to protect his face, pounded back against the wall again and slumped to the floor.

"Wait! Stop!" Lefty tried to scramble away.

Then Scotty seemed to come to his senses and he grabbed Dominic's arm. "Look, we're all in this deep now, but we're sailing outta here come daybreak two days from now. These blokes have to take any heat that comes down." He scowled at Lefty. "You keep your mouth shut if you know what's good for you, right?"

Lefty hustled to his feet. "I'm no rat."

Dominic looked hard at Lefty and then agreed. "Yeah, we have to lay low. We can hide here, but one of us has to go up and get supplies and it ain't gonna be me." They both turned and looked at Lefty.

A groan followed by a couple of unrecognizable words came from the cot. The three of them turned toward James. James was struggling to reach into the pocket of his jacket, which was draped over him like a blanket. Lefty knelt down to help him.

"What's up, buddy? How ya doing?" he asked.

Lefty moved in closer. "He's trying to tell us something." As if he were playing an awkward game of charades, James willed his control over his flailing arm and pointed to his damaged jacket on the floor. "Inside pocket," he grunted. Lefty reached in and to his surprise and that of the others, he pulled out four thick stacks of bills, each held by heavy rubber bands, along with a wad of loose bills. When he saw James grin, they all started laughing and the tension dissipated into thin air.

They had forgotten the booty, assuming it was left behind in the melee. "Ya one tough bastard, Lawson. Yes sir, one tough bastard."

Lefty put one stack back in James's pocket, along with the loose bills, then threw one to Scotty and one to Dominic. He peeled some bills off the top of the last stack and put the rest in his pocket. "Look, I'm going up to get some bandages at the mercantile when it opens up. I'll bring back some food and supplies for a couple of days and we'll hunker down here."

Dominic's hand shot out, landing a flat palm on Lefty's chest. "We'll give you one hour. Be back or we're out of here without him." Lefty leveled his eyes on Dominic. "I don't desert my friends."

James heard Lefty. This loyalty was foreign to him, but he felt reassured and allowed himself to succumb to the blackness creeping over him.

Dominic murmured something unintelligible that Lefty took as an agreement. They sat in silence, at times nodding off. Four hours passed before Lefty ventured out.

The bulkhead belched a mournful creak as he lifted it slowly to make sure the area was clear to leave. There was no activity outside except a mangy dog that was startled as he foraged for scraps. The dog cowered and ran off carrying a treasured morsel in its mouth. Lefty emerged fully from the safety of the cellar. He carefully scanned the area as he made his way up the alley to the main street. The early morning sky was an ominous gray, foretelling a snowfall which would not be good for them. He had to get supplies and get back without leaving footprints for anyone to follow. He reached the street, pulled his jacket collar high up on his neck and hurried along as fast as he could without looking suspicious. Most people were still warm in their beds and the streets were eerily quiet.

**

James stirred to consciousness and oddly enough did not feel too much pain, but he knew he was in deep trouble. Struggling to stay awake, he tried to go over every detail in his mind to see where and when it all went wrong, but he couldn't think in an organized timeline. Jumbled images flashed when his eyes closed and once again he lost his battle, drifting into blackness.

It was an hour later when he came to. He remembered being propelled by a force through the air, up and over the eight-foot wall. At the time his mind couldn't register what was happening. When he landed hard on the ground on the other side of the wall, out of the corner of his eye he saw a ball of fire back above the alley and knew it was some sort of explosion.

The flames were licking the air, searing the branches of the overhanging trees. His ears were muffled. The men were firing at him. He couldn't hold his body straight. When he finally got up on his feet, he listed sideways to the right as he tried to run, making him look like a drunk after a three-day binge. Disoriented, he plunged forward, stumbling over rocks, roots and debris in the empty lot that abutted the alley. Dizziness and nausea overtook him. He held his arms out horizontally in an attempt to compensate for the vertigo and stay upright, but he fell twice more. He knew something was wrong with his back, but didn't know what. James vaguely remembered Dominic wrapping his large burly arm around him. He knew they were back in the hideout and he tried to muster the energy to sit up on the cot, but like an ebb tide, he could feel consciousness recede, leaving him helpless.

**

Lefty returned as the snowflakes started to fall. According to plan, he knocked a signal of two knocks, stopped, and then three more knocks on the bulkhead, opened it and climbed down the stairs. Scotty took the bundles from his arms as Lefty turned and secured the door.

"How is he?" Lefty asked while rubbing his cold hands together to get the circulation going. Once he could feel the tingling in his fingertips, he ripped open a bandage and opened a bottle of whiskey to use as antiseptic.

"He passed out not long after you left and woke up once, briefly." Dominic's brow creased. "He don't look too good."

Lefty knelt down and gently turned James over. Blood had soaked through to the dirty cot but it looked like active bleeding had stopped.

"Help me get these clothes off of him and clean him up." They stripped him, cleaned the wounds with a jug of water and poured some whiskey over his back. After he was bandaged up, they wrapped him in a blanket.

James lay on his side, unmoving on that cot through the day and late into the next night. It didn't take a doctor's eye for his friends to see that the shrapnel wounds on his back were already showing signs of infection. His back was peppered with numerous, small wounds that looked like craters with angry, red, raised sides of flesh surrounding each entry point.

"God only knows how much metal is lodged inside of him," Lefty noted to no one in particular.

Lefty watched him, deeply inhaling on his cigarette and exhaling as slowly as possible, as though the answers he was seeking would come to him during this ritual. Suddenly he stood up and looked at Dominic and Scotty.

"What'll we do, boys?" His voice was loud and gruff.

Dominic shrugged. "Look, we have to be on that ship that's coming in tomorrow morning. We've already signed on. We can't help you do anything with him."

"I'd be surprised if he made it until then," Scotty added.

Lefty had always felt a connection with James. Lefty hadn't always done the right things in life, but he was a good friend and family man. He always said those were the two things that made an Irishman rich. And he'd be damned if he'd leave a friend in need.

"What's the name of the ship you two are signed up on?" he asked.

"USS *Lejeune*, it's coming in from Southampton, England with wounded. It'll be a quick turn-around. We'll be heading back out as soon as she's stocked back up."

"Wounded?" Lefty rubbed his forehead. "Wounded." He murmured to himself. He got up and paced furiously, walking back and forth over the dirt floor. Dust kicked up and Scotty coughed, but he didn't interrupt Lefty.

Suddenly he stopped and looked at them. "That's it," he yelled. "That would work."

"What would work? What are you talking about?" Dominic asked.

Lefty proceeded to tell them about the plan he was formulating in his head.

"Look, we have to get him down to the docks in the morning while it's still dark, before the ship comes in. All you guys have to do is help me do that and during the disembarking of the wounded, we slip James on a stretcher and off they take him to the hospital with the other boys."

"It's not that simple," insisted Dominic.

"Sure it is." Lefty's voice was charged with adrenalin.

"We're going to pass him off as a wounded soldier? He's kind of old."

"Why not? It's not like he wasn't one once. James fought in World War I, you know. He could have been in the–Merchant Marine like you two on a transport ship. This way, we get him to a hospital, get him help and no one's the wiser about how he got his wounds."

Dominic shook his head, "No, it won't work. Each ship has a manifest with the names of who they're carrying."

"So, one of you adds him to the list. That can't be that hard to get your hands on. I've been down there when they bring the wounded back. There are hundreds of litters lined up on the pier. Believe me, one extra wounded man won't be noticed. It's organized chaos, but it's still chaos."

Scotty whined, "Why should we jeopardize our jobs?"

Lefty looked at him in disgust. He leaned toward Scotty, his accusing finger poked Scotty's doughy chest. "Because of loyalty to a fellow sea mariner, because of the wad of cash he put in your pockets. You need anything else?"

Dominic and Scotty exchanged looks and nodded silently in agreement.

"Ok, that's better. Now let's go over the plan." Lefty proceeded to tell Dominic the information he needed to add to the USS *Lejeune's* manifest.

"Another one of your great plans, Lefty?" Scotty retorted sarcastically.

Dominic muttered, "Let's hope this one works better than the last."

Lefty nodded. "Aye, boys, let's hope."

Chapter 27   The Plan

During the first three months of 1945, the average number of wounded WWII soldiers returning to US soil each month reached 28,000 to 30,000. One of the ships carrying the wounded home was the USS *Lejeune*, which was scheduled to pull into port before dawn on February 10th. This was the ship Dominic and Scotty had signed up to go back out on. She was a German cargo carrier that was converted to a US Navy troop transport, renamed the USS *Lejeune* after USMC General John Archer Lejeune and fully commissioned in the spring of 1944.

During the night, James floated in and out of consciousness. He exchanged a few words with Lefty, but kept dozing off. His fever raged and Lefty knew his plan had to work, because without medical help, James was a dead man. He knelt down beside side James's head and called his name.

"James, can you hear me? Jimmy boy, James."

"Yeah," James answered weakly, "Hey, Lefty."

"Listen closely, James. You're hurt bad. We have a way to get you to a hospital, a military hospital where the mob won't find you."

James's mouth turned up slightly, "Don't have a choice now, do I?" His eyes rolled back in his head and his lids lowered.

"James, stay awake. There's a ship coming in with war wounded. They set up hundreds of litters on the docks and there will be so much confusion, it'll be easy to slip you onto one."

James licked his lips. They were so dry. His skin was burning from the inside out. His voice cracked as he said, "Have no papers. They'll know."

"No, they won't. Look, Dominic already left for the docks. Dominic is in charge of adding you to the manifest. Me and Scotty...," he hesitated, "Well, we're going to get you down there. Don't you worry. We'll get you on a litter and they'll take care of you."

James grinned, "You always have a plan. Take my cut."

"No, James, you earned it. Keep it."

"Don't need it where I'm going, Lefty."

"You're gonna make it, James. I'll hear no guff from ya."

James struggled to pull the money from his shirt. "Then keep it safe for me."

Lefty hesitated and then took the money. He held it for a moment before whispering, "Okay."

Lefty and Scotty had to find a way to get James down to the docks. He thought about getting a taxi, but due to the fare wars and past troubles with cabbies, James's face might be easily recognized. They couldn't trust any of them. It was a rough, dog-eat-dog business and any one of those hacks would sell out their mother to survive. His mind was racing and Scotty was bugging the hell out of him as he tried to think.

"Scotty, shut ya trap and let me think!"

Scotty frowned and sat in the corner pouting, reminding Lefty of one of his kids. He couldn't help but yell at him. "Aw, stop looking like ya at a funeral, will..." Lefty's face cracked into a huge smile as he stopped mid-sentence.

"What?" Scotty asked.

"I've got it. I know how we can get James down to the docks. The morgue has a 1940 Packard ambulance for pickups. No one will give it a second look down on the waterfront."

"Can you get it?"

"Sure, I know where they hang the keys. Sometimes they have me do some tinkering with it. You know, to keep it running smooth-like."

"Ya, but it'll be light out when you bring her back here. Someone will see you."

"Not if I hurry, it's a Saturday and they come in late on weekends." He turned to James and reassured him. "I'm going now, James. I'll be back with a ride and we'll head to the docks."

The streets were deserted when Lefty made his way to the city morgue a couple of blocks west. He was careful to stay away from the street lamps. It took him twenty minutes, but he finally reached the building. Lefty looked around to make sure no one was around, and then he slipped down the alley and around the back. He remembered a misaligned window casing on one of the windows in the back office of the morgue. Lefty placed both hands on the sash and pushed the window up. He hoisted himself up and over the sill, falling head first inside to the floor. He didn't move for a minute trying to catch his breath.

I'm getting too old for this, he thought.

Even though the sky was starting to lighten outside, inside the building was dark, but he couldn't risk turning on any lights. He held his hands out in front of him and patted his way around until his knee caught the side of a desk with a thump. The file cabinet he was looking for would be on the left side of the desk. He fumbled around and found the latch handle on the top drawer and pulled it open. Extending his arm up and into the drawer he let his fingers feel around for the keys. He heard them jingle and snatched them.

Got them!

He retraced his steps, climbed over the sill, this time feet first, and shut the window behind him. Crossing over the back side of the building, opposite the alley he came down, he found the ambulance parked in an overgrown dirt lot.

Now for the hard part. The engine purred and he drove quickly back to the hideout. He didn't care about tracks in the snow because they wouldn't be coming back. He parked the ambulance in the alley between the buildings, got out and hurried around back to the bulkhead. He rapped the code on the door, opened it and descended the stairs.

Scotty was sweating more than James. Nervously, he asked Lefty. "Did anyone follow you? You got the ambulance?"

"Told you I would, it went off without a hitch. You got a piece of paper on you?"

Scotty reached in his billfold, took out a piece of paper, ripped a blank portion off the bottom and gave it to Lefty.

"Do you think you can spare it?" Lefty said sarcastically.

Scotty's face darkened and his jaw squared off defensively. "I have a dame's number on that paper. I may want to look her up."

"Do her a favor and lose it," Lefty muttered. On the small piece of paper, he wrote Charles A. Lawson, Boston, 49 years, *Cutty Sark*. He folded it in half, walked over to James and he stuck it deep inside James's pants pocket.

Scotty looked puzzled. "What's *Cutty Sark*? Are you writing down his booze preference?"

"Look, I have to leave him something. He's got his last name, hometown and age. But we have to change the first name and the *Cutty Sark* was a British ship I've heard about. Maybe they'll think he's from over there. He ain't talking much and he always did have a bit of an accent from his Da. In any case they take care of him long before they start questioning anything."

"Is that what Dominic is writing on the manifest?"

"Yep, right down to the last letter. Now help me get him up."

Getting James up and out of the cellar was not an easy feat. Lefty had re-bandaged him and dressed him in a field uniform shirt and pants he pilfered from a soldier's duffle in the bar where he had gotten the whiskey to clean his wounds. The uniform was a good addition to his list of supplies. He got what he could and it would have to do.

Gently, they laid James on his side in the back cot of the ambulance. James looked at his friend Lefty, and tried to speak. Lefty bent closer to hear him.

"Thanks, you stuck by me." Struggling to speak he added, "No one has ever done that before."

Lefty put one hand on James's shoulder and tipped his scally cap with the other. "As we say in the homeland, James, you and I will meet again. When we're least expecting it, one day in some far-off place, I will recognize you, so I won't say goodbye, my friend. For you and I will meet again. I'll never forget what you did for my baby girl."

He shut the back door and climbed in behind the wheel. He looked at Scotty riding shotgun. "Come on, we have a ship to meet."

Lefty drove down to the harbor. "She's already docked."

Scotty sat up straight. "It's okay, they're securing her now. See? No one has disembarked. The gangplank isn't out yet."

Lefty pulled behind a military convoy truck, took in a deep breath and let it out in a low whistle. As far as he could see, the docks and the yard beyond were covered with canvas stretchers.

"That's a sight to raise the hair on your arms."

Scotty looked back at James. "I've seen it too many times."

Soon the yard swarmed with nurses, medics and doctors. They moved like pieces of well-oiled machinery, each doing their job deftly with precision timing and skill. Their goal was to move their patients safely and quickly out of the elements to the nearest hospital.

Lefty waited until the first two rows of stretchers were full. The men being tended to required such undivided attention, no one noticed when Lefty and Scotty carried their friend James between the parked vehicles and laid him on the last litter at the end of the third row.

The short trip had taken a toll on James, who at first seemed vaguely aware of voices and then nothing as he slipped into the abyss. Lefty shook hands with Scotty and watched him board the USS *Lejeune*. When he turned to head back to his "borrowed" ambulance, he caught sight of Dominic Spinelli. Dominic was going from man to man with a clipboard checking off names. They made eye contact and nodded to each other before going on their way, knowing they would never cross paths again.

Chapter 28   Identity Switch

The work was overwhelming and the waves of patients were endless. They kept coming. So many wounded men, so much blood and trauma. The doctors and nurses worked day and night with no end in sight. They would close their eyes for an hour of sleep only to see maimed boys with missing limbs in their nightmares.

The US Beacon Marine Hospital provided health care for military and maritime laborers from ports all over the world. On a day like today, when a ship carrying wounded docked in Boston, one could see all the goodness and evil of humanity play out on one stage.

The smells were the worst. The stench was bad enough when the body was dead, but these men were alive and some were experiencing their own decomposition in unimaginable ways. Casts had been purposely put on thick and tight in the field to prevent the swelling that comes with gangrenous gases. Nothing helped disguise the smell of decaying flesh that permeated hospital worker's nostrils. Some men's limbs had been hastily amputated in field hospitals. Every horrific vision a person could imagine walked or was carried off these ships, and the compassionate medical personal worked endlessly and still felt helpless against the tide of macerated human flesh. Sometimes a kind word, a pat on the shoulder, a warm hand to hold was all they could offer, and so this is what they did. In private, they wiped their tears and moved on.

James was still unconscious upon arrival at the hospital. He was triaged and wheeled down a crowded corridor into a treatment area to be examined and prepped for surgery. Once there, the stark, white lights of the operating room revealed the extent of James's wounds.

The OR team, under the guidance of Dr. Thompson, worked diligently debriding and cleaning the multiple holes in his torn flesh. It was tedious, backbreaking work and they were mercifully grateful for his lack of consciousness. Many of his wounds were infected and one of the entry wounds was dangerously close to the spine. The doctors were not sure if he would walk again.

Their job was to clean, sew up, hydrate, bandage and stabilize the patient and then move him into a ward or room. One of the nurses would document belongings and identification.

On that first day, a nurse found the piece of paper Lefty had placed in James's pocket, but skepticism remained about whom this soldier was because he was older and the information incomplete. Most likely, he was in the Merchant Marine, she thought, but for now his welfare was imperative, not his identity. The nurse wrote "Lawson, Charles (unverified)" on the chart and started to put the note in his file. She stopped and looked at the scrap piece of paper and was suddenly awash with sadness. She picked his chart up again and wrote "Call by nickname – Charlie," then she put the note in a sealed yellow envelope in the otherwise empty box marked, "Belongings."

Another nurse observed this and asked, "Charlie? Did he talk to you? Is that his name?"

"No, but he needs to have something, I don't know, something friendly, I guess. Charles is so rigid. I like the name Charlie."

The second nurse smiled at her, "Then Charlie it is." She understood this. As little as it seemed, this was important to both personnel and patient.

All questions were put aside for another day. A day that would be a long time coming.

It took nine months for James to stay conscious for any length of time and for the infections that ravaged his body to finally be conquered. In those nine long months, the world saw two atomic bombs drop and the second Great War end. The postwar housing market exploded with returning vets, and communities hungered to return to their lives and put the war behind them. Children born in those postwar years would come to be known as the "baby boomer" generation.

James was also born again and his life was forever changed. In Gloucester, he had been known as James, a wolf among sheep. Now, here in this Boston hospital, he was Charlie, an unknown, living alone, trapped in a lie as time marched on.

***

James's first consciousness of where he was, that he remembered, came ten months after the day he arrived at the hospital. Each of his senses awakened slowly, challenged by his surroundings. A sharp, antiseptic smell seemed to shrink the membranes in his nostrils and felt like a feather was tickling him, trying to entice him into a sneeze. Eyelids shielded him from the bright lights and would not open immediately on command. His ears picked up one noise at a time until they all merged into an annoying background hum. James struggled to distinguish any words out of the conglomeration of muffled noises and voices. He felt strange, detached from his body. The eyelid of his right eye seemed to open a little and, through the slit, he saw a blurry figure standing over him. His left eye suddenly opened wide, doubling the blur. He willed them together to bring the blurred images into focus. It was a woman dressed in bright white standing over him, and for a moment James wondered if she was an angel.

An astute nurse noticed the awareness in James's eyes. She hurried over to check on him. He had opened them before, but now he was present in the chocolate-brown irises.

Softy, she called to him. "Charlie? Can you hear me?"

James searched her face as she bent over and leaned closer to him. He understood the words, but they were spoken in slow motion, long and drawn out. *And who was Charlie? Was she taking to him? She called me Charlie.* His mouth opened and closed numerous times like a goldfish gulping for air. Thoughts formed in his head, but no words came out. A tear rolled from the corner of his eye as he gave up. The nurse comforted him and wiped the wetness on his cheek. "It's okay, give it time."

He tried to smile at her. The muscles in his face felt tight and unresponsive, but his grimace must have resembled a smile because she grinned back.

"Welcome back." She smiled.

"Back? From where?"

***

Three days after James regained full consciousness, his memory rushed back full force and hit him like a surprise left hook. He remembered the heist, Lefty, Dominic and Scotty. He remembered the two families he had deserted. He remembered it all, his entire, miserable life and decided he wanted to forget it all.

On the second day, the doctor had told him most likely he would never walk again, but reassured him that, in time, he may remember things. The doctors thought Charlie showed remarkable improvement from the day he woke, with the exception of his legs and memory. They feared Charlie may have suffered a concussive brain injury, but weren't sure how much of the brain was involved due to Charlie's inability to answer any questions. Their prognosis was up in the air because he either couldn't or wouldn't answer them.

A month passed before the doctors confirmed he was an invalid. The words clobbered him like a concrete slab. Panic overtook him. His heart pounded and sweat formed on his brow. He heard fragments of the conversation between the doctor and the nurse, about giving a sedative, accepting one's fate and other bullshit. He'd lost the only thing he had ever owned, his independence.

A lyric ran through his thoughts. *Dark clouds are gathering, a storm is coming, my wandering ways will soon be done.* Bridey McConville was a witch. A good witch, but a witch nonetheless. She had prophesied his fate. He was no longer a wandering man. If he had no control over his life anymore, he might as well be dead. Faces flashed though his mind – his father, Alfred, Macklin. Macabre faces with slack mouths, dead eyes, sinking under the water, covered with white sheets, disappearing in the sucking muck of French soil.

He gasped, trying to get air in his lungs and gain control so he wouldn't suffocate under the weight of his circumstance. Tomorrow, he'll think about it tomorrow. His heavy lids closed and his body succumbed to the sedative.

Tomorrow came, and the next. Eventually, James accepted that every tomorrow would be the same from now on. The same room, the same walls, but he was alive, so he decided the amnesia the staff assumed afflicted him would be an advantage. With no place to go and no one waiting for him, it would make sense to start over. There was a time he wanted to be invisible. This would be a new beginning. Or better yet, his biggest con. The hardest part for him to comprehend was that a full year had passed while he lingered in a twilight sleep. What happened to everyone?

On Charlie's one-year anniversary of waking up, hospital officials made an attempt to confirm Charlie's identity and locate any family he might have. The hospital administration filed a record search with military officials, information that was a presumably known from the paper found in Charlie's pocket. It took a long time before officials stated that no one in the US military forces fit the criteria. The search was expanded overseas to the UK and they eventually came back empty-handed as well. The surname Lawson, first name, Charlie and all combinations were was searched for all spellings – Lawson, Lawsen and Loughson. With Charles, Chuck, Charlie, all to no avail.

A Boston newspaper printed a story of the hospital's amnesia victim with a picture, hoping the public could identify him. Little did they know that three people would recognize him and make the choice to throw the paper away.

Chapter 29   Lefty's Secret 1946

Lefty's youngest daughter, Erin, had grown two inches in the past year. He watched her jumping rope in the street with her brothers and sisters. Her hair, up in pigtails, bounced up and down as she jumped, squealing her delight. Her siblings counted her jumps as she tried to break their records. Freckles stood out on her nose from the summer sun and she no longer showed the sickly pallor that had them so frightened the prior year. He and Bridey thought they would never see her so rosy-cheeked and healthy. *Funny how things work out, he thought. If it weren't for James...*

It had been a long year of watching his back, looking over his shoulder. Dominic and Scotty sailed off on the USS *Lejeune* and hadn't returned to the port of Boston. Lefty assumed James didn't make it through his injuries. For months he checked the death lists the city posted from time to time after the war, but he never saw James's name, or the name he had given him, Charles Lawson.

The poker game, on that night a year ago, was run by the Beneditto family. The family never had a chance to track down the men who robbed them. They had other pressing problems to deal with. The Mariano family took the limelight away from the robbery when they muscled in on Beneditto territory, resulting in a deadly turf war.

Lefty kept his profile low. When he wasn't working his shift at the morgue, he was at home with his family or at Dooley's. Every now and then, he picked up a member of the Beneditto family off the street after a shootout and put him on "ice" in the cooler. One by one, the family was being picked off by the Marianos, eliminating any threat to Lefty and the others.

A couple months after they left James on the docks, half-dead on a litter, Lefty stole a blank death certificate out of his boss's desk. He filled it out with James Lawson's correct information and a burial plot number where he knew a John Doe was buried. He filed the death certificate with the city clerk and applied to the Veteran's Administration to have a marker put on the grave for a WWI veteran.

I don't know what will happen or has happened to you, my friend, but everyone needs a final resting place and if you're dead on paper no one can track you down and harm you. It's the least I can do for you. You helped my Erin and, for that, I'm forever grateful, lad.

Erin's happy squeal brought him back to the present and he listened to her sing. "Charlie Chaplin went to France, to teach the ladies how to dance."

Yes, indeed, life is good, he thought. He snubbed his cigarette out on the stoop, got up, waved to his children and walked a couple of blocks down to the newsstand. He picked up the daily paper and headed to his watering hole for a pint.

Dooley himself was tending the bar, running his dishrag over the richly, varnished wood, back and forth until he reached Lefty.

"You're going to worry that wood down to a splinter, Dooley."

"Aye, but it'll be a shiny one. Top o' the morning. Want your usual?"

"Aye, your early shift didn't turn up this morning, Dooley?"

"Naw, he's done, he was skimming off the top. You can't get good help nowadays." Dooley complained away as he took his time drawing the pint. Finally, he put the beer down in front of Lefty and went to wash glasses.

Lefty opened the morning paper and spread it on the bar in front of him. He took a gulp of the beer, choked and sprayed it over the picture that stared up at him. Quickly he pushed the mug aside, shook the beer off the paper and lifted it up close to his face, squinting at the picture. He read the article under the picture. It was about a "John Doe," an amnesia victim. The only identification was a piece of paper found in his pocket with the following unverified information: *Charles Lawson, 49, Boston, Cutty Sark.*

My God, that's James! Sweet Jesus. He looked around to see if anyone noticed his astonishment. Dooley sensed his restlessness and came down his end of the bar with a concerned look on his face.

"Anything wrong with your pint?" he asked as he threw the dishtowel over his shoulder. Lefty wondered if he had more than one towel. He had never seen Dooley without it. It was like a baby's security blanket.

"Yeah, I mean no, it's fine," Lefty stammered and grabbed the pint, drinking it halfway down to prove it.

Dooley noticed the wet newspaper, reached down and flipped it around to face him. He tapped his finger on James's picture and Lefty took a deep breath in and held it watching Dooley's face for any sign of recognition.

Lefty's heart pounded in his ears as Dooley read aloud the caption under the picture. He watched Dooley lift his eyes to meet his and waited for James to be exposed.

"Would you look at that?" Dooley flipped the paper back around toward

Lefty with a look of disgust on his face.

"What?"

"The poor bloke, no one's claiming him. After serving his country and this is the thanks he gets for the rest of his life. Imagine, not knowing who you are." Dooley make a loud *tsk-tsk* sound, slapping his tongue against the roof of his mouth.

Lefty took a chance. "So Dooley, you get a lot of mariners in this joint. His face not ringing a bell with ya?"

"No, never laid my baby blues on him before." The bell on the door jingled as some patrons walked in and Dooley went back to work shouting out a "Wish him the luck of the Irish though," over his shoulder.

Lefty scanned the picture again. *Well I'll be...I don't think anyone would know James but me.* He read the rest of the article. When he got to the part about how the infection wreaked havoc with his spine and he would never walk, Lefty felt bad but assured James was in good hands.

Well, he was a WWI vet; it's a better place for him now. They'll take care of him. Nowhere else for the lad to go.

***

Lefty had a second pint to settle his nerves before he headed home. Back at his house, Lefty found his pretty baby girl sitting on the front stoop, head on her skinned knees, lips pouting.

"What's wrong, honey?" He wiped the tears trickling down between her freckles.

"Shelagh, Daniel and Declan didn't want to play with me anymore. We were jumping rope and they went inside."

"Well, they don't know the nice, fresh air they're missing. Do they?"

Erin angrily crossed her arms and stamped her foot. "Right!

"How would you like to go for a walk with your Da?"

"Just me and you?" Her voice trembled.

"Yup, just you and me."

She jumped up and threw her arms around his neck. "Where are we going, Da?"

"To the graveyard, little one."

Erin stepped back, her shoulders slumped with disappointment. "Why there, Daddy?"

He winked at her. "It's a good place to think. Everyone there listens. They don't talk back."

She backed up, her hands high in the air, out in front of her. "No, I don't want to go there. The ghosts will get me. I'm scared."

"No, no ghosts will get you. There are no ghosts. Who told you that?"

"Declan did," referring to her older, by three years, brother.

165

"Oh, well then, I'll take care of your brother when I see him for scaring you, little one. But for now, you're with me and nothing will ever happen to ya, right?" He held his hand out, reassuring her.

Erin puffed her lower lip out and bravely stomped forward like a little soldier. "Right, Da. Let's go."

Lefty liked the solitude of walking around the graveyard, but today he wanted to see if the stone had been placed on James's grave yet. He took his youngest child's hand in his, amazed at how the warmth of her little hand melted his heart.

Many times he thought of his friend, James. He would go and sit by the faux grave, which had become more of a symbol of Erin's life than a memorial to James. In the quiet of the cemetery, he sorted out any problems that plagued him, such as his decision to abandon his life of crime and go straight. Lefty remembered telling James that it was a jus matter of time before something would go wrong. When a man faces mortality or anyone close to him faces mortality, it does strange things to him. It makes him look differently at the man he sees in the mirror.

Bridey told Lefty a hint of sorrow lived in James's eyes each time he saw Erin and it grew exponentially as time passed. They approached the plot and he saw the grave marker was finally in place. To Lefty's surprise, tears fell from his eyes. Erin looked up with concern when a tear fell on her hand. Her eyes squinted as she looked up into the sunlight at her father's face.

"Da, what's wrong? Whose grave is that?"

"A friend, honey. This man was my friend and I miss him."

She looked at the engraving and read the letters out loud, J-a-m-e-s- H-L-a-w-s-o-n. Then she sounded the name out.

"Hey, I know him," she cried out.

Lefty put a finger to his lips. "Shhhhh, yes, you do, little one, and you know what I think?"

"What, Da?"

"I think he was your angel on Earth."

Erin's mouth went round in surprise. She twirled around and around her father, pigtails swinging as she squealed with glee. "No kidding, Da? I have an angel?"

"Yes, and this man made it so you could have your operation and stay here with me and your mum. Come on now, let's finish our walk." Father and daughter walked on up the path between the gravestones, holding hands.

"Da, I wish I could help someone, like he helped me. Maybe when I grow up I can do that." She skipped ahead, singing like an angel

. "I bet ya do, love. I bet ya will," he whispered.

Chapter 30 Esther's Secret

E sther Gadda waited for the trolley car that would take her home after her long day of cleaning houses. Her grueling day started before sunup. Six days a week she worked her fingers to the bone scrubbing and cleaning other people's houses before going home to care, cook and clean for her aging parents. Her two children were now adults. Doris was working and James Robert was serving his country.

Those years since her husband deserted her had been financially challenging, but peaceful all the same. Life was hard but she never complained. Being from hardy Swedish stock, she accepted the bad with the good and was equally proud, passive and private as she kept her troubles to herself. Hard work wouldn't kill her, but he might have.

It was dusk but lingering streaks of sun still danced through the shadows of Boston's buildings. She closed her eyes to soak in the warm rays, until she heard a news hawker, circling the edge of the crowd that waited at the trolley stop.

"Newspapers, newspapers, step right up. Come and get your headlines. 'Mystery man lives at Beacon Marine.'" The young man danced up and down the curbstone, like a vaudeville tap dancer, tipping his scally cap to the "ladies and gents," as he called them when they bought a paper.

Esther opened the clasp of her pocketbook and took out the exact change for a paper. She always brought a paper home every night to read to her father. He never learned to read English, even though he could speak and understand the language. She enjoyed this time with him in an otherwise busy household. They started this ritual, years ago, when her children were young. She would tuck them into bed, her two sisters would be out on the town with friends after working the day at the John Hancock building, and her mother would retire early. When the house was quiet and the tea brewed, she would sit in the front room and read to her father.

"Come and get your paper. John Doe is a war mystery!" The newsboy

167

continued his chant as she handed him the change. She folded the paper under her arm as the trolley pulled up and everyone rushed forward to board the car.

When the dinner was eaten, the dishes done and the house picked up, Esther sat on the hassock in front of her father's large, well-worn, leather chair. There were no children to tuck in anymore, which saddened Esther, but she was content knowing they were strong, healthy adults. It had been no easy feat bringing them up alone. If it hadn't been for her family, who knows how things might have turned out? Even though there were years of struggling financially, she would have love to have little ones again, but now she looked forward to grandchildren in the future.

Edward Gadda loaded his pipe as he always did in preparation for their nightly ritual. His pipe was his most prized possession and he would often speak of pipe-smoking as an experience, explaining that his mouthpiece was made in Germany from the highest quality ebonite rod. He would add that the key to that experience was the briar that was used, and that the diameter of the smoke channel was imperative. The passionate pride in his voice displayed his appreciation for the skill it took to craft a quality pipe.

Esther didn't think of all those details. The smell of pipe tobacco and leather of her father's chair meant the comfort of family. For her, the aroma was the best part. She would close her eyes, breathe it in and be transported back to a time when she was a child on her father's knee, listening to stories of the old country. It was during those precious moments that she could feel secure and relaxed, without the weight of the world on her shoulders.

Tonight she waited until he held the match to the bowl, and watched his bearded cheeks suck in and puff out. His eyes would close as he savored the richness of the tobacco and that was her cue to begin reading.

Esther sat sidesaddle on the edge of the large hassock and laid the paper out flat so the soft light from the lamp beside Edward's chair would shine on it. She read the headline aloud to her father, but when she glanced down at the accompanying black-and-white picture of a man sitting up in a hospital bed, she froze.

It can't be...no, it is him. I would know him anywhere.

"Are you all right, *flicka?*" Concern had etched its way deep into her father's face as he watched her. He routinely fell back on Swedish words, more so now that he was getting on in years. Esther liked it; *flicka* sounded lyrical and softer than the English word, girl.

"Yes, I'm fine. Just a little catch in my throat." Esther rolled the newspaper and tucked it under her arm. She stood up.

"I'm going to get a glass of water before I read. Can I get you something to go with your tea?"

"No, I'm fine. *Tack sa mycket.*" He set about relighting his pipe while she went to the kitchen.

"You're welcome, Father."

The scent of vanilla from the rice pudding on the stove wafted past her nose. The oven was still warm and she leaned back against it, took in a deep breath and shuddered. She slowly expelled the air from her lungs in a controlled attempt to still her heart which threatened to pound out of her chest.

It is him. How long has it been? Let's see…1929. Seventeen years since I've seen James.

Esther went in the pantry and climbed up on the stepstool. Her hand searched blindly on the top shelf for a metal box where she stored her important papers. She opened it on the counter and took out a piece of paper. Her divorce decree she filed in 1932. The grounds were written as follows: "Three years of utter desertion. Whereabouts unknown."

Now I know where you are.

Last year, she heard an unsubstantiated rumor that he had died, but she kept that information to herself. Not even her children knew. But now that was all wrong. He was alive. He can't walk, can't remember. Esther thought of all the years she spent alone, the embarrassment, the hurt. She thought of the difficult questions young Bob asked about his father's whereabouts night after night. And then there was Doris, who never asked. She became quieter and took on the role of protecting Esther. James had a way of killing someone's spirit, but Doris figured this out and was stronger for it. Thoughts raced through her head.

No, I won't go to the authorities. Some things are better not remembered. Now you are the living dead, James, and I choose to keep you that way. Yes, my choice. Dead to me and dead to my family.

"*Mina läppar är förseglade,*" Esther whispered softly. *My lips are sealed,* her mind translated. A deep intake of air filled her lungs and on the exhale seventeen years of uncertainty released their hold. She had never fully realized until this moment that her memories had held her prisoner. A renewed identity coursed through her blood. She filled a glass with water and went back to read the paper to her father.

Edward Gadda looked at his daughter's face as she entered the room. "Is everything all right, *flicka?*"

"Fine, in fact, everything is nifty." And she meant it.

Chapter 31   Rose's Secret

Rose liked California, but she missed her family. Recently, she had been entertaining the idea of moving back to Boston, but was hesitant in doing so because of her fear of James. Even though it had been many years, this was a major factor whenever she considered a move back east. Rose wanted their child to have nothing to do with him and had even told her James had died. As far as she was concerned, they were both better off to believe this, especially since she had remarried a wonderful man and the three of them made a normal, happy family.

She poured herself a cup of tea and sat down with the morning paper, relishing a few quiet moments before she walked her ten-year-old daughter to school, a ritual they both loved. Especially for Rose who thrived on the consistency of a daily routine. No more surprises, no more drama. The party girl was gone. That was all behind her now and she loved her life. Motherhood had tamed her wild side and matured her into a responsible woman.

Despite the failed marriage, Rose felt that, when she had reached a crucial crossroads in her life, she had chosen the right path. Goosebumps rose on her arms whenever she thought about how her life could have gone, or for that matter, ended.

James ended her habit of keeping bad company. Now she craved normalcy. Even to the point of being boring, it was an acceptable lifestyle.

Rose thought about how James sought normalcy at times, but the more he tried, the more he feared, and the further the separation widened in their relationship.

The headline, *Mystery Solved in Boston,* caught her eye. Under the byline was a picture of a California woman with her arms wrapped around a man propped up in a hospital bed. The caption read. *"At last, I found my brother."*

Rose stood up so abruptly her chair hit the wall. She knew at once, this woman was either a publicity hog or a liar, or possibly mistaken, because the man pictured with her was not her brother. Of this fact Rose had no doubt, because that man was Rose's ex-husband, James Lawson.

The memories of their time together torn through Rose and her knees began to shake. She reached behind, groped around and found the seat of the chair with one hand and lowered herself onto it. She studied the black-and-white photograph and thought maybe she was wrong. James was seventeen years older than she was, and it had been a few years.

Maybe it's someone who looks like him.

She held onto this thought until she turned to the continued article on the inside page, and there was no longer any doubt. A second picture showed the man sitting up in a hospital bed being handed something from a nurse. He was missing his index finger on his left hand.

Rose gasped. It is him. It's James.

Rose thought back to when James worked at the shipyard for her Uncle Alouche. His finger was crushed as he attempted to remove a piece of equipment that held the suction arm from the slide on a hopper dredge. The doctor couldn't save the mangled finger so they cleanly amputated it. James was unfazed by the whole ordeal and told her it was a rite of passage for a yardbird. Like an unspoken acceptance into the inner circle of shipyard workers.

At first, Rose felt unsure, but here it was in her hands, the truth in black-and-white print. Her daughter's memory had mercifully sifted out the bad ones of her father, keeping only ones she cherished.

Rose remembered when she was young, her grandmother told her what you don't say is even more harmful than what you do. *Secrets can be like a disease, Rosie. Choose wisely what you keep to yourself and what you spread to others.*

It took only a second to make her decision after she watched her little girl bounce happily into the kitchen and announce she was ready for school.

"Mama, I need help putting my hair up. I want a ponytail. Can you do it?"

Rose looked at her daughter's sparkling, rich, brown eyes. She never realized how much she looked like James.

"Mama, hurry."

"Sure baby, turn around and hold still." Rose pulled her little girl's thick mane back and tied it with a pink ribbon.

"Let's pretend, Mama. Are you ready for an adventure on the way to school this morning? I want to pretend I'm a pirate," Helen shouted.

Rose smiled at her daughter as Helen whipped her pony tail from side to side. She turned her around to face her when she was done and hugged her. "You're not a pirate, baby, you're my treasure. Let's go."

Rose knew at that moment she would go to her grave before she revealed the truth about James being alive to her daughter or anyone. She would hold her secret close to her heart, so that it could never be broken again.

Chapter 32 Charlie

The news of a mystery patient in a Boston hospital reached across the country to the west coast. A California woman desperately hoped Charlie was her long lost brother and even traveled to Boston, had her picture taken with him and was interviewed by the newspapers, but her claim was never substantiated. She also never returned to visit Charlie despite promises to do so.

Notoriety-seekers came out of the woodwork in the media flurry, their real intentions never known. Maybe they wanted to see their own names in print or maybe it was wishful thinking that he was their long lost loved one who had never returned home after the war. It didn't seem to matter to Charlie, who also seemed to enjoy the limelight or needed something to brighten the dark, monotonous days.

During the evenings, Charlie rolled the halls in his wheelchair, smiling and nodding to patients and staff, and adorned in his gentleman's maroon smoking jacket, a gift from a sympathizer. He often wondered how many miles he had put on that chair. Years passed, nurses and doctors came and went. Charlie marveled at the inventions he observed in the hospital as well as the changes in society, such as the clothing and hairstyles. But the changes that intrigued him the most were the ones within him.

Many nights, he would sit in the chair in his room until after midnight, looking out over the lights of Boston. But what he loved most was an opened window in the good weather, so he could hear the hustle and bustle of cars rushing by in the outside world. The sounds incited a rush of adrenalin to flow through him like the old days. Life itself, the way it should be. The way his life should have been. He ached for the smell of the sea, the sound of halyards blowing in a stiff wind and even the screeching of gulls circling above a hefty catch, which he once hated, would be music to his ears now.

Charlie's body became his autobiography, which he read nightly as a silent penance. He would look at his missing finger and think of the shipyard and Rose, his useless legs would remind him of Lefty and the night of the heist, the tattoos would bring flashes of World War I and Macklin, as well as France and his brush with death in the flu epidemic. Each night he would read a chapter made evident at that moment by his physical pain and inability to care for himself and revisit his life and think about the way it should have been, if he had made better choices.

Is there anything good I've done with my life? Is there anyone who thinks of me in a good light? Where are the children I brought into the world?

Charlie wheeled his chair down to the common room to see the new television everyone was talking about. He didn't know what was so special about the box until a nurse came in and showed him how it worked.

Amazing, he thought.

A children's show was on and, as Charlie heard the children laugh, he closed his eyes and drifted back to many years ago. He thought about his son and daughter from his first marriage. When they were three and six years old, they would play jacks in front of the triple-decker up on Ashley Street. He could hear them calling out, "Onesies, twosies!" They'd be adults now, maybe married with children of their own. He could be a grandfather.

No, he couldn't be a grandfather. How could he be if he had never accepted being a father? The pain of the emptiness at that moment was worse than any physical pain he had ever endured.

For Charlie, the earth stood still since the night he was shot and this world around him now was like that box-like contraption called television that was in the common room. It was surreal and sometimes he found the best way to handle his surroundings was to tune out and turn off.

Chapter 33   Charlie's Last Years

Charlie rolled his wheelchair down the hospital hallway, waving and greeting the staff like he was royalty strolling on the red carpet. These days, most of his time was spent in the common room, which was a popular place during the day. It provided the closest environment to a family living room for convalescing soldiers who lived at the hospital. A spot near the windows was the most sought-after preference because, once there, you were parked for the day. For some, the windows offered hope of the outside world in the future, while for others they provided a wistful memory of days gone forever.

Today was a warm summer morning and the sun's rays pierced the middle of the room like arrows shot through the large floor-to-ceiling windows. Charlie stopped at the door's threshold watching the dust particles float through the air, riding the beams of light, but what startled him was a memory from long ago that flashed in his brain.

In his mind, a scene from the distant past was building in pieces. This happened more frequently to him now. He thought maybe it was due to his isolation. Charlie could be awake and living a scene inside his head, which proved to be a useful technique to transcend the pain in the early years after his admission. The scary part was not knowing which side reality was on and at times he teetered on the threshold. It was hard to come back to the confinement of these drab hospital walls when he could stay in his head.

He saw himself as a young man with a family back on Ashley Street. The house had a small, fenced-in back yard, perched on a rocky hillside above Boston. At night he loved to stand by the fence, have a drink and smoke a cigarette while looking out over the city lights. It reminded him of being on a trawler out at sea and seeing the coast lit up, guiding the way back to port.

On this particular night as he sat in the velvety blackness of the shadows of the yard, he watched his little girl, Doris, move deftly through the tall wildflowers in the moonlight. She was catching fireflies in a glass Mason jar. Hundreds of lightning bugs blinked on and off as she twirled around and around, giggling softly. He didn't mean to startle her when he spoke, but he did, and before she ran back in the house, he recognized the look on her face. It was fear. She was afraid of him, like his own mother had been afraid of him, so could he blame the child? *Probably not*, he thought. In anger, he threw the empty liquor bottle over the fence where it shattered on the rocks below.

The fireflies turned back to floating dust particles. Charlie waved his hand in front of his face as if he could shoo the memory away. He rolled across the room and positioned himself to look out one of the large windows. He hadn't noticed the young man in the overstuffed chair. He thought he was the first one in the room since he had commandeered the premiere spot, until he heard the voice.

"I've heard about you, you're the one who has been here since '45," the man called over to him. Charlie ignored him and looked straight ahead.

He addressed Charlie again. "Hey, you there, man?"

Charlie closed his eyes. He didn't want to discuss his life with anyone.

The young man continued talking. He didn't need Charlie to acknowledge him. He needed to know that someone else who was in the same boat would listen without judgment or pity. "I don't know how you've done it, man. I've been here four months and I'm going nuts. The name's Tillman, Rudy Tillman."

Charlie moved his chair around to get a better look at the man. At first, he didn't see anything wrong with him and he wondered why he was in the hospital. Maybe he was a mentally ill patient. There were many of them around. They were the ones with invisible yet crippling wounds and the amusing thing was, each war had their own little name for the affliction they suffered. In his war, the first big one, it was shell shock, WWII and Korea had combat or battle fatigue and now the new horror show, Vietnam, had stress response syndrome.

Foolish, he thought. Charlie knew it was all the same. It was HELL with capital letters. Pure hell.

The man leaned sideways in the chair to position himself before he stood. He straightened his back and turned to face Charlie, and that's when he saw the man's horrific injuries. The whole right side of his face was scarred from burns. His right ear was missing, leaving a gaping hole in his head. Small, wispy patches of hair plastered the burned side of his scalp and he must have chosen not to shave the left side of his head, which was covered with wavy brown locks giving him the bizarre appearance of two people glued down the middle, in a macabre attempt to make one body. Also missing on his right side was his arm, all the way up to his shoulder, which was why he had a little difficulty getting to the edge of the chair to stand and balance his weight..

Charlie didn't know what to call how he was suddenly feeling. It hit him

175

so fast. Flashbacks of the horrors of war he witnessed many years ago in the trenches. Flashes of Macklin in mid-sentence, blown apart as he stood helplessly nearby. Sweat broke out on his brow and he thought about going back to the sanctity of his room.

The young man shuffled toward him, "My looks scare your voice away?"

Charlie recovered quickly and extended his hand. "Naw, it takes a lot more than an ugly harp to scare me."

The young man shook it with the only hand he had. "My name is Tillman," he repeated.

Charlie nodded and, sticking to his reputation of being a man of few words, he answered, "Charlie. They call me Charlie."

Charlie spoke only a few words a week to this soldier. What he did do was listen and that made all the difference. He realized through his own trials, listening doesn't cost anything. It comes down to giving a little time. Most people say they don't have the time to listen to other people's troubles. Charlie couldn't say he didn't have the time. Time was all he did have. He found himself drawn to the common room every day at the same time, and every day he would find the soldier sitting in the same chair, waiting. At first he would pull his wheelchair up alongside of him, like two boats rafted together so they couldn't drift away. They would look out the window and enjoy the quiet.

In time, Private Tillman began to talk and the dam that kept him from moving forward with his life burst. The staff watched this special bond mesh and they granted this odd friendship the time and privacy needed to heal.

The priest and the staff all noticed Charlie was the catalyst that started the gradual change for the better in Private Tillman. The young soldier seemed to be interacting with people more and generally showed a much more positive attitude regarding his new life. He was even trying to smile, which he had been self-conscious about, because his mouth was severely lopsided due to scar tissue, but when he did, his eyes sparkled and the doctor knew he had accepted his future.

It was a bittersweet day when Private Tillman informed Charlie he was finally being discharged. Tillman started to say it had been a long thirteen months when he realized thirteen months would be a short sentence for Charlie in this hospital. They went to shake hands and laughed when Charlie's right hand went automatically to the private's missing arm before finally connecting. Charlie would miss his friend, but he was happy for him. The young man could see a life beyond war. It was the one he fought to protect.

***

Dr. Templeton made it a point to do rounds in the common room daily. He was pleased that Charlie was the one who made the positive effect on Private Tillman. After Tillman was discharged, Dr. Templeton went to check on Charlie and found him sitting by the window in his own room, not in the common room.

He cleared his throat as he sat on the edge of Charlie's bed. "I came by to see how you were doing. I thought it might be tough on you when Tillman left."

"The boy got a bum rap, but war will do that. You don't let them get to you and you never let it show." Charlie spoke while staring out the window. He rarely made eye contact with anyone.

"Is that the way you feel, Charlie? Being on guard all the time is no good. You need to let people in. Charlie, did you hear me? Tillman's family said you were instrumental in getting him back among the living again, you know."

Charlie suddenly looked up at him, eyes twinkling, "Looks like I'm good for something."

Smiling, Dr. Templeton agreed, "Yes, what you did was a good thing."

"How much *good* balances the scales, Doc?" Charlie asked.

"The scales? What do you mean?"

"You know, the scales of justice. I want to know how many good deeds offset the bad things one does in life."

"Sorry Charlie, I'm a doctor. If you're looking for redemption, I think you want the other professional, the priest." He laughed as he got up and started for the door. He stopped, looked back at Charlie and when he saw his face, he stopped laughing. He realized Charlie was serious and he began to wonder about the man. What bad or evil things could he have done that he punishes himself so?

The doctor felt like he had to say something to him before he left. He walked back to Charlie and said, "Charlie, keep doing what you're doing. These young men need you to listen. They need a mentor." He didn't wait for Charlie to say anything, and he left the room.

***

A nurse brought a patient into the common room and parked his chair near the couch. She put the brake on the chair and looked out the window. She shook her head in disgust. "Spring days should be sunny and uplifting. This rain has to stop sometime and when it does, I'll bring you outside to sit in the garden."

The patient said nothing. He stared out the window. Visibility was poor due to a cold, foggy mist that hung outside the window, hiding the tulips attempting to push up through the earth.

She handed him a magazine. "I'll be back in an hour to bring you to rehab." She didn't wait for an answer. There were a lot of one-sided conversations here. The workers had no time to linger when there was work to be done. Patients dramatically outnumbered personnel.

When she was gone he threw the magazine on the couch, released the brake and wheeled his chair across the common room to park it beside Charlie. Charlie didn't look at him; he waited for the soldier to start talking. Charlie found this happened quite often now. Templeton was right. He was some kind of sounding board to the infirm men. After Tillman left, he didn't want to get close to anyone else, but the days and nights dragged on and he realized he needed them as much as the soldiers needed him. Anything to quell the boredom and maybe this was his road to redemption. To do something good.

The young man spoke in a monotone voice, barely audible to Charlie's damaged hearing. "It was a Thursday when they flanked us. I didn't know the day at the time. Days don't mean much in war. I'm sure you know that, but now that they told me the day, I won't forget it. Probably think about it every time Thursday rolls around," he said.

Charlie turned and looked at him. The young man's left leg was missing. "How'd it happen?"

"Mortar shell."

"Same weapon, different war," Charlie noted.

"Yup," the Vietnam vet agreed, "She's wrong, you know."

"Who?"

"The nurse. I don't want to go out to the garden. I hate sunny days. I like the gray days, the ones with the clouds hanging low, like today. When it was like this during the siege, it was a good day. The enemy couldn't see us; so on those days in 'Nam when low clouds covered the surrounding mountains in thick fog, we didn't get any incoming artillery or mortar fire.

We could breathe a little easier on those days. Yes sir, we loved those foggy, gray days."

The next day the sun was out and the soldier from 'Nam didn't show up in the common room. He felt too exposed, too vulnerable. Charlie understood, he'd be back, all in good time.

From the window, Charlie observed a family with young children outside at the picnic table. They were visiting their oldest son and had wheeled him outside to get some fresh air. He thought about his parents and siblings, something that he hadn't done in years. Charlie knew he had made a mess of his life right from the start, but he didn't have anyone to look up to. No happy mentor. He only had anger. Anger that consumed every waking moment. Looking back, he attributed anger as his inheritance, bestowed upon him by his father, but that was James. By circumstance, not by choice, he wasn't that person anymore, so he made a decision to meet with the priest. He needed to purge his mind of the remnants of James before the nightmares that haunted him tore him apart.

***

Father Mulcahy met with Charlie on Wednesday mornings. He wheeled down to the Chaplain's office and nodded at the priest.

"Hello Charlie, I have to tell you, I am encouraged with your interaction with the men."

Charlie shifted his weight in the chair. He looked around the office, avoiding the priest's face. "They just come."

"Why do you think they seek you out?"

"We're the same."

"That's right. You're the sounding board for something they can't harbor inside. Same reason you came to me."

"Yeah, I know what they're going through."

"I know you do, Charlie."

Charlie snorted, "You know, it might only be the fact that they see the miserable state I'm in and it offers them hope. They couldn't possibly be as screwed as the old man who lives in a hospital. Whose only family are strangers. Who will die here."

The priest sat in front of Charlie to confront his anger.

"Your family doesn't have to be strangers. From what you've told me in our meetings, you have people here in Boston."

"No, I don't. Forget about it, Father. "

"Okay, okay, don't worry, Charlie. What you've told me is in confidence and will go no further. So let's move on. Tell me about your father. You hinted that he was a problem."

Charlie didn't say anything for quite a while. Father Mulcahy waited patiently. Charlie thought about his parents. Long gone, they did not tug on his heart when he thought of them, but his brother, Peter, and sister, Catherine, did.

The first time my world changed was due to hesitation with Dad. The last time I acted quickly, on impulse, was with Alfred. How ironic the results were the same, both dead.

It had been such a long time since he allowed himself to think about his family. Charlie believed the last time was when Rose told James about Catherine's visit to tell him their mother had died.

He wondered what their lives were like. Had their lives changed as radically as his had over the years? Peter was the one who had potential. He hit the books, studied and loved every minute of it, whereas James hated school. Peter, his father's favorite, was the serious one, quiet and organized; he was never a troublemaker, unlike James who was known as the "black sheep" of the family. The more notoriety James received with that title, the more he loved to live up to it. So in the teen years, he and Peter went their separate ways, hanging with different groups of friends, but there was a time between the ages of seven and twelve when they were inseparable, and if there were any place in time where Charlie could magically return to, it would be then. What he wouldn't give to live his old life again, running on the beaches of Gloucester with his brother.

Yes, he'd like to go back in time, except for one day. It was on that day, during the summer of 1908, that the brothers' relationship changed forever. Peter and James spent the summer months skipping rocks or fishing at Niles Beach below Eastern Point Light, racing through the woods, and catching tadpoles in the pond. Then one day, they were up to their knees in the water beside the jetty out on the point and Peter noticed a crab scampering sideways, in and out of the mounded gigantic rocks that formed the jetty.

"I'm going to get him," Peter yelled as he crawled over the rocks and lay down on his belly, reaching down deep between the rocks until his armpit stopped him. His face turned red and he grunted and groaned as he searched for the crab, his fingertips barely reaching bottom. His tongue was pressed between his lips and his eyes were searching left to right, as if he could see to the sandy bottom of the hole. Peter felt about with his hand, straining to reach deeper.

James watched the color of his brother's face deepen to a dark red. "Hey, come on Peter, the tide's coming in. That crab's long gone."

Disappointed, Peter resigned. "Yeah." He went to get up and felt a shift in the rocks. His arm was wedged deep in a crevice. The tide was rising fast and his face was low to the water. Peter panicked and yelled for James to help him, but James stood there frozen, not knowing what to do. It was only a minute, but it seemed like forever to James before his father ran up the beach and found them. He had been up on the cliff, saw them on the jetty and was about to yell at them for not doing their chores when he heard Peter's screams.

His father reached the jetty and knocked James out of the way, pushing him backwards into the water and helping Peter relax so he could twist and turn his arm out of the granite vice that was holding him. Suddenly free, Peter held his hand, which was bleeding from abrasions. Their father picked Peter up to carry him home, but not before throwing James a distasteful look.

James felt awful, not helping Peter, but then he thought for a brief moment what his family life would be like if he were the only son. Maybe his father would like him. As the thought hit him, he looked at the back of his father walking away from him. Peter peered around the strong arms wrapped lovingly around him and James knew right away, without a doubt, that Peter had read his mind.

Young James slumped down on to the wet sand, shame eating at him, until the rage hit him. It mounted in him, rising so fast. His heart pounded, his body pulled itself up by the sheer force of his anger into a standing position, and a howl ripped out of his mouth. A crab made a run for the safety of the rocks and without a thought, James picked up a rock and smashed it down on the back of the crab's shell until it was pulverized pile of dust, indistinguishable from the sand to be washed away on the next tide.

"Charlie!" The priest's big hands gripped Charlie's wrists.

Charlie tried to move, but he couldn't. He was stuck like Peter. He opened his eyes and looked up at the priest who was standing in front of him. "Charlie, stop. Stop. You don't have to talk today if you don't feel like it."

The old priest is stronger than he looks was Charlie's first thought. Then he asked, "What happened?"

"I didn't want you to hurt yourself. You were pounding your fists on the arms of your wheelchair. What horrors are you going through my son?"

Charlie pulled away and turned his chair around. "Nothing, forget about it. I'll see you next time. Open the door, Father."

Father Mulcahy obliged and watched Charlie roll down the hall until he turned the corner, out of sight. A shake of his head accompanied a heavy sigh. He looked up at the water-stained ceiling and said a prayer before muttering. "Hey, how about sending a little help down here. I'm sure you have a divine plan in mind."

Chapter 34 Redemption 1975

Although the hospital took good care of Charlie, the last couple of years had been rough on him. Being bedridden for so long had taken its toll and he felt his body growing weaker every day. Life was leaving him, but he had to wonder at times if he had ever lived life. He kept these thoughts, all thoughts, to himself now and this had proven to be corrosive, eating him alive from the inside. After Father Mulcahy passed away in the mid-sixties, Charlie rarely spoke, awarding his visitors mute acknowledgement in the form of a look, a nod and at times, a smile.

Over these many years he had watched people come in and out of his life. Most of them were doctors, nurses, curiosity seekers and reporters who wanted to revive the search for his identity, like Myles Bingham, the reporter who attempted to identify him back in the fifties. Charlie wondered what happened to him. Sometimes people came and visited out of their need to feel good about themselves and others were genuine in their attempts to make the patients feel good.

During the first couple of years, Charlie had regained his memories a little at a time. No one knew this. They said he had amnesia and took pity on him and now, thirty years later, once again the tables had turned; now they had the amnesia. To them, Charlie was no longer a mystery. He was just an old man.

Charlie took pity on himself when he remembered who he was and the mess he had made of his life. While others slept under the cloak of darkness, Charlie bathed in thoughts of clarity, pure and raw in nature and void of the cloudiness of everyday life. As a wandering man, he avoided things he didn't want to deal with by staying in constant motion, but now he could not escape his reality. His thoughts bounced off the walls that imprisoned him and forced him to face the man in the mirror he had successfully avoided in his youth. He could hide no more. He was a shriveled shell of a man, a tortured lost soul with no redeeming light in sight.

The irony of it all. Amnesia would have been a blessing, he thought.

Charlie watched the years go by, people marking each decade with its own unique time stamp of change in music, clothing, hairstyles and philosophy; all exclaiming this was the best or worst time to be alive. But Charlie's years as a military hospital inpatient were marked by the wars of different generations and the soldiers who moved through the medical system.

They were the same, he thought, maybe different types of weapons were used, but the results were the same. After World War II came Korea, and the Cold War, whatever the hell that meant, and then there was Vietnam. Well, they said Vietnam wasn't even a war. It was a conflict. Bullshit! Tell that to the twenty-three year old who will never walk again, the nineteen year old with a severe brain injury, or the families of the ones who never returned, like Macklin. I was lucky to get out of the First World War unscathed and what did I do? Got myself messed up in an alley in Boston, during a heist, no less. I wasn't even young enough to be called a punk.

The hardest times in the hospital for Charlie were watching the military officers come in to place medals on the young men's chests in recognition of their bravery and service. They lay there maimed, some sightless or worse, and they still could muster up a smile with a salute, if they still had an arm to salute with. Charlie was embarrassed that people assumed he was in this group of men of moral fiber that made up the most heroic of humanity.

But this day would ease Charlie's mind, because on this day the woman who walked into his room made his day different than all the others throughout all his years at Beacon Marine Hospital. At first, he didn't know what it was about her. It wasn't something he could put his finger on, but it felt like a swath of comforting familiarity surrounded him.

The staff insisted on placing him in the chair so he could look out the window. A simple gesture he used to crave, but even that had dwindled. He was tired of watching the world pass him by. This is what he was thinking when she walked into his room. All this time, no one has invoked any emotion other than remorse in him, until now. He watched the nurse, he guessed to be somewhere in her late 30's, approach him with a lunch tray. She laid it down gently on the bedside table and pushed it close so he could reach it.

"Hello Charlie, my name is Mrs. Lynch. I've heard a lot about you. I'm going to be your nurse for a while."

The afternoon sunlight filtered through the window, gently bathing her face in the glow. He looked up at her and noticed a sprinkling of freckles peppered the bridge of her nose and upper cheeks. Her starched, white nurse's cap sat upon an unruly mop of long, auburn-red curls.

She's an Irish angel. Look at those sea-green eyes.

"I'll be back for the tray and to change the linens before we get you back into bed. Enjoy your lunch."

His hand shook as he picked up the fork off the tray and brought a bite of fish up to his mouth.

"I'll check in on you before I go off shift, Charlie, and bring you some of my mum's lamb stew. It goes down easy and tastes like Heaven's own ambrosia. I brought a batch in for the nursing station the other day and it was gone before I turned around."

Charlie watched the nurse leave the room. He managed a half dozen or so bites before he dozed off into a deep sleep and dreams of a past life overtook him.

***

Mrs. Harrington, the charge nurse, pulled the Kardex cards for the past three days and reviewed the nursing notes. Mrs. Lynch, her newest staff nurse, had recently transferred from City Hospital and she seemed to have a profound effect on Beacon Marine's longest-residing patient. Charlie had even responded with speech. Only one sentence here or there, but it was more than anyone had gotten out of him in the last few years.

Mrs. Lynch tentatively stepped into her supervisor's office, not quite sure if she was going to be reprimanded for something. She approached her desk "Hello, Miss Harrington. You wanted to speak to me?"

"Yes, I did, Mrs. Lynch. Please sit." Harrington's eyes directed her employee to the chair opposite the desk as she continued thumbing through and reading the chart on her desk. The new nurse's eyes widened as she looked at the seat, like it was an electric chair waiting to electrocute her. Her supervisor watched with a little smirk on her face and said, "Mrs. Lynch, it's not going to bite you. You're not in trouble if that's what you're thinking. Now sit down. I have a meeting soon, so I'll be brief."

Mrs. Lynch sighed, her relief visible. As she lowered herself into the seat, she noticed that it was Charlie's file that Miss Harrington was studying.

Miss Harrington finally straightened the papers neatly inside the folder and closed it. "Mrs. Lynch, in the past few days while our oldest patient, Charlie, has been in your care, many people noted there has been a marked difference in him. He's been more interested in his surroundings, more vocal."

Mrs. Lynch thought about this and she knew something had sparked in the old man. "I'll have to admit, I believe that is true. I have noticed he seems more engaged."

"Well, the difference was enough that Dr. Templeton noticed it and he is truly amazed. Charlie has been his patient for a long time and this is the first real breakthrough he's seen in him in quite a while. Therefore, in following his directive, you will be his primary nurse and devote more time trying to get him to communicate."

"I'd like that, but the workload..." Mrs. Lynch said, but was interrupted.

"That's our problem, Mrs. Lynch, not yours." Miss Harrington stood up and walked over to the window, her eyes glued to the street as she spoke, "Look, I'll be honest with you. Occupancy is slowing down and budget allocations are always a problem, especially these last few years. We rely mostly on government funding, so cutbacks will most likely be made by the end of this year." She turned back to look at her staff nurse and then back to the window, clearly not relishing the future of the institution.

"Dr. Templeton and I have been through decades of changes here and if there's anything we'd like to see before our reign is over, it's seeing something make a difference in that old man's life. We have become extremely fond of Charlie. He has mentored many young soldiers over the years. Now it's his time." Once again she turned toward Mrs. Lynch and then sat down behind her desk, exhaling heavily.

Mrs. Lynch's own father came to mind, and if Charlie ever had any children and the tables were turned, she would want someone to be there to comfort her father in his last days.

"Of course, Miss. Harrington, I'll do my best," she said, reassuring her in a quiet but firm voice.

"I know you will, dear. I have complete faith that you will. You're that kind of person, Mrs. Lynch. It shows in your nursing skills. I must admit I was a little reluctant hiring a married woman, but you've been exceptional."

As sweet as she could be, Mrs. Lynch bit her tongue on the way out.

***

Mrs. Lynch stood in the doorway of Charlie's room watching the old man sleep. She thought he must be about seventy-nine if the information in his chart was correct, and he had been here for thirty long years. Suddenly, she had doubts about what she was expected to do. How could she possibly make a difference if there hasn't been anything changed in all this time? It would be a miracle? But her father always said you never know how something so little as a kindness could make the world of difference in someone's life.

Charlie stirred from his sleep and opened his eyes as the nurse walked in.

"Charlie, it's me, Mrs. Lynch. Do you mind if I sit with you awhile?"

Charlie smiled, but didn't answer her. She pulled up a chair beside his bed and fluffed his pillows before she sat down. This sitting in silence had gone on for a few days because she didn't know what to say. She knew nothing about this man and had no common ground on which she could begin a conversation.

She thought about her father who had passed away two years ago. She guessed he and Charlie were close in age. She had once heard that writers should write about what they know so she decided that was a good place to start. And what she knew best was her life growing up and her family. A subject that was true and dear to her heart.

"Charlie, how are you today?"

He nodded and she continued, "You know, I was thinking my father would have been the same age as you, maybe a little older. He was a kind man, a good family man."

Charlie winced at that. The sentence cut him like a knife. Here she is comparing her father with me? Would she do that if she knew I deserted two families, three kids?

Mrs. Lynch noticed the flinch, but said nothing and continued. "I miss him dearly. I know my father did many things in his life that were not right, but he always loved us. Oh, and believe me, there were a lot of us to love." She was staring out the window, lost in some past memory that brought a twinkle to her eye.

With the ways I went wrong, is it possible my kids could love me?

"How many?" he whispered. She turned back quickly and looked at Charlie, surprised that he was asking her a question. She moved closer to him, hoping to keep him engaged.

"Nine, there were nine of us. My mother made ten. My father, God rest his soul, made sure he provided for us even in the worst of times. When you have nine children, you're playing the odds and some things don't always go well. I wasn't as healthy as the rest of my brothers and sisters. I guess you could say I was the runt of the litter." The words suddenly flowed out of her with ease.

Charlie's eyes sharpened as he listened to her voice, her words had struck a familiar chord. There was something he was struggling to bring to the surface.

He repeated part of what she said. "Runt of the litter?"

She pulled her chair even closer to him and leaned in to speak. Now, she needed and wanted to keep that connection they had made.

"Yes, I was the runt and I needed to go to a specialist for an operation. My mum didn't know how that would happen because we had no money. We were poor, but Da was my hero. He came through and found a way. And here I am today!" she announced, her smile lighting up the room.

Charlie listened to Mrs. Lynch's voice animate with the lilt of an ancient storyteller as she reverted to a young Irish girl.

"My Da would take me for walks to the cemetery to visit his friend's grave. He told me his friend was my own special guardian angel and that he would watch over me." She laughed, "I remember that day vividly because I stopped being afraid of ghosts and my brother couldn't tease me anymore."

Something stirred in Charlie. His voice was weak and he struggled to get out the words. "Grave? Whose?"

"His name was James. My father talked about him a lot. He thought of James as his brother."

"What was your Da's name?"

Mrs. Lynch straightened up in the chair, squared her shoulders and proudly responded in a thick Irish brogue, "Robert Michael McConville."

Charlie said nothing. He waited, knowing with concrete certainty it would come.

The young woman's face brightened with the thought of her father. She looked at Charlie and her smile grew wide and she chuckled, "Oh, but his friends? His *good* friends ... they called him Lefty."

"Lefty," Charlie repeated in a whisper. He exhaled before he closed his tired eyes, suddenly feeling at peace as stillness washed over him. That's when he knew this compassionate, young woman was little Erin, Lefty's baby girl. And Charlie also knew, right or wrong, he had been instrumental in Erin receiving her lifesaving operation.

Over the following days Charlie listened to Erin's life story. She spoke of her childhood, her aspirations and dreams, and her marriage to a good man. He shared his truth with her and each day they spent together he felt the weight lift from his existence, like a snake shedding its skin. In some strange twist, he felt she was his redemption.

A week later, with Erin McConville Lynch by his side, Charlie passed from his fractured life, but during his last few moments, he remembered the day his life changed and Lefty's last words. *I won't say goodbye my friend, for you and I will meet again. Whether it be in heaven or hell, we will meet again...*

Chapter 35   Myles 1975

Forty-six year old Myles Bingham was in the prime of his career with his own column in a prominent Boston paper and two novels under his belt. He sat in the IHOP sipping his coffee, waiting for breakfast as he read the morning paper in front of him.

The waitress knew his daily ritual and didn't disturb him to refill his coffee cup until he folded the paper in half and settled on the page with his column. You save the best for last, he told her. But this morning she noticed he was still stuck on the first page of the metro section.

Boston's Mystery Sailor Dies

An unidentified man who went by the name of Charlie, Beacon Marine Hospital's longest inpatient resident, has died.

Charlie was admitted with traumatic wounds at the end of WWII in February of 1945. His identity was never discovered even though the infamous story was printed in newspapers around the world. A world that passed him by.

Charlie became a symbol of patriotism for many people, as well as a mentor to infirm soldiers from several wars. He became known as the living, unknown soldier

Funeral services will be donated by the Seaman's Bethel, New Bedford, MA. Burial will be in the veterans section of Mount Rural cemetery, 9:00 a.m. on Tuesday, January 21st.

Myles stared at the picture, the same one that had caught his attention years ago.

It had to be back in '57 when I investigated Charlie, so that was eighteen years ago. My life has certainly changed in that time. I wonder what Charlie's life was like living most of it within the walls of a hospital.

He had never forgotten Charlie's story and, suddenly, everything came rushing back in pieces. Pieces of a puzzle that never fit.

There has to be someone out there who knows who this man's identity. He decided to go to the funeral. *Maybe that's where I'll find the integral piece.*

***

On Tuesday morning, Myles made the trip from Boston to New Bedford and arrived at the services early. The small chapel was packed and he estimated about one hundred or more people were in attendance. He looked around in amazement. Not a bad turnout, considering Charlie's identity was unknown.

Who are these people? Now this was a story. Myles wondered if the symbolism these people bestowed upon this man towered over the type of man he thought Charlie to be.

Military officers, fellow news reporters, and nurses in uniform, as well as past patients filled the pews to show their respect for Charlie. Myles took a seat in the back and looked around at the historic bethel, settling his eyes on the famous bow-shaped pulpit jutting out high above the congregation, immortalized by Melville's famous novel, *Moby Dick.*

This is where sailors about to set sail would visit to pray for a good catch and a safe return to port. He wondered about the ones who didn't return and their stories. Myles never stopped looking for a story. The murmurs around him quieted as a priest climbed the steps up to the pulpit.

Myles's eyes settled on the casket as the service started. He sat dumbstruck, listening to strangers from all walks of life eulogize the unknown soldier. He looked around to see if Dr. Templeton and that head nurse had attended, but he didn't see them.

Doubts set in. Could I have been wrong about everything I had suspected about Charlie all these years? Myles wondered.

A young man in dress uniform made his way from the first pew to the pulpit. One would be shortsighted to see only the trauma this soldier had suffered; but they would be completely blind not to see the pride this man wore with his uniform. He approached Charlie's casket and saluted. With a crisp turn he proceeded to the pulpit, reached into his pocket and pulled out a small piece of paper. He quietly unfolded it and gazed out over the many gathered to say a final goodbye to the unknown soldier before he spoke.

"Good morning. My name is Sergeant Daniel Fleming. We gather here today to pay our respects and say goodbye to Charlie.

"'Taps' is played at the end of the day, at solemn ceremonies and at military funerals, as it will be today. Most people are not familiar with the lyrics. The first three words 'Day is done,' speak of an ending. Charlie's life has ended. But his deeds are not done. They will live through all he has touched. This man we came to honor today will not be forgotten, because I am living proof of the legacy he leaves behind."

"Charlie was a living casualty of a war that wiped him of his memories, of his footprint in life. We don't know who he was, but I know the place he had in my life. He was my lifesaver. I met him in the common room of the VA hospital when I was at the end. I had given up hope. I was broken. A shell of my former self, closing out my loved ones, not only because they couldn't understand what I was going through, but also because I didn't want them to get close to the horror and ugliness of war. I needed to protect them from that. But Charlie knew, he had experienced it and he lent his ear to us and quietly listened. The men talked freely to him and received back understanding without judgment or pity. Charlie had the formula. Time and listening equals a priceless gift."

"In time, Charlie became a legend at the VA and new patients would catch wind of his story and eventually seek him out. Maybe we saw that he was worse off than we were. We would recover in time. Most of us had good memories in our lives. We returned to our families to love us and help us through. He would have none of these. What he did have was time and his capacity to listen, which he gave unselfishly to returning soldiers from wars and conflicts for three decades, helping the lost find their way. Sir, I pray your adversity is over and a rewarding journey lies ahead. I thank you and salute you for service to God, your country and your fellow soldiers. May you rest in peace."

The soldier stepped down from the pulpit, approached the casket and saluted before returning to stand with other representatives of the Armed Forces.

Myles, the hardened reporter, felt his eyes well up with tears that threatened to spill over. A conflict fueled within him as his face burned with embarrassment. No one noticed. Everyone was struggling with their own emotions, exposed and raw, their own thoughts of life, accomplishments and mortality.

When the service concluded, the Reverend invited everyone to accompany Charlie's casket, carried by local fishermen who volunteered to be pallbearers, to the cemetery just a short walking distance away. Once outside, Myles hung back, watching the people exit the church doors and line up behind the casket.

The procession led by the Reverend and the military personnel moved slowly up the quaint, cobblestoned street. It was a bitter cold day, but they walked eastward in silence, voicing no complaints.

The Reverend spoke a few brief words at the graveside, something to the effect that this was Charlie's last sail, as they lowered the simple, wooden casket into the grave. Myles struggled to hear his words from where he was standing. He watched the faces of the mourners.

Myles was beginning to lose hope that there was anyone attending who could shed light on Charlie's identity. Why he thought today was any different than the last thirty years was beyond him.

The crowd began to dissipate. Myles buttoned the top button of his wool suit coat, leaned up against the cold stone wall adjacent the grave plot and lit up a cigarette. From the corner of his eye, he noticed a woman stop, turn back and approach the open grave. She tightened her wool wrap-around coat, under which he assumed was a white nursing uniform since she wore a nursing cap specific to a Boston school.

The sun was higher in the sky now, warming the frost that covered the ground. Sunlight filtered through the wisps of condensation, giving the grassy knoll a mystical look. The woman reached the edge of the grave, slightly bent her right knee and leaned gently forward. She threw a long-stemmed rose onto the top of Charlie's casket. He heard her whisper a few words aloud that sounded like Gaelic.

Throughout his career, Myles's approach to people had evolved, gaining the decorum some young men lack in their enthusiasm. So out of respect, he waited until she had a moment of silence and until she turned away from the grave before he approached her.

"Miss, may I speak to you a moment?" She stopped and tightened her grip on her purse. Myles quickly introduced himself to ease her discomfort. His eyes searched for a warm place for them to talk.

"It's nice to see the sun out, but it's still cold. Do you mind if I ask you some questions inside the coffee shop on the corner? It's within walking distance and a public place." He pointed to the intersection outside the back gate. Before she could answer or object, he added, "I'll buy!"

She glanced at her watch. "All right, I believe I have enough time to get back before my shift. I don't make a habit of speaking to strangers, but coffee wins out. I'll need a cup before that drive back to Boston."

"Great, shall we go then, Miss? I'm sorry. I didn't get your name?"

"It's Mrs. Lynch, Erin Lynch. Nice to meet you, Mr. Bingham."

They walked in the solemn silence that envelops people after sending a fellow soul off to eternity, two strangers, each of them thinking about the man who was eulogized, the common denominator between them. The reporter and the nurse both ordered a hot coffee and sat on the stools at the front window, overlooking the street, adjacent to the cemetery.

Erin removed her scarf and gloves and laid them on the stool beside her. "You said you're a reporter, Mr. Bingham?"

"Yes, I am. You've probably read my daily column, 'The Last Mile with Myles'."

Erin measured two teaspoons of sugar from the glass shaker and took her time stirring her coffee. "Yes, I have read it. Are you doing an article on Charlie?"

"Well, I already tried that back in '57, some eighteen years ago now," Myles said.

"Oh, I didn't know that. I think Charlie deserves a legacy. A human interest article would be nice. He was an inspiration to a lot of fellow patients over the years."

Myles cocked his head to one side. He knew Erin noticed the strange look on his face when she said, "What? You don't think so?"

"I can't say, Erin. Charlie has been a mystery. I always thought I would discover who he was and when I saw he died, I came here hoping someone would come to the funeral with information."

"And you picked me?" Erin's left eyebrow arched. She remembered her mother telling her that signaled she was getting her Irish up.

"Well, you stayed behind at the graveside and I read real emotion on your face when you left your flowers. I figured you got to know the real man."

"I was Charlie's nurse. It's hard to lose a patient."

"And?" Myles prompted.

"And my father once told me, 'Erin, always go to the funeral.'"

"Why? What did he mean by that?"

"He taught me that it means that I have to do the right thing even when I really, really don't feel like it. I should never be too busy. It may inconvenience me, but the small gesture could make all the difference to someone else."

"But Charlie is dead and no one knew him. What difference? To whom?"

Erin's green eyes flickered with something, but Myles couldn't quite place what it was. Her voice was stronger when she explained, "Maybe the difference is in me. Maybe when I saw all the people who took time out of their busy lives to attend my father's funeral, it made a difference to *me*. It was a powerful thing to see what people mean to others, not just to you. For instance, take those soldiers who came to say goodbye to Charlie. Charlie said something that made a difference to them. He changed their lives. He changed how some of them perceived themselves and maybe for that he deserves some respect."

"Did Charlie open up to you?"

"No, but we had a connection of sorts." Erin's eyes drifted somewhere beyond the café's front window. There was a moment of silence before she continued. "He reminded me of someone my father knew when I was a child."

"Some people thought Charlie had something to hide. Was he a good man in your opinion?"

"Mr. Bingham, that's an odd question. Do you often speak ill of the dead?"

He noticed her green eyes had sharpened and he surmised she didn't like him very much. "No, I'm asking your opinion."

"I don't judge, that's not up to me. You know, even a man who hasn't lived an exemplary life has a redeeming quality somewhere. Don't *you* think so, Mr. Bingham?"

Myles caught the innuendo and knew Erin was a vibrant young woman who didn't mind showing her intelligence and strength, especially in her convictions. He had learned the hard way, over many lonely years, to appreciate these qualities in a woman, even though he felt it was too late for him. Befuddled by the whole woman's liberation thing at the time, now he conceded that he was a recovering chauvinist.

He pushed back with his answer. "I don't believe Charlie was who he pretended to be. People looked at him like he was a war's symbol of strength and courage. I'm not so sure. There are black and white questions to be answered, plain and simple."

"You're wrong, Mr. Bingham. Human lives are not just black and white. Quite the opposite. They're colorful, but sometimes they get muddied and there are gray areas. So, if Charlie instilled that patriotism and strength in others, how is that bad? And who are you to say that's bad?" Erin stood up and slipped her gloves on. Myles understood that this was her cue that she was going to leave. He stood and reached for his wallet to pay the check.

Erin waited until he was ready before proceeding to the door. Myles fell into line behind her. He didn't want to lose her before a chance to argue his point. "In answer to your question, Erin, I believe it was under false pretenses and that's why it's bad," Myles answered.

"You don't know that for sure. That man spent thirty years of his life inside those four walls. You're a writer. Can't something bad turn into something good? What does the word 'redemption' mean to you?"

Her words struck him like a slap in the face. He walked along beside her, studying her. He stopped abruptly, grabbed her arm and turned her to face him.

"Erin! You knew who Charlie was. Didn't you?"

His eyes held her eyes as she answered, "Not right away I didn't. It took me a while."

"Who was he?"

Erin's eyes chastised him as every good Irish woman could do with a look. "Mr. Bingham, there an old Irish proverb my mother used to say. It goes like this: 'Good as drink is, it ends in thirst.' I believe it's the same for knowledge. You see, the thirst for knowledge could be so great in someone they don't see that sometimes, just sometimes, some things are meant to be left alone." Erin squared her shoulders in defiance, then relaxed a bit. "This is one of them." In a softer voice she said, "Thank you for the coffee, but there's no Pulitzer here,

Mr. Bingham. Go home."

Myles's shoulders slumped and his eyes widened in astonishment. "You're not going to tell me, are you?" It came out more like a statement than a question. He followed her out of the coffee shop, on her heels like a puppy dog waiting to be thrown a bone.

Erin didn't hesitate to answer. She smiled, "No, you're right, I'm not. Would you betray a trust, reveal a friend's secret or divulge the mystery ingredient in a family recipe? My mother taught me better. She would roll over in her grave. Goodbye, Mr. Bingham." She turned and started to walk away but stopped suddenly and looked back at him.

"Mr. Bingham, I'm sure you've heard Napoleon's quotes."

"Which one?"

"The one where he said, 'History is a set of lies agreed upon.' I hope you and I can agree on Charlie's mark in history. I'll look forward to reading your article. Good day, Mr. Bingham." Erin left him standing alone on the sidewalk.

Women! What in the hell did that mean? Myles watched her go and then ripped his page of notes out of his notepad, crumpled it and threw it in the trash basket outside the coffee shop entrance.

Maybe she was right. You can't change anything by digging up the dead. They go on in the memories of the lives they've touched and whatever good they did in their life will surface to the top, like oil in water. The rest will sink and decay with the ages. People remember the good, Myles thought, and that might not be too bad.

Myles Bingham's human interest story topped the next day's paper. It was eighteen years late, but under the byline the headline read,

The truth of the man lies not beneath the granite gravestone but somewhere in the gray area between.

EPILOGUE

On a cold January day in 1975, Charlie was memorialized at the Seaman's Bethel with all the pomp and circumstance due a veteran. He had been a living "unknown sailor" for thirty years and an infamous symbol of the strife of a world war. Charlie was laid to eternal rest in a small New England oceanside cemetery in the seafaring town of New Bedford. He would have thought it a fitting place.

The following excerpt is from the 1975 eulogy given by Everett S. Allen, author and assistant editor of the *New Bedford Standard Times*, for an unknown sailor, Charles A. Jameson (name unverified). The words summed up the importance of the man and who a man is, even though he is not known by a name.

"Sailors may not know your name or even ask it, or think it important, for there is within them a persistent tendency to ignore the semicolons of a landsman's life."

ABOUT THE BOOK

This story began back in 1975, with a visit to my mother on Cape Cod. Little did I know, crossing the Sagamore Bridge would bring me into the past, and begin a fascinating genealogical journey to discover my ancestral roots. She showed me a Boston Globe article beseeching the public's help to identify a recently deceased John Doe, an amnesiac who had lived in a Boston hospital for thirty years. "He's your grandfather," she stated. The subject was not up for discussion, but this picture planted a seed in me which would later grow into years of research.

Thirty-Seven years passed before I looked into my maternal ancestry. During my search, I met wonderful people from all over the country, including two WWII cadet nurses and a ninety-year young United States Justice Department investigator.

Research is similar to turning over a rock to see what crawls out from beneath it. You dig deeper, because things hide in the dark crevices, in the twisted roots of another world and off the radar. So I dug and before I knew it, I found a rogue root growing sideways like an impacted wisdom tooth.

Originally, I thought *The Dark Root* would be a good title for this book, but as my writing ran parallel to my journey's uncovered secrets, I realized there are gray areas in my protagonist, as there are in my family. Life is not black or white and so I believe *The Gray Area Between* is a fitting title.

Ask about your family heritage, before the relatives with first-hand knowledge are gone, and their stories are lost forever. Today's technology provides many searchable archives and although not a replacement for a one-on-one conversation, there is still much to be learned.

Enjoy the Journey

Join me on *The Gray Area Between* page on Facebook

Patrice M. Perrotta

Made in the USA
Middletown, DE
01 December 2017